Tracy M

Keeper's Lodge

Michael Terence
Publishing

First published in paperback by
Michael Terence Publishing in 2022
www.mtp.agency

ISBN 9781800942936

I would like to dedicate this book to my husband Ian.

He has been incredibly supportive during the writing of Keeper's Lodge, often taking on my share of chores, so that I could devote my time to write. Putting up with me burning the midnight oil and never complaining when I woke him in the middle of the night to add to a chapter and then sharing it with him through excitement.

So, a very big thank you, I'm truly grateful ♡

Prologue

Fire, Victoria's Retreat – 2023

"I don't know why you keep asking me that question, Nurse Bowman," Rachel queried, turning round to look out of the window. "It's like I keep telling you, Rachel isn't available for her session today and has left me in charge."

"I see," said Nurse Bowman, stepping over to close the blinds to distract her gaze away from the car park outside. "Seeing as she has left you in charge, perhaps you would like to sit in on the session today in her place and, if Rachel returns, she can join us?" suggested Nurse Bowman.

"Are you expecting her back anytime soon?" Nurse Bowman continued, trying to ascertain how long Rachel's more dominant personality trait was likely to be in residence. She had nursed Rachel for a number of years, ever since she was handed over from Doctor Gyllensvan's psychiatric unit in Holden and had been trying to unravel her complex dissociative identity disorder ever since. Her disorder comprised four different alter egos ranging from a five-year-old child called Amy, who was actually a rag doll memento from her childhood. Helena, a caring and mild-mannered woman in her mid-twenties, who she had developed a strong bond with during her childhood captivity, an aggressive, unpredictable senior personality trait, whose characteristics were more often than not confrontational, hostile and violent. This ego was called George, who appeared to be masculine but had actually refused to co-operate in any type of consultation process, only coming to the fore when Rachel was highly emotional or unwell. Then there was Sarah, who was usually available for comment simultaneously alongside Rachel. Rachel did not switch into this character but often spoke to it like she was standing next to her, engaging like a friend. Sarah was seldom around without Rachel, so this situation was quite rare.

"Do you know where Rachel has gone this morning?" asked Nurse Bowman, wondering where her mind had slipped off to.

"Yes, she mumbled something about food supplies and Anika," said Sarah, reopening the blind, as if she was searching for her.

"I see," said Nurse Bowman, retaking her seat behind her desk and shuffling her papers. Anika was the name Rachel had been forced to adopt during her ten-year captivity at the hands of Joseph Treville, her psychotic father figure. Rachel, along with her sister Linda, had endured the most horrific confinement and were forced to re-enact moments their father figure had cherished of his own children, before they sadly died in a tragic car accident. It was becoming more and more obvious that Rachel could not accept that her name was Rachel and could not relate to this person at all. The only name she could remember, the name she had been called for almost half of her life, was Anika, and despite this name being attached to her almost inconceivable confinement and starvation it was the only name she could connect to. She frequently refused to accept that she was called Rachel, often shelving this identity like it was a burden, discarding it to one side, like an intrusion.

"Do you know why she was checking in with Anika?" Nurse Bowman asked, wondering if today's session would include her main character statue.

"Yes, she wanted to check on her food supplies," said Sarah, turning away from the window and taking ownership of the chair in the far right-hand corner of the office.

Nurse Bowman nodded, acknowledging her understanding as to where this was leading and what the outcome was likely to be. "Ah, I expect she will be back any minute then," Nurse Bowman concluded, "as I know she has plenty," she confirmed, opening her folder.

Nurse Bowman watched as Sarah started shuffling in her chair, crossing and uncrossing her legs. She sat on her hands and then stood up and sat in the chair immediately opposite her. Nurse Bowman watched on, observing her swing round in her chair to face the chair she had just vacated and then she saw what appeared to be an exchange of hand gestures, implying that Rachel was back in the room.

"Hello Rachel," said Nurse Bowman, pre-empting the current state of play.

"Hi," said Rachel, a smile unfolding on her face.

"Nice of you to join us today," Nurse Bowman added. "How are you feeling? Is everything OK with you this morning, after your period of absence?"

"Yes," said Rachel, turning to face the empty chair. She scowled, which signified she was cross at having her outing revealed and then turned to face Nurse Bowman again. "I was just checking on the food situation," she clarified, patting her bulging pocket to confirm to herself that the cupboards were well and truly stocked. Rachel carried small deposits of food around with her everywhere, layering on extra clothing to gain extra pockets. Today she was wearing three cardigans to max out on available storage and Nurse Bowman could see that she even had something concealed in her sock.

"Right," said Nurse Bowman switching on her voice recorder, "let's continue from our last session." She glanced down at her notes to refresh her memory and then began to wonder whether it was wise to mention Linda again, so early in the session. She decided to work up to that and shifted her focus onto her day-to-day habits. "Rachel, we've spoken before about you being able to take part in some communal activities with other patients. How do you feel about that?" said Nurse Bowman, reaching for her coffee.

Rachel started to fidget in her chair and then turned around to face the chair in the corner. "Well I already share my room with Sarah," said Rachel, smiling across at her, "and then there's Helena who often joins us," she added. "Also Anika," she continued, turning away from Miss Bowman to avoid eye contact. She knew that Nurse Bowman would follow this comment by reminding her that Anika was the name she was forced to assume and was not a separate person.

Nurse Bowman sighed, she was becoming increasingly concerned that Rachel was identifying with Anika as a second self in parallel, which together with her four additional identities was now emerging as a fifth. She decided to say nothing for the time being, moving on so that she could encourage Rachel to take part in some group activities. From experience she knew how this benefited rehabilitation, allowing more fragile patients to integrate with a live person in contrast to an hallucinating presence. "Would you like to join our talking circle?" suggested Nurse Bowman, thinking that this would be a good introduction to integration. "It's a very small group where we sit and discuss how we are feeling, what we have done during the course of the week, what we would like to do and much more. It's a way of sharing our emotions and fears but it's also a place where we can share happy thoughts. There are only a few members currently," Nurse Bowman continued, making it sound like a social committee, "and we do have a session scheduled for this afternoon." She paused, looking up to see if Rachel was still on the same page. She could see that Rachel was looking a little dazed, a trait often exercised when she felt she couldn't cope with what was on offer. It was a withdrawal process, shutting down so that she didn't have to respond or comply with anything that was offered or expected of her that she wasn't comfortable with. "Well why don't you think about it for a while?" Nurse Bowman offered, thinking that perhaps she had pushed the boundaries a little too far this time.

Rachel looked across at the empty chair in the corner of the room as if she was looking at Sarah for reassurance and then announced that she wasn't feeling very well. "I really want to go back to my room now," said Rachel, reaching out for her imaginary presence like a comfort blanket. Nurse Bowman nodded in agreement; there was no point pursuing anything further once Rachel had put the shutters up, as this usually had a way of escalating to something far greater, leading to further obstacles to be broken down.

Nurse Bowman sighed, switched off the recorder and rose to her feet. "It would be good for you, Rachel, to join in with some of the other patients," Nurse Bowman offered, as she turned the handle on the door and stepped out into the corridor.

She watched as Rachel scurried down the corridor holding her hand out to the side like she was clutching onto Sarah for guidance and reassurance. Rachel turned the handle on her door and she followed her into her bedroom, observing her typical behavioural pattern that she had adopted and performed like a ritual on a daily basis. Rachel's main focus was television. It was a window to the world, a world that had been stolen from her and was now a way where she could experience life safely from the confines of her room. She had a full itinerary of programmes to follow and specifically loved family-based soaps and romantic films. She had no interest whatsoever in day-to-day news feeds as the wider picture was far too daunting, she merely concentrated solely on family life like a magnet as to what she had missed out on within a loving family environment. She also liked game shows which she found fun and loved solving mathematical equations.

Rachel also displayed mild symptoms of autism. She counted everything, multiplied it, divided it and then started the process over again. Nurse Bowman noticed she often reverted to this when she was anxious, like it was a diversion away from her troubles. Her 'go-to' actions.

She often quoted lines from adverts if she saw a product, such as toothpaste or bath products. Her brain was like a sponge and it was quickly becoming evident that she was exceptionally intelligent. Her brain had been starved as well as her body and now she was thirsty for knowledge.

"Is there anything I can get you?" Nurse Bowman asked, as she watched Rachel settle into her arm chair and reach for the TV remote.

"No thank you," said Rachel, setting herself up for an afternoon of viewing. She had everything she required piled up on the table next to her armchair. Numerous packets of biscuits, crisps, cakes and sweets. She had an exceptionally sweet tooth and candy was her thing. She wasn't greedy, she just needed to see them. She had to ensure they were there should she want them, should her need arise. Nurse Bowman closed the door.

"So what did you think of that session?" said Rachel, flicking through the channels to see what the afternoon would bring.

"I think they are trying to break us up," said Sarah, lying down on the bed. "They want you to find new friends, so that you don't mix with us anymore. That's what I think. They are trying to get rid of us," she added.

"Yes, they make it appear that you are a bad influence, not good for me and that I should make new friends," said Rachel, turning to face the bed. "But we've been friends for so long, there's no way I'm leaving you behind," Rachel confirmed. "Don't worry Sarah, I'm not sharing my room with anyone else but you."

Her attention was then drawn to her usual afternoon soap opera, which featured a married couple who had the ideal marriage, two children and a small dog. Rachel was fascinated by their lives and thought it was real. The concept of acting didn't feature in her world, despite Nurse Bowman explaining daily that it was a representation and that the couple were not really called Bob and

Sue, were not married and the children were born to another family. They were merely acting/pretending for want of a better expression, Nurse Bowman had told her, for the purpose of the cameras to entertain viewers. Rachel was convinced that Nurse Bowman had this completely wrong and that they were a real family and were just allowing people to view their lives. Anyway there was no way she was going to miss any episodes for the sake of the bloody talking circle, she thought, making herself comfortable by plumping the cushions and stretching out her legs to prop them on the edge of the coffee table.

Rachel's world was very limited and was basically conducted within the confines of her bedroom. She had no desire to venture further, and put up real resistance when it came to any outdoor activities. Her room was bright and airy but sadly the view was only of the car park but this had its benefits as she liked to observe the comings and goings of doctors, nurses, visitors and new patients. She was on the fourth floor and had a corner room. These rooms were considered superior, as they were larger and were usually assigned to full-time residents. Rachel liked her room, especially the wall which was covered in pictures of meadow flowers. If she was to leave her room for any reason then she wanted to go there to pick the flowers, she decided. She looked across at her bed, which had a teddy bear duvet cover, and then she stared at the metal headboard. She hated that headboard, if she could get rid of one thing, it would be that.

"Now, Rachel, you really need to calm down if you want me to undo the restraints," Nurse Bowman had advised during one of her episodes. Yeah, she really hated that bloody thing and felt like ripping it from its hinges. She looked across at Sarah, who was stretched out on the bed snoozing, and studied her profile. Sarah looked angelic but Rachel knew she could be controlling and often encouraged her to do things out of character that often got her into trouble. She hated the fact that Nurse Bowman kept encouraging her to take part in things and mix with the other people that resided here. She still didn't fully understand why she was here, but she knew she liked it, as there was plenty of food and she could watch TV.

She had very little memory of what went before but she knew she was always hungry and she knew she never wanted to feel that way again. She kept dreaming of a little girl in a pink tutu that she felt connected with who danced ballet continually, but she just couldn't place her in her everyday life and thought perhaps she was her sister. No that couldn't be right, could it, she thought, remembering her sister was called Linda. No, that's not right either, she decided, her sister was called Roberta, of that she was certain. Maybe she had several sisters, she concluded. She looked back across at Sarah trying to work out if she was her sister too, they seemed to be multiplying. She counted them on her fingers one by one. Linda, Roberta, Anika, Sarah, Helena and Amy. Then there was George, she thought, wondering where he fitted into the family tree. She must have a brother, she reasoned. In any case why did she need anyone else when she had counted seven people instantly on her fingers who she spoke with most days. Her world was full to the brim and if she was to take on anyone else in here, she thought, looking around her room, she would need to move up to the penthouse. She giggled at this thought. She knew there wasn't really a penthouse above her but she liked to pretend there was after watching a movie about a wealthy couple who had checked into a glamorous hotel in New York.

Rachel was under twenty-four-hour supervision with her every move scrutinised by CCTV. Her room was devoid of anything that could be reinvented as a tool for harm and the windows were shut fast. The air was circulated by air con to suit the climate and the door was alarmed. Rachel had little or no understanding that she was being monitored for her own safety and thought that, when she was alone in her room, she was independent of any intervention. The only thing that irritated her was that she had to ring the bell when she needed the bathroom. This was a real nuisance and she hated the way one of the orderly staff escorted her as though she was a small child.

Rachel also had little understanding of time and as her mind had basically shut down, anything that went before did not exist in her world now. To Rachel, with the exception of her time spent with Julie Somers, her psychiatrist, and Doctor Gyllensvan, her memory was what existed now. Therefore, the prospect of growing older didn't feature, so it was as if this was what life was. Routine was critical to Rachel and everything needed to be done in the same order each day. The only time she appeared to relax and focus was her time in front of the TV, where she soaked up information absorbing it like she was at a lecture, stockpiling it and presumably filing it for later use. For now, though, she had no plans to act on any of it and refused point blank to mix at all outside of her sister collection. She glanced up at the calendar on her bedroom wall where she was encouraged to mark off each day as it was spent. Today was Tuesday and she knew that after lunch Julie Somers would be here again.

She didn't understand the purpose of Julie Somers' visits and she certainly didn't like the probing questions she often asked. She found her a nuisance and hated the way she always felt groggy after she left, like she was in a transfixed state. She had begged Nurse Bowman over and over to stop her from coming but she was told that it was part of her rehabilitation process,

whatever that meant. She wondered whether the talking circle might be less intrusive. After all, she could just watch from the sidelines, she didn't have to contribute unless she was feeling brave. It might be better than looking at the stars on the ceiling with Julie, which often made her feel sick. She pondered momentarily, then sighed. Why did she need to see anyone? She had everyone she needed already.

She stood up and rang the bell and then sat down again to wait. She had made the decision to attempt to swap one for the other and wondered whether this might be possible. Nurse Bowman seemed desperate for her to take part in her talking circle, so maybe if she told her she would take part if she would cancel Julie Somers' visit this afternoon. An orderly called Rose answered her call, assuming that she needed the bathroom and entered her bedroom with a cheery smile. "Hello Rachel," said Rose, in her usual upbeat manner, "need the loo?" she asked, pre-empting this to be the case.

"No, I would like to speak to Nurse Bowman please," she requested in her nicest voice, used when she wanted to get something her own way. Rose nodded, stepping back out of the room to check if Nurse Bowman was still on-site. She returned moments later informing her that she would be along shortly and then scurried away as quickly as she had been summoned.

Rachel rehearsed in her head her negotiation technique and then sat meekly in her chair, like butter wouldn't melt in her mouth. She was getting smart at getting things her way. She looked across at Sarah who was now snoring and wondered whether to wake her. Could she handle this herself or did she need Sarah as backup? A light knock on the door indicated that there was no time to wake Sarah and fill her in, so she called out gently, positioning herself in her chair, as if he was about to star in one of her soaps. "Come in," she said, looking down at the floor.

"You wanted to see me, Rachel?" said Nurse Bowman stepping inside.

"Yes, I was thinking about what you said earlier, about me joining your talking circle and was wondering if I could do that today instead of seeing Julie Somers?"

"I see," said Nurse Bowman, curious about this sudden change of direction. "And why have you changed your mind, Rachel, when you were so adamant earlier that you didn't want to mix with anyone?"

"Well, I see Nurse Somers every week and I don't think I feel well enough to see her today but I think I might be OK to sit in on your circle, if I don't have to say too much and I can listen in, as it's my first time," she said, with pleading eyes. Nurse Bowman nodded, advising that she would check first to ensure that she could reach Nurse Somers before committing to anything else. She stepped out of the room confident that Rachel was now up to something, as there was no way that she would volunteer herself for anything that would involve others, but if cancelling a session with Nurse Somers was a way in which to integrate, then that's what she would do.

Rachel couldn't believe her luck when she received a message later that morning that she would be collected from her room after lunch to join the group. She had managed to pull it off without Sarah's help and now didn't have to look at stars on the ceiling with Nurse Somers. She did, however, have to sit with people she didn't know and she knew that would be a problem. Perhaps she should fill Sarah in after all. She deliberated, thinking that she would prefer it if she went too. She sat staring at Sarah watching her snore, wondering what to do. She hated mixing with others, they were nosy and always asked lots of questions. She hoped she could just listen, as that would be really good. It would be like watching one of her soaps, she suddenly thought. She stood up and walked over to the bed, looking down at Sarah. She studied her features and then turned to look at herself in the mirror. She was quite similar to Sarah, she decided. They both had honey-blonde hair, shoulder length, dark eyes, and were both very slim. They could be twins, Rachel contemplated, perhaps they were. Maybe that's why they were such good friends and went everywhere together. She tried to remember when she first met her but just couldn't work it out. Maybe it was because they were born at the same time. It was quite confusing having so many sisters, she decided.

She looked at the clock on the wall which confirmed she had ten minutes left until lunch was served, before realising that she was five minutes late for her afternoon quiz. She took a deep breath and sat down in her chair again, agitated that this was the case. She liked to do everything in the right order and now she wouldn't be able to meet the contestants and hear about their family life before the game started. She could feel herself unravelling as the first contestant, a man with a balding head and shabby beard picked the first number. "Oh no, you can't start yet," she yelled, "I don't know who you are," immediately waking Sarah from her slumber.

"What are you yelling at?" Sarah quizzed, sitting up and rubbing her eyes.

"It's the quiz master, he's started without me and now I don't know who anyone is," she explained, pacing back and forth in front of the TV. "Sarah, how can I tell him to wait and go back to the start, he must have known I wasn't ready?" she questioned. "Why did he start without me?"

She could hear the lunch trolley making its way up the corridor which would be yet another intrusion. She usually tolerated this as it happened at the same time each day during the quiz and Rose knew not to disturb her, laying her food down on the table without so much as a word. Food was also something that she welcomed eagerly, so there was no way she was going to interfere with its arrival. "Rose, can you help us, we want to get the quiz master to start again," she asked, holding the door ajar, so that she could wheel the trolley into the room.

Rose sighed, knowing that this was going to be tricky to explain, as the entire viewing schedule had been set for the day, carefully chosen to give maximum benefit to Rachel's rehabilitation and was on a loop, set 24 hours in advance. It was devoid of anything violent or what might be considered inappropriate, so that Rachel could be educated and fulfilled gradually without her being subjected to anything that might be upsetting or hard to explain after being confined for half of her lifespan. Sudden exposure to something unmonitored would be detrimental to her recovery. Therefore, normal smart-style intervention could not be applied. "Ah sweetheart, that's not possible I'm afraid but let me sit with you for a couple of minutes so I can help you catch up," she offered.

"But I need to start at the beginning," she said, starting to feel anxious.

"Look," said Rose, "I'm sure we can sort this." Rose had a way about her and quickly assessed the situation. "Look, the man is called Peter and the lady is called Rita, as the booth they are each standing behind has their name on," Rose pointed out. Rachel wiped her tears and stared at the television. "And look," continued Rose, "they are now having a little chat about where they come from," said Rose, feeling pleased that the host was revisiting his earlier questions.

"Now it looks as if Peter has answered the first question incorrectly, so they are going to ask the same question again so that Rita can have a turn," she said, turning back to her trolley. Rose could now see that Rachel was completely tuned in and no further intervention was necessary, so she handed her a plate of sandwiches and swiftly left the room. She had become accustomed to Rachel's outbursts during her time here and, despite her having no official medical training, she seemed to be able to defuse situations she often witnessed while serving at mealtimes. Rose had worked at Victoria's Retreat for over seventeen years serving meals and assisting with some of the recreation activities. Her soft tone and mild manor was a magnet to a lot of the patients, which made her popular with everyone. She was due to retire the year after next and was becoming deeply concerned about what her life would be like afterwards. It had become her world too.

Rachel sighed, as she wandered back and forth in her room after lunch contemplating. Why the hell had she agreed to take part in the bloody talking circle? Maybe Julie Somers would have been the better option, she deliberated. No, she decided, sitting back down in her chair. She hated Julie Somers' visits. They made her feel sick and she never wanted to look at stars again. She took a deep breath and rose to her feet in readiness as the hand on the clock clicked into position. It was 2pm, time to go. She looked across at Sarah, who was brushing her hair in the mirror and watched as she tied it up into a matching ponytail, identical to hers. They were definitely twins, she decided as she stood behind her in front of the mirror. Everything about them was the same and they were exactly the same height and from where she was standing she couldn't tell them apart. She glanced over to the corner of the room at Amy sitting up on the shelf, lifeless. What was wrong with her today? She hadn't said a word all morning. Her woolly braids had been tied in a knot across her eyes like she was hiding from the world. Oh well, she'd deal with her later.

She felt her body stiffen in response to the faint knock on her door. "Are you ready?" said Nurse Bowman, popping her head around the door, smiling. She had purposely decided to collect Rachel herself to escort her down to the session, as she felt certain that Rachel would either delay her visit or bail out completely. This was definitely not her thing and she knew that Rachel was very clever at causing some sort of situation/diversion that would bring an end to everything that had been put in sequence.

"Can Sarah come?" said Rachel, reaching out and then clasping her hand firmly around Sarah's.

"Yes, I see no reason why she can't come to the first session," said Nurse Bowman, grateful that this was the only concession.

She stepped to one side so that Rachel and her imaginary confidant could exit and watched on as they made their way down the long, dimly lit corridor towards the winding staircase. Rachel stopped at the top of the stairs and then pushed her hands out as if she was shoving Sarah forwards, ensuring that she led the way down the mahogany clad staircase. She was using her like a shield, following her down each step, holding her arm up like one hand was resting on her shoulder. Nurse Bowman sighed as she placed her hand on the banister rail to aid her descent; Rachel's multiple personality disorder was so ingrained that it was proving increasingly unlikely that she would ever recover sufficiently to have any sort of independent life outside of these walls.

Rachel stopped directly outside the doors leading to one of the small recreation rooms that had been designated for today's talking circle and peered through the right-hand circular window. She wanted to see who was there. Despite her keeping herself to herself, curiosity had allowed her to observe some of the other patients from a distance and she could see that Maizy-Jayne was sitting in what was presumably Nurse Bowman's chair conducting the meeting.

"Good afternoon all," said Nurse Bowman, opening the door and greeting everyone with enthusiasm. "Ah, thank you for filling in for me Maizy-Jayne," she said, indicating that she could now vacate her chair. She nodded at Rachel to take a chair and then watched on bemused, as Rachel walked across the room to claim an additional chair for Sarah, which she placed next to her own without a gap. The room was fairly small, modestly furnished but there was a picture of a meadow on the wall. Rachel smiled, likening it to the one in her room. If she felt too nervous, she decided she would lose herself in the meadow, her safe place.

"As you can see we have a new member today," Nurse Bowman suddenly announced. Rachel, would you like to introduce yourself?" she said, gesturing towards her. Rachel looked across at Nurse Bowman horrified. Why was she singling her out when she strictly said she wanted to sit on the sidelines and observe? Rachel could feel herself start to unravel, pushing her hand out to the vacant chair, as if indicating that Sarah should go first.

"I want to go first," said Maizy-Jayne standing up with her hand in the air, waving like she might be missed from the back row.

"Fair enough," said Nurse Bowman, realising that putting Rachel under the spotlight so soon was a rookie mistake to make and with all her years of experience was rather stupid. Relief flooded through Rachel's body like she had been saved from walking the plank and her attention turned to the opening scene of today's production. Maizy-Jayne was more than happy to take centre stage and did a little pirouette twist and curtsy before retaking her seat. Rachel observed this move with anxiety. She had performed the move incorrectly and she knew more than most that an incorrect pose would mean that there would be no food again.

"You need to do it again," shouted Rachel, startling her new audience. "You did it wrong. Quickly redo it before Father sees," she begged.

The three other girls started laughing loudly. "Yes, do it again," they yelled in unison, badgering the girl to repeat her pirouette move.

Rachel looked around the room watching the girls chant. Her head was reeling and she felt awash with adrenaline and they now appeared to be swaying back and forth, their faces coming in at her. She felt sick and immediately looked up towards the ceiling to see if the stars were out. Was Nurse Somers here after all, she wondered, searching frantically for the meadow picture? She dropped to her knees and shielded her eyes. "Make her do it again," she yelled, curling up into a ball on the floor. "Make her do it again," she whispered before her trembling body became lifeless.

The girls were now jumping up and down in their seats and one was dragging Maizy-Jayne by her ginger curls, shouting "do it again". Two of the girls were rushing around the room, knocking things off the table and tipping up the other chairs screaming, "do it again, do it again."

Nurse Bowman had completely lost control of the session and was now sounding the emergency alarm. "Eileen, Sandra, stop what you are doing right now," instructed Nurse Bowman, as she witnessed them emptying the book cabinet in the reading corner at record speed. Eileen, a small-framed, dark-haired Irish girl then dropped to her knees and proceeded to rip the pages from the book she was holding like she had scissor fingers. Sandra took great delight in this and proceeded to throw the ripped pages up into the air like confetti. Beverley had now lost interest in Maize-Jayne and released her grip on her hair and was heading towards the piano. Before you knew it the sound of classical tones was belting out from the piano, making the whole scene extremely eerie.

"He's here," whimpered Rachel from her curled up position. "It's too late," she whispered gently, before going completely inside herself.

The door burst open and the nursing team attempted to defuse the situation, sedating Eileen and Sandra who were now completely out of control. Two orderlies were wrestling Beverley away from the piano and were desperately trying to muffle her operatic tones, while Maizy-Jayne hid under the table with her hand over her ears and her eyes closed. Rose was observing from the sidelines watching Nurse Bowman help Rachel to her feet and then helped assist her back to the safety of her own room. She had heard the commotion from the kitchen as she was putting on her coat to leave for the day. A scene not dissimilar to many she had witnessed over the years.

"Thank you for your help, Rose," said Nurse Bowman, indicating that she would take it from there. Rachel was comatose, completely withdrawn and was lying on her bed staring up at the ceiling. Rose nodded and exited the room not knowing that that would be the last time she would see Rachel again. Nurse Bowman stroked Rachel's brow, while she stared at her deadly white gaunt expression, as Rachel continued to gaze upwards. She knew with absolute certainty that the pirouette manoeuvre that Maizy-Jayne had demonstrated had sparked a memory from her time in captivity, where she had to perform a ballet scene that was held dear to her perpetrator. If she got it wrong, she would have to repeat it over and over until it was performed correctly or it would result in starvation. Nurse Bowman turned and looked at the empty shelf in the corner of the room that she knew had been assigned to Amy, her imaginary doll and then quietly left the room.

Rachel woke to the sound of sirens and flashing lights outside her bedroom window. Where was she? she wondered momentarily, before realising that she was in her bed, in her room, next to her meadow picture. What were those flashing lights, she pondered? curiously climbing off the bed and heading to the window. Maybe it was a new person being brought in by an ambulance she considered, something she had witnessed on numerous occasions. No, she could smell burning, something was burning and the sirens she could hear were coming from within.

She could hear the sound of feet rushing up the corridor and people yelling instructions as her bedroom door burst open. One of the night staff was instructing her to follow him, as she reached for her coat on the back of the door. "We need to evacuate immediately," he shouted, as he pushed open the other bedroom doors collecting patients from her wing as they went.

Patients were screaming and crying all at the same time and the night staff were struggling to contain any sort of order to the evacuation process amongst the smog. Smoke had engulfed the hallway making it impossible to see and the sound of coughing, spluttering and gasping could be heard everywhere.

"How do we get out?" sobbed Rachel, staring at the central staircase that was now engulfed in flames. Tears were running down her cheeks and onto the coat she was still holding, which she then discarded on the floor. "How do we get out?" she yelled, while gagging for air. Prestigious looking paintings that graced the stairwell were now melting onto the maroon carpet and Rachel could just about make out the remains of its founder as his eyes melted and then merged with his mouth making it appear that he was being swallowed by himself. The screams were getting louder and more and more piercing and Rachel could hear people sobbing uncontrollably as they were being led towards the back staircase. She was struggling to breathe, would she make it outside, would she see Linda again? Where was Nurse Bowman she wondered all of a sudden? She could just about make out the wording Fire Exit glowing green above the fire door that the night nurse was now shoving open.

"Down you go," he ordered, "and don't stop," he spluttered trying to shield his mouth and nose from the smoke, as he pushed her forward.

The stampede of people behind her pushing and shoving, made her lose her footing. "Stop pushing me, you cow," she yelled trying to see who it was that shoved her violently in the back.

"Then get out of the fucking way you looney," hollowed an extremely overweight man who must have been at least seven foot tall, wearing a ladies nighty.

"Oh no, where is Sarah?" she yelled, "I have to go back," she shouted, turning in an attempt to go back up the staircase. People were shoving against her, forcing her down. "No, get out of my way," she yelled, pushing someone to the floor and then trampling over them. "My sister is in there. I have to find my sister," she yelled, fighting against the onslaught of bodies. She felt a hand grab her arm forcing her back down, dragging her onwards.

"Let go of me," she yelled, struggling against his firm grip. "I have to get to my sister," she screamed as she was pushed out into the open. Why was he glaring at her like that? "Why are you looking at me like I am an idiot," she questioned, heading back towards the door.

"You're all bloody idiots," said the man who had basically saved her life, "and you're not going back in," he yelled, dragging her away from the door so that the others could get out.

"I'm here," said Sarah suddenly coming into focus. "I was right behind you all the way," she said, sweeping her up into a tight hug.

"Bloody nut case," said the orderly, as he watched her hug herself while kissing and talking to thin air.

Fire Engines and ambulances were everywhere and people were running back and forth screaming and crying in complete chaos. Flames were leaping from the windows and screams could be heard from within. Staff were trying to contain the patients and were rounding them up onto the coach that they usually used for outings. Was that Nurse Bowman she could see being carried out of the front entrance on a stretcher? She must get to her. She must see if she is OK. "Nurse Bowman, Nurse Bowman," she screamed rushing across the car park. It was her, she could see her distinctive white hair dusted with soot down one side of her profile. Her kind but worn expression, aged by years of harrowing work. Her eyes closed. Was she dead? Was the nurse, the only nurse she trusted, dead?

"We've got to get on the coach," said Sarah pulling her away from the ambulance. Rachel turned to face the coach where staff were desperately trying to do some sort of registered role-call amongst the pandemonium. She could see Eileen, Sandra and Maizy-Jayne, her tormentors, boarding the coach, suddenly remembering her ordeal from earlier. She turned to face the building wondering if her father was still in there. Would they save him or would they let him burn?

One

Three years later…

"How's she doing," said Mike, as he joined Paul in the waiting area outside Doctor Leeson's Office. "Has she said anything yet?"

"I've just arrived," said Paul, adjusting his navy blazer so that the collar and lapel were straight. "Haven't even seen the usual receptionist, who's normally very informative," he added, deciding to remove his blazer and lay it across his lap. The reception area was exceptionally hot and he felt clammy and uncomfortable. He stood up and moved over to the window and then turned to face Mike. "I can't get the image of her trussed up like that out of my head," he said, tossing his blazer over his shoulder.

"Yeah, I know what you mean. It was a hideous sight, one that will haunt me indefinitely." Mike thought back to the afternoon they burst through the door of Linda's new apartment and found her bound and gagged, a few days earlier. She had been tormented and assaulted by Joe Treville who was still at large. They had an APB out on him but as yet he had avoided capture.

"Gentleman, sorry to keep you waiting but it's been an exceptionally busy morning," said Doctor Leeson striding into the reception area and reaching out to shake both their hands.

"Good of you to fit us in," said Mike, acknowledging how busy the doctor was. "How's Linda doing?" said Mike.

"Well, as you can imagine with everything that went before, her amazing recovery and reintegration back into society has been undone somewhat but I do believe she has the tools and understanding to pull back from this," he said, gesturing for them to follow him into his office.

He motioned towards the two seats that were placed side by side in front of his bureau-style desk and then walked across to the cabinet where a water jug and glasses were set out on a small round tray. He filled the glasses and passed them across without question and then took his seat behind the bureau.

"Has she been taken to the observation suite?" Mike asked, wondering if he would be witnessing any more hypnosis sessions moving forward.

"No, I have decided against that for the time being but she is being monitored twenty-four seven," he confirmed, reaching for his overfilled glass.

"Is she talking yet?" asked Paul, curious as to whether they would be right back where they started seven years ago when she first escaped the clutches of Joe Treville's father, her childhood perpetrator and captor.

"Yes, this morning her assigned nurse was able to converse with her and I am able to confirm that she is no longer in her enforced trance, which is a trait both sisters adopted as a means of escape."

"Has she given any details of her ordeal?" Mike quizzed, eager to have as much information as possible to assist with the arrest.

"Snippets, I would describe them as at present but I'm certain we will piece it all together as her recovery progresses."

"Can we see her?" asked Mike, wondering if this would be possible at this early stage. "We do have a psychopath at large," Mike pressed, emphasising the importance of getting some vital clues as to where he might be heading.

Doctor Leeson sighed, knowing how difficult it was to balance the needs of his patients with law enforcement. "Perhaps just one of you for now but keep it brief," the doctor advised. Mike rose to his feet and nodded at Paul, calling rank over the decision. He thought back to all those years ago when he had first found her wandering the street of Gordon Square. The agony of not knowing what had happened to her. He felt compelled to see this through. He couldn't let it go.

Paul nodded, completely understanding that this case was deeply ingrained in Mike for numerous reasons and had taken its toll on his dear friend.

"Lead the way, Doc," Mike said, eager to move things along.

"Ah, well not so fast, Sergeant, we need to prepare Linda for your visit," he said, rising to his feet. "We can't just pop in unannounced, like we were popping round for coffee," he said, stalling Mike's over-enthusiastic need for immediate answers. "Give me a moment to inform Nurse Hatten and she can prepare her and check that she is willing to be questioned," the doctor advised as he stepped out of the room.

Mike sighed, as he stretched out his arms and placed them behind his head. "I know, I know," he said, glancing at Paul, realising that he was, as usual, rushing full steam ahead. "I just want to catch the bastard before he carries out any more of his father's sick rituals," he said, clicking his knuckles and then folding his arms firmly in front of him.

"Yeah, I know, it's so fucking frustrating sitting here waiting while that monster is out there planning his next psycho escapade, but we are going to have to be patient, Mike. This deranged maniac has been planning this for years. He has carefully thought out and possibly practiced these ceremonial acts before and he's going to be really pissed off with the interruption and is now possibly at his most menacing and unpredictable. Basically he's a time bomb."

"You're telling me," he said, switching his gaze to the door which Doctor Leeson was now entering.

"Right, I've briefed Nurse Hatten and she seems to think that a short visit, without too many invasive questions would be permissible, but, Sergeant, Linda is in a very frail state, so go easy with the questioning," he said, indicating with a gesture that they were ready to proceed.

Mike followed the doctor down the long corridor, wondering if, after a period of observation, she would end up back with Doctor Gyllensvan. He truly hoped not. After his last meeting with him he had lost all faith in the doctor's ability to make rational decisions and believed he was close to the edge himself. His thoughts then turned to Julie Somers, wondering how she was doing in his care. So many troubled people, all scarred by the same hands, broken into thousands of fragments, some damaged beyond repair.

Niko, the man who raped his wife, flashed through his mind like a sharp instrument, causing a stabbing pain down the left side of his forehead. His stomach wrenched and he felt his heart race as he quickened his pace behind the doctor. Niko, yet another victim of the same perpetrator, beaten, tortured and humiliated, finally losing his own grip on reality, turning him into a vicious violent hater of all women, to which his own wife had been viciously subjected. God, how he hated that man and fought with his own conscience daily about how he wished he had killed him that night, knowing that he was back out on the streets. Yes, Joseph Treville's list of victims was continuing to grow, despite him dying of a heart attack some years earlier, and now his son Joe was carrying on his father's crimes almost as though he was a reincarnation of him, reinvented with the same thirst.

"Before we go in, Sergeant," said the doctor, turning to face him with one hand on the door handle, "I want to warn you of an observation I have made over the last twenty-four hours." Mike stared directly at him, wondering what on earth he had uncovered now, as he laid all his earlier thoughts to one side. "Linda doesn't appear to be reacting well to male doctors and the only nurse who has managed to break her silence is Penny Hattan. I can only assume that she has now lost all faith in men and sees them as executors of violent, sadistic acts of inconceivable punishment. Therefore, please keep to the far side of the room and don't attempt to encroach on her personal space. Penny Hatten is with her and will assist with any questions you may have, which may have to be filtered through her. I guess we will see how this pans out, as we go," he added, finally turning the handle on the door.

The room was bright and airy, and Mike felt relieved as he took his seat next to the doctor. He had felt hot and clammy and the weight of everything that he was carrying emotionally was starting to suffocate him. Linda was sitting on a stretcher bed facing the wall and Nurse Hatten was brushing her long blonde hair, talking to her in a soft voice. Linda had made no effort to turn to see who had entered the room and Mike found this really unsettling. After the doctor's update he had expected some form of frantic behaviour but she hadn't even flinched. Doctor Leeson gestured to Nurse Hattan that they were ready to be introduced, so that she could pave the way.

Nurse Hatten held Linda's hand as she informed her that the nice policeman who had rescued her would like to speak with her and ask her a few questions. Mike could see that Linda was trembling, as the nurse sat down next to her on the bed. "Would you be able to answer a few questions, Linda?" said the nurse as she stroked her brow. Linda nodded, as she held on tightly to her hand. "Would you like to turn and face him, so that you can see him?" the nurse asked in a soothing tone, while smiling. Linda shook her head, indicating that she wanted to face the wall and didn't want to speak face to face. A tear rolled down her cheek, splashing down onto the nurse's hand. Nurse Hatten reached for a tissue and gently wiped Linda's cheeks and Mike felt like his heart was breaking.

She looked so fragile and he suddenly felt like he didn't want to ask her anything. He didn't want to bring back the memories of being bound and gagged and held against her will by Joe Treville. He wanted to make it all go away, wipe out everything that had happened to her and give her the fresh start she deserved but instead he needed to ask her the most intimate invasive questions, bringing it to the fore so that she had to relive it all again. He took a deep breath wishing she would turn and face him, while wondering how she could remain so still knowing they were there. She was blocking out the vision of him, so that she could cope with the invasion. If she didn't have to see him then he wasn't really there. She was going to get through this. He felt like they were on the telephone, each in their own private space.

"Hello Linda," he said as the words slipped out of his mouth before he was ready. He swallowed, a lump forming in his throat almost making it impossible for him to say his next line. What could he say, where could he start? What could you possibly say to someone who had been imprisoned for almost half of their life, starved and neglected, someone who had managed to escape only to be hunted down by the son of her perpetrator and held against her will, once more imprisoned by a psychopath? 'How are you?' was definitely not going to be his next line.

He swallowed again in an effort to clear his throat and then stuttered his next few words. "Linda, I'm so very sorry that this has happened to you," he said, thinking how pathetic the words sounded after such a horrific ordeal. "Unfortunately we had Joe Treville down as a missing person under the pseudonym of Jason Topaz. His identity was only uncovered after we arrested his mother in connection with another case we were working on, which unexpectedly merged with this one." He paused, wondering how much information he should give her at this stage. She had the right to know everything that had materialised but how the hell could he explain after what she had been through.

"Linda, I don't know the full extent of what happened to you at your flat, I can only imagine the horrors that you were subjected to, but for now I would like to try and answer some questions that I think may be running through your mind." He had made the split decision to focus on the events leading up to her capture, as he suddenly realised that she would have very little understanding of what had transpired before her sickening and vile hostage-style torture. If he focused on everything that went before, he could build the picture for her, filling in the gaps, and hopefully give her some understanding of what had subsequently happened.

"Linda, your mind must be awash with questions, wondering how this preposterous situation took place and why it took place. You remember the night you reported your sister missing at Holden Police Station and the following morning I made the call to you informing you that we had located her and that she was already known to us under an assumed name? Sadly, it wasn't Rachel after all but was in fact your psychiatrist Julie Somers. Well, since that day we have uncovered the truth behind why Julie Somers was posing as Rachel and we also identified that the missing person case we were working on relating to Jason Topaz turned out to be Joe Treville, the son of Joseph Treville, your childhood captor. It's a lot to take in, Linda, but I am going to carefully explain to you what we have uncovered, so that you have an understanding of what led up to your capture.

"Joseph Treville Senior remarried several years after the loss of his first family in a traffic accident back in the seventies and had a son with his new wife, Diana. They named him Joseph after his father, which was quite a fashionable thing to do back then but he was referred to as Joe and they lived in California. When Joseph Treville senior died, his estate went to trial after the Gordon Square case and his family were financially ruined. According to his mother, Diana, Joe was a difficult child, didn't mix well with other children and was different from his peers growing up. As the years passed she noticed his fascination with his father's history and basically made it a case study. He had a dark side and became totally fixated with the Gordon Square case and it became an obsession. He also felt that he was robbed of his inheritance as the majority was paid out to you and Rachel as compensation to help rehabilitate you and cover the cost of ongoing psychiatric care.

"In his sick, twisted mind, he had decided that you were responsible for his financial loss but was also fascinated by your plight. Sadly, he had a taste for his father's darker side and wanted to continue to pursue his father's legacy of crimes through his own doing."

Linda sat staring at the wall listening intently. She made no effort to turn but she desperately wanted to know more. She blinked, wiping the tears from her eyes and then slowly turned to face Mike.

"Linda, Joe Treville has spent the last seven years following the rehabilitation of you and Rachel and has been carefully planning his revenge."

"I don't understand why he would hold us responsible," she suddenly blurted out. "Surely he knew the pain and suffering we went through during our captivity," she added, reaching for another tissue.

"He's a sick twisted individual with a dark psychotic mind," said Mike, "and sadly he has a really weird and deranged view of what transpired. He basically worships his father's crimes and wants to recreate them. He wanted to see his father's crimes first-hand through your eyes, I suspect," he said, wishing he had better news.

"Yes, I expect that's it," she suddenly announced. "He definitely wanted to see things from my perspective, as he asked me to describe things to him in excruciating detail, such as what Helena looked like and how she smelt and he wanted to know about Mary and whether I had met her. He really got off on it, receiving the information like a drug," she said, looking up towards the ceiling, as she recounted that horrendous afternoon.

"Sergeant, have you got him in custody?" she asked, looking up and facing him head on so her eyes bored into him. Mike swallowed, trying to clear his throat. He felt like he was choking and hated the fact that he had to inform her that Joe was still out there. It could be her undoing if she didn't feel safe.

"No," he said, looking down at the floor, feeling ashamed that they hadn't managed to do the one thing that would make her feel secure. "Linda, we do have an APB out on him, he won't get far but anything you could tell us that might lead to his arrest would be extremely helpful at this stage," he said, as he twisted his hands, aggravated by the fact that they hadn't managed to achieve this.

"And my sister, Sergeant?"

Mike shook his head. Again he had failed her. "Julie Somers is now being cared for by Doctor Gyllensvan," he informed her, hoping that at least she could see there was some progress amongst this hideous situation.

"I don't really understand her involvement and why she was posing as Rachel," she asked, thinking that she really couldn't get her head around this.

"Julie Somers became fixated with your case after spending several years working on your rehabilitation, especially that of Rachel. When Rachel was moved to Victoria's Retreat, she continued with her visits, I guess trying to unscramble Rachel's tortured soul. She became fixated with your sister's development, especially the plight that went before. She started to re-enact some of the horrors, stopped eating for several days at a time, her weight plummeting by at least five stone. I guess after working amongst such mania with some of the patients most severely affected by multiple personality disorder, her mind became unhinged and she developed schizophrenia, or should I say dissociative identity disorder, which it's now called and encompasses both conditions. In the end she thought she was Rachel," he said, trying to bring some sort of order and understanding to the case.

"Why did she call herself Emma and not Rachel?" Linda asked, turning back to face the wall.

"From what we understand from her psychiatrist, one of the domineering personality traits, known as Julie, tricked her into taking on this identity, so that she could move to a new town and carry out her fantasy lifestyle. Her identity disorder consisted of numerous personas made up from Rachel's and your own identities and imprisonment."

"Linda, Joe Treville misidentified Julie Somers, assuming her to be Rachel. Their identities fused somehow with her ongoing visits and he followed her to Holden. We believe that he still thinks that Julie Somers is Rachel."

"I see," said Linda, turning back round to face him. "I guess I was next on his list," she said, finally understanding why he had entered her world.

"We will find Rachel," Mike guaranteed, making a promise he wasn't sure he would be able to fulfil. "Our research suggests that she has been missing for quite some time but we are following up on all our leads," he reassured her.

"Sergeant, was Joe Treville responsible for burning down the Victoria's Retreat?" she suddenly asked, spinning around to face him.

"Yes," Mike confirmed. "Linda, is there anything you can tell us that might lead us to him?" he asked, desperately wanting to avoid any questions that might bring back horrific memories of that day.

"Sergeant, until that day I had no idea who he even was or where he had come from, let alone where he was heading but I do know I never want to be confronted by him again," she said, with absolute certainty. A tear rolled down her cheek, which she wiped away as though she was annoyed that it had interrupted her anger and then she turned to face the nurse.

"That will be it, gentleman, for today," Nurse Hatten advised, gesturing towards the door.

Mike rose to his feet alongside Doctor Leeson, who hadn't uttered one single word during the entire interview.

"Thank you," said Mike, nodding at Nurse Hatten. "And thank you, Linda, for agreeing to speak with me today."

Doctor Leeson closed the door, turning the handle firmly and led him back to his office where Paul was waiting.

"So how did it go?" Paul asked curiously, as they headed down the steps outside the front entrance of the hospital.

"She doesn't know anything, Paul, and to be honest why would she? I mean until that day she didn't even know he existed," he said, pulling at his hair.

"Did she elaborate on what happened that day?" Paul questioned, wondering how Mike had handled the interview.

"No, I steered clear of any invasive questions, following the doctor's orders, so I decided to fill in the gaps for her and explain who he was and why he was persecuting her and Rachel. It had occurred to me that she might have no fucking idea who he was."

"How did she handle it?" Paul questioned, thinking that that was probably the best way to approach it.

"Well, I got the impression she had worked out who he was by the questions he was asking her during her ordeal. He was asking her stuff like, 'what did Helena look like and how did she smell'. He even questioned her about Mary. She must have been absolutely petrified when she realised he was Joseph Treville's son, knowing that the nightmare was about to be commemorated like a re-enactment of the most unimaginable horrors known to her."

"We've got to find him, Paul, so that we can offer her some kind of hope for her future."

Two

Mel stared at the cabinet where the parole letter was wedged between two glasses and sighed. She had placed it there last week, removing it from its resting place three times to read it and then replacing it in the exact same spot. She couldn't quite work out why it needed to be there and why she didn't put it out of sight, so that she didn't have to keep being reminded of it every time she opened the cabinet to retrieve a glass. She just knew it needed to be there until she decided what she needed to do with her emotions. Her emotions seemed to be the only thing she had any type of control over. She had no control over the decision to release Niko on parole and no one would listen to her pleas to keep him behind bars.

Yes, she had filed for all the usual restraining orders but what use was a piece of paper to ward off a vicious rapist. She knew he would try to find her after losing seven years of his life behind bars. He hated all women and she suspected that she now stood alongside his mother who he despised with venom and held responsible for the death of his father. She rose to her feet and opened the cabinet door, retrieved the letter from its envelope and reread it for the fourth time.

Her victim liaison officer, Alison, had reassured her over and over that he had been GPS tagged and was on an extremely rigid curfew. He was also banned from entering certain surrounding towns, which in turn would shield her whereabouts and increase her anonymity. To her it all seemed pointless. To her, he should never have been released. She didn't care that he had to report in regularly and that his allocated offender manager would ensure he followed the conditions imposed or he would be recalled. Basically, he was out on licence. But he was still out and that sickened her. Eventually his GPS would be removed, it was only a matter of time. As far as she was concerned she was the one sentenced. Sentenced to never ever feeling safe again and always remembering what he did to her on that dreadful day. She wondered what he might look like now. Seven years was a long time to rot in a cell. She liked to think of him rotting and imagined him decaying beyond all recognition. Bits of him dropping off onto the floor, being squashed into the flooring by the other inmates as they strolled past. Yeah, she liked to think of him plastered across the flooring, unwanted and forgotten. Her sensible side obviously realised that this would not be the case and that he had probably spent the last seven years playing pool or table tennis with the other inmates and was highly likely to be in good health. He probably had an excellent diet and a reasonable amount of fresh air and exercise, striding around the yard where the prisoners were exercised, possibly playing football. No, he would be sitting on a wall, she decided, smoking a roll up, spitting on the floor, planning something evil, his revenge attack.

She wondered if he still had his jet black hair with his quiff. She guessed it was probably dyed in an effort to make him look Greek. Changing his name from Nicholas to Niko, all part of the charade. Perhaps he might even be grey by now. He would recognise her though, she figured, turning to look in the small mirror, resting on the breakfast bar that she had quickly done her makeup in that morning. She hadn't really changed outwardly but her insides were twisted in a knot that she just couldn't undo. Her thoughts then switched to the cabin where he had almost met his death, at the hands of Mike. He too wished Niko was dead but she truly didn't want it to be at Mike's peril. No, she wanted him to suffer for what he did to her that day, often thinking of ways she would like him to meet his comeuppance. One day she would get her retribution, she had promised herself that.

She rolled the letter up and popped it inside the vase on the kitchen window ledge. What was the point of seeing it every time she opened the cupboard, she reasoned. It wasn't going to change anything, it was only causing more anguish and anxiety, she decided. No, she needed to get a grip and concentrate on her family and her job. She had taken the day off to chill. The news of Niko's release had really taken its toll on her and she was finding it hard to concentrate, despite everything that needed to be done on the case she was working on. She stared at the vase with hatred and then likened the shape of it to that of an urn. Yeah she would leave him in there, she decided, she might even burn it.

She glanced at her watch and then stared around the room at all the jobs she had intended to do. The day had basically dissolved and very little had been achieved. She had lined up a list of simple chores to keep her mind off Niko but he just kept interfering with her thought process. "Damn," she yelled, jumping up from her seat, suddenly remembering that Jack was bringing Henry, his buddy from the playgroup back for tea. She set to work bringing his little arts and crafts table out to the centre of the kitchen diner and reached for his Play-Doh set. She tipped it out on the table and set it out ready for their return and then scrambled through the contents of the freezer in search of chicken nuggets or fish fingers. Phew, she had both, she sighed relieved that she didn't have to do any last-minute dashes to the corner store en route to Jack's nursery.

She quickly brushed her hair and tied it back in a ponytail and then looked around for her trainers. "Where the hell are they?" she yelled, suddenly feeling frustrated that Niko had cost her yet another afternoon of her life. She spied the tip of one poking out from under the sofa and then dropped to her knees to retrieve them. "I won't let you take up any more of my time," she yelled, pulling them on at record speed, addressing her anger at the urn. She grabbed her keys off the side and then headed out the front door.

She took a deep breath and exhaled, gripping the steering wheel like she was about to wrench it from its column and then turned to look over her shoulder before reversing off the driveway. She needed to stay focused on the good stuff she told herself and, right now, Jack and Henry needed her full attention for the rest of the afternoon.

She pulled up beside Henry's mum's white Mercedes in the little car park outside the nursery, giving her a cheery wave before climbing out of her car. "Hi Liz," she said, opening the passenger door and climbing in beside her new friend. Their friendship had been born out of Jack and Henry's union at nursery but they found that they had a lot in common and Mel really enjoyed her company. She liked the way Liz always had a cheery disposition and had something to say about all topics known to man and never had a bad word to say about anyone. She always saw the good in everything and was total heaven to be around and Mel knew that if there was anyone to cheer her up Liz was definitely the girl for the job.

"Hey, how are you doing?" said Liz, glancing at her watch and then scrambling through her bag for her ciggies. "Just enough time for a quick one," she said, opening the car door so that she could stand by its side while getting her nicotine fix.

"Yeah, not bad," said Mel, knowing she was lying but she really didn't want to burden Liz with her thoughts about Niko.

She hadn't really touched on the subject of her assault seven years ago, as it was something she was desperately trying to forget, although deep down she knew that that would be impossible. Still she didn't need to discuss it with everyone she met. It was a private matter and she had managed to keep it secret from everyone with the exception of her colleagues at Holden Police Station where she worked alongside her husband Mike and his partner Paul. She didn't want to be known as 'the woman that got raped', so whenever she went anywhere, stepped into a shop, or restaurant or Lord knows where else heads would turn. No, she wanted anonymity, she didn't want to be that person.

"Hey the door's opening," said Liz, stamping on her cigarette butt and throwing it inside the hedge. She watched Mrs East opening the nursery doors to let in the queue of parents, together with a sprinkling of grandmas that had formed outside. Mel climbed out of the passenger seat and closed the door so that Liz could lock it with her fob and then she strode towards the entrance with her arm interlocked with hers.

She smiled and her heart melted as she saw Jack come into view, behind a little girl with pigtails. He was holding Henry's hand, leading the way and looked chuffed to bits that his little friend was coming back to his house to play. Yeah, this was what she needed to concentrate on. This beautiful little boy that she had been blessed with. She was going to invest everything she had into being the best mum possible and that scumbag was not going to get a look in.

Mel watched on as Jack and Henry confidently retrieved their jackets from their coat hooks and then smiled as they haphazardly tried to put them on. They had been encouraged by Mrs East not to interfere and to let them tackle this task by themselves so that they would be equipped for the next stage of their schooling, but it was so hard not to intervene when they often set off with their coat on inside out with the label flapping or with a sleeve rolled up so tight they couldn't move one of their arms. They did look cute though, she figured, then noticing, as she looked down, that his trainers were on the wrong feet.

"Mummy, Mummy," Jack yelled, suddenly seeing his mum's face pop out from behind a woman with wrinkles. He pushed Henry forward so that he couldn't be missed and then reminded his mum that Henry was coming back to play, like she might have forgotten. Mel bent down to swap over his trainers, looking back over her shoulder to check that Mrs East was out of sight then whispered in his ear. She told him that she couldn't possibly forget two very special little boys, that she was going to make a very special tea for, while they played with the Play-Doh.

Yeah, she had a wonderful life with Mike and Jack. She had a great job she loved, albeit she would prefer to be out in the field working alongside Mike like the old days, instead of working as a desk-base constable at Holden but she still got to see some of the action and this little treasure that was now skipping along in front of her with his best buddy Henry needed to be her primary focus. "Yes, all eyes are on you, little fella," she said, swinging him around, as she swept him up to pop him into his car seat.

They arrived back at Westbury Fields ten minutes later and were soon engrossed in watching the boys make snakes out of the Play-Doh, each seeing who could make the longest one. "Coffee Liz?" she questioned, holding up the coffee pot, knowing full well that this was a silly question. Liz's main diet consisted of coffee, wine and cigarettes and she was always moving from one fad diet to another. Her weight was her only gripe in life, which really bothered her and Mel knew that her three vices were her way of keeping her focus away from the strongest vice of all, food. Liz made a lot of wrong food choices. Chips and doughnuts being her go-to favourites. Then she would worry herself to death after devouring three doughnuts on the trot and then another diet would start. She was pretty, auburn shoulder-length hair and had the most amazing green eyes that complemented her porcelain tones to perfection but her weight bothered her and she claimed she needed to lose three stone. But boy, apart from that she was the most fun person to be around and had a wicked sense of humour. Although Mel did wonder if it might be a front to cover how she was really feeling.

Mel switched on the oven, settling on fish fingers after a unanimous vote, and then decided to peel some potatoes to make some mash. "Heard from Rob?" Mel questioned, while hunting down the potato peeler from its hiding place in the kitchen drawer.

"Yeah, he called last night and should be home by the weekend," she said, a smile unfolding on her face.

"Hey that's great news," Mel said, knowing how desperate Liz was to get her man back safe and sound and in one piece. Being married to an army officer must be hell on earth and Mel had often wondered how her friend coped with not just the loneliness but the fear of him not coming home again ever. It was bad enough working as police officers and all the risks attached to that but at least she was by Mike's side daily. Yeah, she really did wonder how Liz managed to keep such a cheery disposition.

She tipped some peas into a saucepan and then wondered whether to offer Liz a doughnut. She had bought them fresh that morning on her way back from the nursery drop-off and they were now sitting in full view, right under Liz's nose. She knew she should have put them away earlier, knowing how Liz struggled with this area of her life but she had been so distracted with Niko she had completely forgotten about them. "See you've bought my favourites," Liz interjected, saving Mel from further deliberation.

Mel smiled, "Of course," she said, suddenly feeling really guilty as she handed the plate across to her friend.

Liz's spirits were now in an extremely heightened state of euphoria as she licked her lips, savouring every mouthful, as she tried to shield her treat from her son. "You having one?" Liz questioned, suddenly feeling conscious of over indulging yet again and as usual being the only one sitting with all the candy. Mel smiled knowing that a doughnut was the furthest thing from her mind and the thought of eating anything at the moment made her feel sick to the pit of her stomach but she picked one up knowing it was what her friend needed to see and took a big bite, making it look like she was relishing the moment.

The boys, by now, were running around in the garden and were racing Jack's cars back and forth on the patio squealing.

"Dinners almost ready, boys," Mel called from the kitchen, as she slid the fish fingers from the baking tray onto their plates. "Liz, will you just clear their little table for me as it's almost ready?" she asked, giving the boys a generous scoop of mash and a spoonful of peas each before carrying the plates over. Squeals of delight filled the house as they came rushing in to take their place at the table, each checking out the other one's plate to ensure they both had the same. She set a beaker of juice down on the table for each of them and then joined Liz on the sofa to continue their natter.

"Tell me more?" Mel requested, knowing that she would rather hear all about Rob than have to search for something else to talk about from her side of things, knowing that all she had to offer at the moment was Niko and that that was off limits.

"Well, he can't wait to get back, obviously," she said, suddenly looking all agush with excitement. "And," she said with a pause, grinning like a Cheshire cat, "this time he's staying for quite some time, possibly two months," she added, folding her arms as if to say that was the icing on her doughnut and nothing could top that.

"Oh that's brilliant news, Liz, I'm so pleased for you," Mel said, knowing that her friend had been so lonely and really needed the comfort of her man. Mel had never met Rob, as their friendship was too new but Mel could tell from the things Liz had told her that he was a great guy and she hoped that perhaps the four of them could hook up for drinks and get to know one another, as he sounded like someone Mike would get along with.

The afternoon passed quickly and it wasn't long before Mel watched on with her heart melting as Jack tried to help Henry into his trainers and assist with his jacket. They didn't really need a jacket this time of year, to be honest, as they were experiencing a really lovely May, masquerading as a balmy July, but it was hard to explain to the boys that they only needed their jackets when it was cold. They had been told that their new coat hooks at nursery were for their personal belongings such as coat, rucksack whatever they brought with them must be hung on their own personal hook identified by their sticker, and somehow this instruction had merged with 'you must hang your coat there' and if they must hang their coat there then they needed to have it with them at all times. Kids logic, I guess.

She watched on bemused by Jack's overly enthusiastic wave, which then made him topple backwards and then she scooped him up into a bear hug informing him that it was bath time and that Daddy would be home any moment. She blew a kiss to Liz, shouted "see you tomorrow" and then headed back indoors to deal with the little man in her life that was so important she could barely catch her breath at just how much love she felt for him. She then made a promise to herself that nothing was going to come between them and that she must carry on sensibly and try to block out the intrusion of Niko from her amazing life that she had built with Mike.

They made their way up the staircase singing "I'm a little tractor," when Mel heard the key turning in the lock. "We are up here," she yelled, ensuring that there was no doubt that they were home, despite her Golf being present on the driveway. "Just running Jack a bath," she added as if he wouldn't have guessed the obvious.

"Be up in a minute," he responded, striding into the breakfast diner and discarding his jacket over the back of the sofa. He reached into the cupboard and retrieved a glass and then selected a bottle of Merlot from the wine rack, without too much consideration. He just needed a drink, as it had been one hell of a day interviewing Linda and he was still on edge. He then turned and opened the cupboard again. It was gone, the parole letter was gone. He paused momentarily and then opened the cupboard to the right and then breathed a sigh of relief. She had finally moved it, after a week or so of haunting and now she had laid it to rest. He poured himself a glass and then put it down to one side.

"On my way up," he yelled, suddenly feeling just a little bit lighter that his wife may have decided to put the letter away, so that it didn't keep constantly reminding her every time she opened the cupboard. One step at a time, he decided, as he raced up the stairs. He knelt down beside the bath after giving Mel a peck on the cheek and then tickled Jack under the chin. "So how're my two favourite people doing this evening?" he said, deciding to perch on the toilet after all. He was feeling his age this evening and his knees couldn't handle the strain. "Well?" he said, waiting for one of them to launch into song.

"Henry came," said Jack, starting the evening chat off perfectly.

"Indeed he did," said Mel, really pleased at just how much Jack's speech had improved since he had been mixing with other children.

"We've had a very exciting afternoon, Daddy," Mel added, filling in for her son who was now trying to teach Dhillon the dinosaur how to swim.

"And how are you?" Mike asked, staring at his wife, hoping that her day off hadn't been spent dwelling on the past and that she had managed to relax and get some benefit from it.

"Yeah, not bad," said Mel, wanting to save anything deeper until she had settled Jack for the evening. "Let's get this little monkey into bed and you can tell me all about your day," she said, turning the tables so that she didn't have to make any more decisions today about how she was going to manage her emotions moving forward.

Mike watched on as Mel coxed Jack out from the bathtub with the promise of a dinosaur story before sleep time and then he made his way back down the staircase back to his wine.

"So how did your day go?" Mel asked, stepping off the bottom stair and noticing that Mike was already devouring his wine. He pointed to the glass that he had filled for her and then gestured for her to join him on the sofa. "Interviewed Linda today," said Mike, looking up at the ceiling wondering where to start.

"Oh my God, I forgot you were doing that today," said Mel, suddenly sharing the pain that she wasn't the only one suffering at the moment from this horrendous ordeal. "How's she doing?" Mel quizzed, her police officer inquisitiveness kicking in alongside her personal emotional attachment to the case.

"Well, after a brief meeting with Doctor Leeson it was agreed that one of us could interview her in a sensitive non-invasive manner. I obviously took rank over the decision and spent about fifteen minutes with her, together with her nurse and Doctor Leeson, of course."

He took another glug of his wine and placed the glass on the table, staring down at the floor. "It was so painful, Mel, it was gut-wrenchingly heartbreaking, watching her try to comprehend just what had happened to her. I was advised by the doctor, well instructed really, not to ask anything too sensitive and to be mindful of the fact that the observation team had noticed that she wasn't responding too well to male intervention. Doctor Leeson feels that this is indicative of the fact that both her predators, for want of a better expression, were male and he feels she has lost faith in that gender."

"Yeah, I get that," said Mel, "I mean when you think about it logically, she has led such a restricted life, imprisoned and then supervised in an institutional environment, she has had very little involvement with the outside world. Her father figure starved, neglected and basically tortured her and then she was held in a hostage-type situation by another male, yeah it's not really surprising at all. Did she have any information as to where Joe Treville might be heading?" she asked, reaching for her wine.

"No, she didn't even know who he was at first, until the realisation dawned on her with the questions he was asking?"

"Questions," Mel quizzed, wondering if Linda had been under some sort of interrogation during her ordeal.

"Yeah, from the brief conversation I had with Linda, she said he was asking all about Helena, how she dressed, what she looked like, even how she smelt. Apparently he appeared to be getting off on her telling him these facts which were genuine from the actual scene itself, like he was reliving it through her eyes. She didn't elaborate about all the questions but she did touch on the fact that he was also asking questions about Mary and whether she had met her. Basically this appears to be his thing, Mel, he is so besotted with this crime and wants to recreate parts of it for his own sick pleasure."

"Can you imagine for one second how she must have felt when she realised he was Joseph Treville's son," Mel said, standing up and walking over to the patio doors. She stood by the open doors staring up towards the sky. "By God she must have thought she was going to have to relive it all over again. She must have been paralysed with fear."

"Seems so desperately sad that after all her efforts to rehabilitate, her university course in psychology and her thirst for survival that this bastard may have undone much of what she has managed to achieve," Mel added.

"Yeah, but she's strong, I saw something today in her that tells me she will get through this. I could almost see the cogs turning in her mind as I was filling in the gaps for her. She was psychoanalysing the situation and I guess will now break the information down piece by piece and then use it to build a bridge back to normality."

Mel turned from the patio door and stared directly at her husband. "That's quite an analogy, Sergeant," she said teasing, thinking that Mike was getting really good at analysing situations and foreseeing possible outcomes.

"Ah, all part of the job," he said, resting his hands behind his head, realising that his wife was mocking him. "Can you bring in my next patient please, Nurse Brugge?"

Three

Mike stood staring at the two pictures of Joe Treville on the crime board, one completely unknown and the other posing as Jason Topaz. It was probably a cutting from another magazine, he decided, likening the circumstances to the portrait plot. Yeah, he was a bit of a master at assuming identities and had probably taken on another one now to avoid capture. His attention was then drawn to Rachel, wondering what she looked like now. Did the picture on the board resemble her, or has she disguised herself to prevent being found. I guess it would depend on which one of her multiple personalities was in charge, he decided. He sighed, took another swig of coffee and then headed back to his desk.

He looked across at Mel in the corner who was busy typing up case notes from audio and then spun round to stare out the window. How the fuck was he going to solve this, he pondered, wondering where Rachel had been for the last year or so and how she had managed to survive outside of her heavily supervised institution. Maybe she hadn't survived and that's why she hadn't been traced, Mike suddenly considered, wondering if they should be checking death records of unknown Does. Or maybe she had been picked up by some sleazy pimp who was selling her assets to other unsavoury characters. The image of her switching personalities during a session with a customer made him shudder, remembering vividly his car journey with Julie Somers to the hospital when she switched into her father and demanded that he stop the car. It was pretty terrifying and would be even more so with your pants down, he thought, conjuring up the image and thinking that they would be getting far more entertainment than they had paid for.

He seriously hoped that she had been taken in by someone kind and caring but then of course you would have to question her saviour's sanity as to why they hadn't made it known to officials, unless they too had a secret to hide. His mind switched from one possible conclusion to another, none of which held any sort of reputable standing. Where would a young, pretty, unstable girl go and who would be looking out for her or exploiting her. He turned to face his desk with the word 'exploiting' running through his mind and then switched on his laptop to run through missing persons again. He looked at his watch and then at Paul's empty chair, wondering where he was. It was almost 10am and Paul was never late, you could set your watch by him.

He turned his attention back to the missing persons, when he heard Paul greeting Bridget at the front desk with a cheery good morning.

"Morning," Mike said, looking up and adjusting his glasses, so they were now on the tip of his nose. "You're late on parade this morning."

"Yeah, I stopped by the old bakery to pick up some breakfast and got chatting with Fred and Sheila," he said, sitting down and checking that everything was straight on his desk. He fiddled with his pen collection and then passed over a box, informing Mike that Sheila had sent him and Mel their favourite cakes, along with her best wishes. Mike opened the box enthusiastically and yelled across to Mel to come and claim her coconut slice, before he ate it and then proceeded to stuff his face with his iced bun, saving the cherry till last.

"So what kept you?" he quizzed, noticing that he had nothing else with him and had presumably eaten his breakfast at the bakery.

"Well, I stopped by for a bacon buttie and a coffee," he said, as usual setting the scene.

"Yeah, we get that bit," said Mike, winking at Mel, as she opened the box and took up residence on the edge of Dave's desk opposite. "And?" he said, wishing he hadn't interrupted, as he knew that Paul would start again.

"Well I stopped off for a bacon buttie and got chatting with Sheila, just about Jane and letting her know about our good fortune with the pregnancy, etc. and one thing led to another, so I had a second coffee and we moved on to how the bakery business was going and how everything was for us here at Holden." Mike took a deep breath, looking across at Mel and then took another bite of his bun. "Well she mentioned that a few weeks ago they were giving the bakery a deep clean, out of hours and were still at it around nine o'clock in the evening when they spotted a girl standing across the road outside the gates to The Sanctuary. Apparently she stood there for ages, just staring into space and then suddenly she turned and headed over to the bakery. Sheila said that while they were actually closed to the public, as the lights were on, the young girl assumed they were open and Sheila didn't have the heart to turn her away. She said the girl looked terrible, so skinny, dark circles under her eyes and looked like a lost soul.

"Well you know what Sheila's like, she always wants to mother everyone, so she put the kettle on and ushered her over to a table. She was there for hours and devoured a whole rice pudding, intended for at least six, Sheila claims, anyway," he said, opening the lid of the cake box to retrieve his scone, "she said the girl claimed to have been a resident at The Sanctuary when she was a small girl."

"Was it Emma?" said Mel, "or should I say Julie Somers," she corrected.

"Yeah, almost certainly," said Paul. "But that's where it got interesting. Sheila said the girl really started to open up but the stories she regaled were rather jumbled and confusing and Sheila felt that they were made up of several people's experiences. Sheila said it got really weird and then she realised that the girl was extremely troubled and was displaying signs of some kind of identity disorder, as she kept switching until Fred decided enough was enough and chose to shut up shop."

"They didn't just show her out onto the street, did they?" Mel questioned, thinking it was most unlike them.

"No, they called her a cab and paid the driver to take her home."

"Did Sheila tell you anything that might give us a clue as to where Rachel might be now?" Mel continued, thinking this was also unlikely if she believed her to be Rachel.

"Not really, but she did mention Danbury Manor and Casio Grange, so my guess is that Julie Somers did visit Rachel in both of those institutions, continuing with her ongoing rehabilitation sessions, so right now Julie Somers is possibly the only person who may know of her next move," said Paul, licking the jam and cream from his lips.

"Well up until that point, anyway," said Mike, wondering where on their flimsy timeline Rachel fell off the grid. "Julie was well on the way to unravelling at that stage but she's probably the best lead we have, albeit completely unreliable and distorted. Lord only knows where her mind is now and what Doctor Gyllensvan has managed to unravel. I'm tempted to pay him a visit," said Mike, looking across at Paul. "Regardless of what state her mind is in, we may be able to extract something from her conscious or even subconscious memory that might just be enough of a lead to…" he stopped wondering where it might lead, then followed it with, "probably down the wrong garden path but right now it's all we've got," he said, standing up to shake the crumbs from his jeans.

He took a deep breath and exhaled as he retook his seat. He was really beginning to hate his visits to the doctor. He had totally lost faith in his ability to analyse in an intelligible, lucid, reliable and convincing manner and now anything he delivered was subject to question, making him the least reliable source of information. However, there were still moments of sanity amongst some really debatable statements. The fact he had felt that Julie Somers would be fit to retake her seat at the table, so to speak, after a short break, was undeniably a major flaw in his credibility and suggested that he too needed time away from all the madness that surrounded him. This totally validated why all counsellors need regular counselling themselves. He wondered how long it had been since the doctor had last been evaluated. Far too long he concluded.

"I guess turning up without an appointment would be foolish," he deliberated, reaching for his phone and scrolling for the doctor's number, but he really needed to speak with Julie Somers, as she seemed to be key to Rachel's timeline from one institution to another.

The doctor answered on the second ring, indicating to Mike that he wasn't busy with a patient and was probably behind his desk contemplating how soon he could get Julie back to work. "Good morning, Doctor Gyllensvan," said Mike, psyching himself up like he was about to go into battle. "It's DS Mike Brugge here," he said, standing up to distance himself from his desk. Mel watched on as Mike pleaded his case to the doctor, reinforcing how crucial Julie was to finding Rachel and then was completely startled when Mike returned to his desk informing them both that they could interview her immediately.

"Yeah he put up no defence argument at all," said Mike, completely perplexed at how easy it was to manipulate the doctor without any effort whatsoever.

"Yeah, I expect he's already left the building," said Paul, sarcastically, in total agreement of Mike's interpretation of the doctor's state of mind.

They rose to their feet in unison, eager to get to Julie as quickly as possible before the doctor came to his senses, and headed for the door. Mel smiled at Mike as she watched him leave and then sat down in Paul's seat. No matter how much effort she put into trying to adjust to her new desk-based role she just couldn't get used to being left behind. She turned and looked over at her desk, piled high with case notes, sighed and returned to her post.

"Do you think she's in one of the observation rooms?" said Paul, remembering the video footage from the Gordon Square case.

"Almost certainly," said Mike, recalling very vividly episodes of mania he had experienced in her company. "Or at least I hope the doctor has stretched his resources to accommodate a full evaluation and treatment plan for her but to be honest nothing would surprise me," said Mike, selecting reverse gear and backing out of his parking space. He looked across at Inspector Dhillon's empty bay pondering his return. He should have been back in the office today but as yet there was no word from him. He would look into that later.

The journey to the hospital was uneventful, albeit the traffic frustratingly slow and Mike made the decision, after circling the car park three times, to park in the bay clearly designated to Nurse Julie Somers. "Well she won't be needing it now will she?" he said, watching Paul raise his eyebrows. Paul nodded, agreeing with his logic, as they made their way swiftly inside and waited for the lift. Mike pressed the green button again, agitated by the wait and then exhaled as the lift doors opened. Paul selected the third floor and then waited again as the lift doors closed. Mike felt like he was in a time capsule every time he entered that goddam lift, reliving the same scene over and over. He hoped today they would get some answers.

"Good afternoon," said Mike, as they approached the desk clerk. "Detective Sergeant Brugge and Detective Sergeant Osman to see Doctor Gyllensvan," he said, looking over at the doctor's door.

"Ah yes," said the clerk, "he said he was expecting you." She pressed one of the digits on her desk phone and the doctor's door promptly opened. "Good to see you," said the doctor, reaching out to shake Mike's hand. He extended his greeting to Paul and ushered them inside, closing the door firmly, dimming the room to its usual amber glow.

"And what can I do for you gentleman this morning?" he said, retaking his seat behind his desk, while gesturing for them to take a chair. He spoke as if he had no idea why they might be there, confirming to Mike that the doctor was losing his grip, and then looked across at Paul with an expression that said it all, when the doctor suddenly recalled that they were there regarding Julie Somers.

"Ah yes, Julie Somers," he said, shuffling his papers into a neat pile and then clasping his hands in front of him. "Julie has regained some clearer thought processes, since her return," he said, smiling as if her recovery was close to the finishing line. "She is responding well to treatment and has now undergone seventy-two hours of constant monitoring by a locum psychiatrist in one of our suites." He adjusted his spectacles on the bridge of his nose, while he confirmed from the paperwork in front of him the psychiatrist's name. "Doctor Armstrong," he stated, placing the paperwork down on his desk. "Yes, Doctor Armstrong is assisting me with my patient load, until such time that…" he paused, before continuing his statement and then cleared his throat, as if pondering his next few words carefully, "until a more permanent solution can be found," he finally stated.

Mike looked at Paul, knowing that the doctor was referring to Julie Somers, implying that the permanent solution would, in fact, be her after a period of recuperation.

"What has been ascertained during her seventy-two hours of observation?" said Mike, growing exasperated at the doctor's lack of acknowledgement to the seriousness of Julie Somers' breakdown.

Doctor Gyllensvan removed his spectacles and placed them on the desk in front of him and then stared directly at Mike. "Doctor Armstrong has seen no evidence of dissociative identity disorder over the period of observation so far. He clearly states in his notes that Julie has pleaded with him over and over that she would like to return to her duties and has appeared lucid and consistent with her request."

"But surely you have briefed Doctor Armstrong that she took on the identity of one of her patients and some of her alter egos," said Mike, shaking his head in disbelief.

"Of course, Sergeant, but the findings so far suggest that this episode has since past. I have worked amongst the most severely ill and, with the correct medication, normal function can be resumed if the balance of meds is reached to its optimum."

"I hope you're not suggesting that Julie will be returning to her post," said Paul, confirming to Mike that he too thought the doctor's analysis of the situation was absurd.

"Not at all," said Doctor Gyllensvan. "Julie Somers has a long way to go, I'm simply reporting that we appear to have been successful in our choice of medication, which is proving effective and has enabled us to see considerable improvement in her demeanour. We will of course keep her under observation for some time yet but I feel it would be detrimental to her recovery for her to remain in the observation suite. She has nursed hundreds of patients in that environment and it is causing some confusion with her rehabilitation, Sergeant."

"Yeah, I get that," said Mike, tuning into the fact that Julie Somers' environment was going to be paramount to her wellbeing and putting her in a fish-bowl environment, which she associates with the most severely deranged patients would be counterproductive.

"Where is she now?" Mike asked, eager to get some time with her before the doctor changed course.

"She has been moved on to Newton Ward, adjacent to Isaac Ward, where we monitor patients in a more relaxed manner. This ward is for the less severely ill patients that are deemed fit to mingle without risk of harm both to themselves or others. They are still under camera surveillance, Sergeant, after all this is an institution for troubled minds, and for some, rehabilitation is unreachable."

"Shall we go?" Mike announced suddenly, like he had had enough of the explanations, which to him were like idle banter.

Mike and Paul rose to their feet eager to move things on and followed the doctor out into the corridor towards the lift. They descended five floors in the lift and then took a further flight of stairs until they were three levels below ground. They followed the doctor down a short corridor, which opened up into a wide open space with the all too familiar nurses station, which was occupied by a guard who appeared to be standing to attention as they entered.

Mike and Paul were requested by the guard to sign in and were then instructed to remove any items from their pockets that could be reinvented as a weapon and to relinquish their mobile phones. "Follow me, gentleman," the doctor said, as he entered a pin code into the door reader, followed by his finger print. Paul had never been down inside the observation suite before and was beginning to feel a bit clammy and apprehensive. Mike was really curious to see inside Newton Ward, only having experienced the internal workings of Isaac Ward before and was right on the doctor's heels. As the double doors opened they stepped inside a small vestibule, which appeared to be a holding chamber while one door closed and the other opened. "Each door is controlled by a separate pin," the doctor explained, emphasising that this was an extra safety precaution as the patients were free to roam.

They followed the doctor down a long corridor and then turned right at the end. This corridor led to an open-plan area, which appeared to be some sort of recreation lounge, as patients were taking part in entertainment pursuits such as dominos, chess, and a group had gathered around a table at the far end playing cards. There was a woman in a long white nightgown singing at the piano, much to the annoyance of a chap who was sitting wearing a red bow tie reading a newspaper.

"Will you shut up," he pleaded, over and over until finally moving to the opposite side of the room. "Bloody racket," he yelled over at her when the distance he had chosen had proved to be insufficient. Mike's eyes were darting everywhere as a man approached him with his nose twitching in a sniffing motion, claiming he could smell trouble.

"Go and sit down, Sidney," instructed the doctor, who appeared to be totally at ease with such an intrusion.

"But I can smell trouble," he said, continuing to sniff all around Mike.

"Trouble," said a petite woman, tuning into the conversation from a nearby armchair. "What sort of trouble?" she said, standing up to get a better view, while sweeping her rainbow coloured scarf around her beehive hairstyle. "Who are you and what do you want?" she questioned, while shuffling forward, as if she was in charge of the recreation room.

"Margaret, return to your seat please," commanded a familiar voice from the sidelines. Mike stepped back totally dumbfounded as Julie Somers stepped forward to shake his hand. "Good to see you, Sergeant," she offered, removing her hand from his grip and wiping it down the front of her apron. "And to what do we owe the pleasure?" she asked, as if she had no idea whatsoever why he was there. She glanced across at Paul momentarily with a puzzled look like she was trying to place him and then refocused her gaze back on Mike.

Mike stumbled back totally blown away by the fact that Julie looked like she was actually working there as opposed to a patient undergoing psychiatric treatment. "Well we have come to see you, actually," said Mike, wondering how to now approach his inquiry. "Is there somewhere we could have a chat?" he said, addressing this question towards Doctor Gyllensvan.

"This way," instructed Julie, as if she was still working by the doctor's side. Doctor Gyllensvan indicated that they should follow as Julie led them into a small meeting room adjacent to the lounge area.

Julie took her seat at the table, like she was in the think tank, assessing a patient's care after observational therapy, and clasped her hands ready to receive new information. Mike noticed that while her hair was still dyed black, she had styled it in her usual bun and was wearing her glasses. "Can we have some coffee in here please?" she shouted into thin air, like she was talking to an orderly.

Mike looked across at Doctor Gyllensvan for guidance, wondering how to bring control to the conversation when quite clearly Julie Somers was now running the show.

"Julie," said Doctor Gyllensvan, taking his place at the table, "Sergeant Brugge and his colleague would like to have a chat with you about what happened during your sabbatical," he said, leading the conversation so that they could get back on course.

"My sabbatical?" Julie quizzed, in a fashion that suggested that she had no idea that she had even been on leave.

"Yes, your sabbatical," said Mike, deciding to take control of the conversation from there. "Your time at Arlington Terrace, which you leased for a period of three months from Hunters Estates," he clarified. Julie sat there staring into space, like she was receiving this information for the very first time and was trying to recall the information from the archives of her mind. Mike looked across at Paul, wondering what his take was on this and whether he felt Julie was being genuine. They had both seen so many different sides to her and she was clearly unhinged but there was something about the glint in her eye that suggested to him that she knew exactly what he was talking about.

"Julie, we would like to talk to you about the psychotherapy sessions you undertook with Rachel Blossom and her ongoing care," said Paul, deciding to go in for the kill. If she was in psychiatric mode then he would treat her in that capacity, extracting what information they needed, after all this was the purpose of their visit. "We understand that after the fire at Victoria's Retreat you continued to treat Rachel in other institutions such as Danbury Manor and Casio Grange," he continued. "Do you have any idea where Rachel might be now?" he said, deciding to get straight to the point. Julie started fidgeting in her seat, obviously caught off guard, and the name Rachel had sparked off some kind of reaction, as she started to twitch, making sharp jerking motions.

"Is there anything you can tell us to help us locate her?" said Mike, thinking Paul had been very clever, striking from this angle. If they could keep her train of thought focused on the professional side of her career, away from the Arlington Terrace saga then they might stand half a chance of getting a lead on her whereabouts.

"Julie, do you know if Rachel was transferred to another institution after Danbury Manor?" he asked, thinking by the level of swaying that they might be losing her in her professional capacity and that she was about to switch.

"Only that she was interested in alternative care," said Julie, suddenly having a moment of lucidness.

"Define 'alternative care'," said Mike, wondering if this was something that Danbury Manor was offering or was this outsourced.

"What is alternative care Julie?" said Paul, kneeling down in front of her, in an attempt to extract as much as possible before she bailed out.

"It's a therapy not recognised by the medical profession," said Julie, starting to tremble.

"Is this something you have sampled and executed?" said Paul, wondering if she had dabbled in this territory.

A tear rolled down her cheek, as she shook her head. "No," she whispered.

"Who was providing this service, Julie?" said Paul, rising up from his kneeling position. "Julie, who was treating Rachel, when you last saw her?" he asked, rephrasing his question. "Julie, stay with me," Paul pleaded, as she swayed back and forth. "Who was treating Rachel, Julie? She must have confided in you," he said, knowing that this question would go unanswered.

"That's enough, gentleman," Doctor Gyllensvan interjected. "Please remember that Julie is a patient here and anything she might offer may not even be creditable," he suggested.

"Yes, we are aware of that, Doctor," said Mike, frustrated at being shut down when they were finally getting somewhere. "But we also have a young, extremely vulnerable young girl out there somewhere and we have a duty to find her."

"My father is treating her," Julie suddenly interjected, swaying violently back and forth. Her eyes opened wide and her head rolled back and then there he was, as if he was taking over her body for his own use like a possession. Her mouth opened and a deep, male voice spoke yelling, "Get out of here," a voice Mike had heard before, as he shuddered from the memory. Julie spun around to face Mike and then she spat in his face, while growling like a wild dog. "Get out of here," the voice repeated.

Mike wiped his face with the back of his hand, quickly siezing the moment. "Where is Rachel Blossom?" he repeated. "Did you take her to Arlington Terrace? Did you take her to Arlington Terrace?" he repeated, as Doctor Gyllensvan ushered them out of the room.

Mike spun round and took one last look at Julie, before the door was closed. A sick smile had unfolded on her face as she mouthed the words "You will never know."

"Doctor, you can't end the session there," Mike pleaded, "she knows something, I'm sure she knows something," he repeated, as the doctor encouraged them along the corridor. Mike turned around as he heard a commotion from the direction they were being edged away from. Julie was being forcefully encouraged to leave the room by two orderlies who seemed to be losing the battle, as she escaped their grasp and was now heading full throttle towards them. Julie flung herself at Mike like a possessed animal and then sunk her teeth into his shoulder.

"For fuck's sake," yelled Mike, trying to force her head back and then swiping her left cheek, so she would release her jaw. She now had a firm grip of his left arm and Mike could feel her fingernails sinking deep into his skin, as she switched to a razer technique using them like a sharp blade running the entire length of his arm. Paul and one of the orderlies grabbed her arms and held them firmly round her back as she continued to spit and snarl, blood and froth dripping from her mouth. Doctor Gyllensvan opened another door and was actively pushing Paul and Mike towards it, giving them instructions to shut the door, while he attempted to coax Julie with the assistance of the orderlies back down the corridor.

"Jesus, Mike, that's a serious bite mark you got there mate. You can see most of her teeth marks along the top edge. Fuck, she's even left a tooth behind," he added, assessing the gaping wound as blood gushed all over the back of his polo shirt.

"Yeah, not a day to be wearing white," he stuttered, suddenly feeling a little light headed, while holding his hand over the wound to stem the flow of blood. He suddenly felt the tooth between his fingers that Julie had left embedded in his shoulder, realising that the swipe he had administered in an attempt to free himself from her attack had knocked it out.

Paul opened the door and peered out into the corridor observing the trail of bloody footprints that were indicating the route that Julie had been taken. He could hear voices, one of which was the doctor's, and then he came back into view carrying a small first aid box.

"I think we are going to be needing more than a Band-Aid, doc," said Paul, thinking the doctor had underestimated the severity of the attack.

"Yes, I realise that, Sergeant, it's merely to cover the wound temporarily," he said, in an angry tone, while unravelling a gauze bandage. He took in the sight of the vicious wounds to Mike's left arm and shook his head unable to believe that he had just witnessed his long-serving colleague behave in such a demented manner.

"I suggest you go via A & E," he advised, "before heading back, as that will need stitches," he proposed.

"Doctor, we will need to see her again," Mike said, wincing as the doctor packed the wound on his shoulder. "There is the possibility that Julie was treating Rachel with this alternative therapy that she describes, switching between her multiple personality disorder under the guise of her father and may not even realise this. Doctor, she behaved like she was possessed by the devil," he added feeling really unnerved by the viciousness of her attack.

"Well, I don't think we are quite ready for an exorcism yet," said the doctor, flippantly.

Paul raised his eyebrows and turned his gaze away from Mike's, biting his tongue. Then unable to keep his thoughts to himself, he turned to the doctor with a look of disbelief.

"Doctor Gyllensvan, while I am aware that you have seen this type of mania many times before, I am sure that even you found that episode extremely upsetting, seeing as Julie is not only a colleague but, I am also sure that after all these years, a good friend. It also demonstrates first-hand that she does suffer from dissociative identity disorder, as described to you, even if Doctor Armstrong hasn't seen any evidence of this during his seventy-two hour observation tests. It also highlights that seventy-two hours was totally insufficient to make a valid evaluation of her mental state," said Paul, slapping all his thoughts right across the doctor's face, like a wake up call.

“I’m not suggesting that Julie hasn’t suffered a breakdown, I’m merely trying to establish the severity,” he said angrily, closing his first aid case firmly and grasping it in his hand like it was a vicious dog on a lead. He then waved it in the air with an exasperated gasp turning back round to reopen the door. “Good day, gentlemen.”

“We will need to interview her again, Doctor,” Mike called out, as the door slammed shut.

Four

"He's a fucking lunatic," said Mike, as they walked out of the A & E department after receiving nine stitches to his left shoulder. "I mean, I realise he hasn't actually set her to work as such but she's walking around Newton Ward under that illusion, so Lord knows what that might bring," he said, clicking the key fob and staring at Julie Somers name plate on the wall adjacent to her parking space.

"Yeah, I think there's a fine line between sanity and madness and I think he's dangling right on the end of it," said Paul, climbing into Mike's van. "And she definitely knows something about Rachel's whereabouts but the scary thing is, there is the possibility that only one of her personalities is controlling this aspect and if the drugs suppress this identity then she could be lost indefinitely."

Mike looked across at Paul, he selected reverse gear as he absorbed what Paul was saying.

"If we don't question Julie now, Mike, sooner rather than later I mean, then the drugs could alter her mindset and the father's alter ego could melt into oblivion," he said, meaning the clock was ticking.

"Yes, I guess it's only a matter of time before the doctor gets lucky with the cocktail and selects the correct combination of drugs," said Mike, thinking that if Julie's sanity is restored then they would be unable to question any other identities. "But it's fucking insane that we are contemplating interviewing someone that doesn't actually exist," he said, suddenly questioning their logic.

"Well he does exist, Mike. He has a presence within Julie's mind and is controlling her body for his own use, so technically as deranged as this is we need to speak to him again. We need to agitate her, so that he comes to the fore and takes over, like he did this afternoon."

"Well, I think we'd best leave that to the professionals," said Mike, thinking that the questioning should perhaps be done while she is under a degree of sedation. "I've seen first-hand what happens even in a controlled environment, it's scary as hell and extremely dangerous," he said, selecting first gear, while recalling some historical hypnosis sessions with the Gordon case. "I do agree that we need to access her multiple personality mindset again but I don't think it's wise to tackle it the way we did today knowing what we know now," he added quickly. "But the thought of doing it under the control of Doctor Gyllensvan makes my blood boil," he said, feeling the rise of pressure flood through him as he tightened his grip on the steering wheel. "Perhaps we can speak with the locum," he suggested, trying to recall the guy's name. "Armstrong wasn't it?" he queried, nudging Paul after a period of silence in an effort to bring him back from wherever his mind had slipped off to.

"Sorry, yeah Armstrong," Paul said, giving himself a shake, while jotting the name down in his notepad for later. He popped it back in his inside pocket and clicked his pen to the closed position. "Do you think they will tighten the parameters surrounding her care now?" said Paul, thinking that after today's performance she should be in an isolation cell.

"Yeah I guess there will have to be some adjustment to her 'free to roam pass'," Mike considered, thinking that it would be unethical for her to remain in Newton Ward after today, "but Isaac Ward is not an option either according to the doc's reasoning, so she may get transferred to another unit."

"Well, so long as it's not Danbury Manor or Casio Grange," said Paul with a smirk, thinking they could be adding another deranged missing person into the mix.

"Hell no," said Mike, "they don't even know how many patients they have, let alone where they are and right now my faith in the medical profession is dwindling somewhat," he said, pulling into his usual parking space back at the station.

"Have you heard anything from Dhillon?" Mike quizzed, noticing that the inspector's parking space was still empty.

"Nope," said Paul, climbing out the passenger side and lighting up a ciggie.

"Maybe I got it wrong," said Mike, "but could have sworn he was due back this morning."

He headed towards the station steps, leaving Paul to finish his smoke and sighed as he entered reception. He nodded at Bridget and then fumbled in his jeans pockets for some change and then selected his usual from the vending machine.

"What happened to you?" Bridget quizzed, taking in the sight of his blood-stained polo shirt and bandage poking out from his collar.

"Don't ask," he said, giving the sugar button a frustrated treble push, before accepting the fact that the machine was devoid of any sugar. He sighed again and headed to his desk, hoping that there might be a random sugar sachet somewhere in his desk drawer.

He pulled out his chair and sat down, placing his head in his hands. What a fucking morning he thought before looking over at his wife. Mel was busy typing up notes from audio and was completely oblivious that Mike had returned from his visit to the doctor. He waited a full five minutes while sipping his coffee before alerting her to his arrival, so that he could gather his thoughts and put them into some sort of order. He couldn't quite get his head around it himself, let alone have to explain to Mel that they needed to interview the father figure inside Julie Somers' twisted mind.

"Hey," he said, walking over to her desk in the far corner of the room, alerting her to his presence.

"What the hell happened to you?" Mel asked, jumping up from her desk and then jolting as the earphones were ripped from her ears. "Jesus, Mike, what the hell happened?" she repeated, taking in the full extent of his injuries.

"Julie Somers' father," said Mike, shaking his head in disbelief as to what he was saying. "During the interview she became agitated and her father figure took over her being like a possession. That's the best way I can describe it to you really, he literally took over her body using it like his own. She leapt at me frothing at the mouth like a wild dog and took a bite out of my shoulder," he said, wincing from the memory.

"Is she in the observation suite?" Mel asked, thinking she should be in a straight jacket in an asylum. "She's in the ward opposite, assigned to less severely ill patients, deemed fit to mix with other patients," said Mike raising his eyebrows, as he perched on the edge of her desk. "You should have seen her, Mel. She was wondering about the place like she was still nursing. She ushered us into one of the side rooms like she was about to undertake some sort of consultation. Doctor Gyllensvan explained that during the seventy-two hours she had been monitored, the locum doctor who had been accessing her had seen no sign of any identity disorder and basically told us that Julie was begging to return to her normal duties."

"Surely that's not going to happen?" said Mel, taking in the sight of the deep razor scratches to his right arm.

"Well, until that point, I think the doctor, although he disputed it, might possibly have considered it. He did cover this off by saying that with the right mix of medication normal function could return but I don't think, even as insane as he appears, that he would have put her to work right away."

"Well not for a couple of weeks anyway," said Paul striding into the room and giving his take on the morning's misgivings. "As horrible as that was to witness, and painful," he said, addressing that part towards Mike, "it definitely brought home to the doctor that his long-serving colleague was suffering more than just a minor breakdown. Problem is, when you work amongst it all the time, it doesn't seem so extreme. He's used to witnessing mania every single day."

"That's why it's unethical to treat people you know," said Mike, clenching his fists and then clicking his knuckles. "Usually because of the emotional attachment but, in this case, it's even closer to home because she's also being treated in an environment she associates with her usual work practices and the two are merging."

"Well I'm not sure we have any influence over where she is treated," said Mel, turning to her computer to check where the line is drawn, "but what we can do is raise our concerns with the Care Quality Commission or CQC as they are commonly known."

"Yes, but that's more for if you feel someone is being neglected or not receiving the care and compassion required for their rehabilitation. Doctor Gyllensvan is not neglecting her, he just can't see the wood for the trees," said Mike, as he paced back and forth.

"Yeah, I get that but if we start making waves, it will start an investigation and usually while things are being investigated the party involved will more than likely be moved."

"Look, you said yourself, Doctor Gyllensvan's judgement is in question. He's way overstretched, exhausted by all the mania, understaffed and he's not making rational decisions. I remember you once said to me that you felt compelled not to leave her in that goddamn institution. Well, here's our chance to get her moved."

Mike sat motionless staring at his wife, knowing she was making sense. He then turned to Paul, "What's the alternative, perform a seance," he said sarcastically, thinking about Paul's earlier suggestion about interviewing the father figure inside Julie's troubled mind, which in comparison seemed totally barking. "Right, let's bullet point what needs to be done here in a logical, police procedural way," Mike stated, taking charge of where things were heading. "Firstly, Mel, can you research a little more about what can be done where there are concerns about the wellbeing of a psychiatric patient. Especially the concerns of us, as police officers, working on a case she is related to and whether that will influence things."

"Paul, let's head to Danbury Manor to interview the staff there. Let's do some digging as to what this alternative therapy stuff is all about and whether they were aware that a patient in their care was being treated by such methods by an independent psychiatrist. They may have no knowledge of the methods that Julie was applying or they may be in it up to their necks, treating patients with methods not recognised by the medical profession, as Julie indicated during her outburst."

"Mel, apply for a search warrant. We will dig as far as we can with immediate effect but my guess is we are going to have to have all the papers in place for this one."

Mel watched her husband do what he did best, take charge, and then turned her attention to the job at hand. Then Mike went to check he had another shirt to change into from his locker.

"So what direction are we heading?" Mike asked as he selected reverse gear and swung his car around.

"Westbury Fields," said Paul, looking up from his iPhone. "It's the manor house at the back of the parkland."

"Jeez, I wondered whether that was some sort of care home," said Mike, thinking about all the times he had pondered the possibilities while out walking in the park at the rear of their new home. It had obviously, at some stage, been a stately home or someone's luxury retreat but so many of them have been turned into care homes of sorts.

"Yeah, I've passed it a number of times," said Paul, releasing the window to let in some air. "It's so goddamn hot," he said, waving his hands.

"It won't last," said Mike, "you know what the British weather is like."

"It has its own little chapel inside the grounds down by the foot of the stream," Paul continued, thinking how idyllic it looked. "It will be interesting to take a look inside."

They pulled up outside a large white electric gate twenty minutes later, wondering if they should have called ahead for an appointment, and waited for someone to respond to the intercom system. Mike buzzed again, irritated by the wait before the sleek white gate slid to one side. "Not very secure," said Mike, as they proceeded without so much as a single word.

"Well they've probably got their hands full," said Paul, imagining all sorts of mayhem going on behind closed doors.

They pulled into one of the parking spaces designated as visitor parking and stared at the small stately home. Mike's thoughts were immediately transported back to their visits to The Sanctuary children's home, seven years prior, and he half expected a stern Miss Rosenburg to step onto the front porch at any moment.

The grounds were devoid of any activity, which seemed rather bizarre to Mike considering it was a beautiful May afternoon and the weather had been exceptionally hot for the time of year.

"You would have thought some of the residents would be outside," said Paul, echoing Mike's thoughts as he turned and stared at the perfectly manicured lawns.

"Perhaps they're out the back," said Mike, thinking that surely there would be the sound of voices but it was eerily quiet.

They strolled along the footpath towards the front porch, the only sound to be heard was the gravel crunching underfoot. Mike climbed the two steps leading to the entrance and rang the bell, curious that still no one had even bothered to acknowledge their arrival, despite opening the gates. He turned to face Paul who was staring up at one of the upstairs sash windows and sounded the bell again. "Someone's coming," he said, listening to the faint footsteps in the distance that were getting louder and closer. The door was opened by a nun who rushed past them on the steps, indicating that she was far too late to stop for anything, as she rushed down the gravel drive towards the front gate without uttering a single word.

"Obviously taken the vow of silence," Paul said, with a smirk.

"I guess she wasn't opening the door to us then," said Mike, taking a peek around the door to see if anyone else was around. "Hello," he called, as he made the decision to step into the hallway. "Hello," he repeated, "is anyone there?" His attention was drawn to the top of the staircase where he could see a white haired woman in a blue nighty kneeling down peering through the slats of the banister rail. She immediately rose to her feet and scurried away like a frightened rabbit.

"Well I guess we are going to be showing ourselves around," said Mike, making the decision to move further inside. The hallway looked extremely sterile with grey tiled floors and white walls, devoid of any pictures. The only feature was the large oak grandfather clock positioned against the wall at the foot of the staircase.

"Not what I was expecting," said Paul stepping inside and taking in the sight of the vast empty entrance hall.

"You would have thought there would be some sort of reception desk or a sign pointing to an office at the very least," said Mike, wondering which way to go. "I was about to say they must be all out on a day trip but I hardly think that's the case here," he said, mocking.

"Yeah, that would be a bit of an ordeal, to take an entire home of mentally disturbed adults to the zoo," said Paul, laughing.

He suddenly stood to attention when he realised that his mocking comment had just been overheard by another nun in a grey habit, stepping out from a doorway that they had just passed. "Can I help you, gentleman?" she asked, making her presence known.

"Ah yes, thank you," said Mike, retrieving his badge from his jeans pocket and holding it out in front of her. "DS Mike Brugge and this is DS Paul Osman, from Holden CID," he said, moving closer so that she could confirm their identity.

"And what can I do for you today?" she asked, gesturing for them to follow her back into the room that she had just exited. This room was furnished quite lavishly in comparison, with a deep-pile beige carpet underfoot and oil paintings gracing the walls. "Please sit down," she instructed, pointing to the two chairs positioned in front of her desk. Mike sat down to order, feeling really uncomfortable. Why was it that whenever they were interviewing someone in charge of a home, they were made to feel that they were standing in front of a headmistress. She closed the door and took her seat behind the desk. "So what brings you to Danbury Manor today," she asked, rephrasing her earlier question.

"We are trying to locate a young girl called Rachel Blossom, who we understand used to reside here as a patient," said Mike, adjusting his seating position. "We are trying to put together a timeline of her whereabouts and Danbury Manor appears to be the last place she resided before falling off the grid."

"Falling off the grid, DS Brugge, is an odd term to use, implying that we may have lost one of our patients," she said sternly.

"Well, we can't account for her whereabouts, Sister…" said Mike, pausing, hoping that the sister would grace them with her name. He glanced down at the name plate at the front of her desk and continued undeterred. "Sister Bernadette, can you confirm the name of the home that Rachel Blossom was transferred to please?" he requested, thinking logically that this question should be easy to answer if everything here was above board, as she implied.

Sister Bernadette rose from behind her desk and headed across to the mahogany filing cabinet positioned in the far corner of the room. Paul looked at Mike and shrugged, thinking it all seemed rather bizarre.

"Very quiet here today, Sister," Mike continued, glancing at his watch, wondering if perhaps the residents were dining.

"Yes, the residents have a nap at this time of day, after lunch," she added, snapping the filing cabinet drawer shut in a sharp agitated gesture.

"Rather civil," said Paul, thinking that a siesta of sorts would be extremely hard to orchestrate with a home filled with troubled minds and was more associated with a nursing home for the elderly.

"Indeed," said Sister Bernadette, returning to her desk and replacing her spectacles on the bridge of her nose.

She opened the file and shuffled a few papers and read what appeared to be the entire case file before looking up towards them. "Ah yes, Rachel Blossom is one of our success stories," she said, a smile unfolding across her stern face. "She was transferred here from Casio Grange in Shelton, for assisted living," she said, closing the file. "Rachel was integrated back into society after a six month stay with us, which proved very successful indeed," she said, rising to her feet.

Sister Bernadette reopened the door, as if bringing the meeting to a close and gesturing for them to leave.

"Not so fast, Sister," said Mike, standing up so he could talk at eye level. "We have first-hand knowledge that Rachel suffered from dissociative identity disorder on an extremely severe level. Not so long back she was deemed to be almost untreatable and was one level away from being committed indefinitely. Who sanctioned her release and when you state 'integrated back into society', I assume you mean some sort of monitored assisted living where there will be a case file of her progress?"

"DS Brugge, Rachel Blossom is no longer one of our patients and I am unable to furnish you with any more details due to patient confidentiality clauses that I am bound by," she said, indicating once more the direction to which they should be heading.

"Sister Bernadette, we have a duty of care towards Rachel and by all sense and purposes you are withholding vital information as to her whereabouts and can be held accountable, I assure you," he said, retaking his seat, as if to say this meeting will now continue and will end when I say it will end.

"Now let's start again in an amicable way that will serve the best purpose to all involved," said Mike, gesturing that she should retake her seat behind her desk. "Sister, we have made an application for a warrant to search your files and all corners of this home, until we are satisfied that Rachel received adequate treatment and that there is a process in place for her ongoing care. So we can deal with this now in a civil, less invasive voluntary fashion, or we can come back with a warrant and a full team of investigators. The choice is yours."

Paul crossed his legs and adjusted the collar of his shirt, slightly loosening his tie. He could see that Mike meant business and that they were there for the duration and that they weren't going to be dismissed until he was damn well ready. "Sister Bernadette, surely there can't be anything unethical about providing two police officers investigating a missing persons enquiry with the next steps of a former patient," said Paul, uncrossing his legs and settling into his chair.

"Who evaluated her prior to her release?" said Mike, wanting to know who was responsible for this ludicrous decision. Sister Bernadette looked lost for words as she reopened the case file and reshuffled the papers until they were spread halfway across her desk. "I take it that she was receiving ongoing treatment for her dissociative identity disorder?" said Mike, looking across at Paul.

"Sister Bernadette, we know that there was fragmented medical history attached to her case notes, due to the fire at her former home Victoria's Retreat but surely she was re-evaluated by a psychiatrist?" said Paul, feeling Mike's agitation at basically getting nowhere.

"We have the information compiled at Casio Grange, her former residence," Sister Bernadette confirmed. "Her evaluation was undertaken by Nurse Ivy Mason, who had been assigned as her case worker and nurse. It clearly states here," she said, tapping her finger on the paper, "that Rachel was always bright, cheerful and co-operative during her stay there. She joined in with communal activities organised by the home and was always compliant and there was never, at any time during her stay, evidence of an identity disorder, no sign of irrational behaviour and, in Nurse Ivy Masons closing statement, which would be her personal view, concluded that her breakdown was possibly brought on by a childhood tragic event to which they have no information. It would appear that Rachel had buried this part of her life, Sergeant." She looked up, closing her file, feeling that she had given an adequate account and clasped her hands on top of the file.

Mike looked over at Paul, unable to comprehend that Rachel or one of her multiple personalities had obviously managed to convince their psychiatrist that they were of sound mind, which influenced her transfer. "Who was Rachel's care worker here?" said Mike, thinking that Rachel had been very cunning to pull this off.

"Nurse Lewis, Karen Lewis," she confirmed giving her full name.

"And Nurse Lewis treated Rachel for how long exactly?" said Paul, wondering what sort of medical training these nuns had for this type of illness.

"Six months, approximately, but it became blatantly obvious that after a six month period here, together with her time at Casio Grange, which together served as over a year of constant monitoring and evaluation, that Miss Blossom's troubles were behind her," she said, looking confident that they had dealt with her stay both professionally and sympathetically. "We were,

Sergeant, unable to establish what went before and by that I mean her childhood troubles but this is quite common and some patients never revisit their earlier years, choosing to bury them indefinitely but this is no reason to withhold their freedom. What we do here is care for moderately troubled minds before assisting them back into society. This is not a prison, so please forgive me if we end this interview now but I have patients to attend to," she said, standing up and opening the door once more.

"Sister Bernadette, I realise that you are extremely busy here," said Mike, thinking that it didn't sound like they had any patients here at all, unless they were all heavily sedated, "but either you can provide Rachel Blossom's next steps or we will need to interview Karen Lewis," he said firmly. "I feel certain that you didn't just open the front door and wave her off."

"Sergeant Brugge, I detect a note of sarcasm in your voice, which is totally unfounded. Karen Lewis has worked here for over ten years and I trust her judgement impeccably. She will at this time of day be on her break but please wait here and I will see what I can muster," she said, closing the door and heading off down the corridor.

"Surely to God the file must contain information about her next steps," said Mike standing up and walking across to the window. He looked out across the vast lawns to the rear of the building and then turned to face her desk, staring at the file. He reached out towards it knowing that he was on dodgy ground without a warrant and then withdrew his hand, as the door handle turned.

"Please retake your seat, Sergeant," Sister Bernadette instructed, pausing momentarily before returning the file to the cabinet. She looked somewhat irritated that she had left it unattended and then turned her attention back to introducing Karen Lewis to the proceedings.

"Sergeant, this is Karen Lewis, Rachel's care worker and nurse," she said addressing Mike, as if Paul was no longer in the room. "Nurse Lewis, this is Sergeant Brugge from Holden CID." She looked briefly across at Paul and then decided to add, "and his colleague. They are here regarding Rachel Blossom's stay with us, as sadly she appears to have gone missing."

"Good afternoon Nurse Lewis," said Mike reaching out to shake her hand and then stepping back so Paul could do the same. "We are sorry to interrupt your day here but, as explained, we are trying to locate Rachel and you are the only lead we have," he said, retaking his seat.

Karen Lewis was the total opposite to what Mike was expecting. Firstly, she wasn't a nun, which really surprised Mike, as he had taken it as a foregone conclusion that the home was run by a convent team. She was much younger than expected too. Mike tried to gauge her age, settling on late twenties, in contrast to Sister Bernadette who looked positively ancient. She looked extremely timid and her slight frame and the trembling hand she had extended out to Mike did nothing to change his opinion – that she looked as nervous as hell. Her short mousy hair and oversized glasses hid most of her tiny face and she was dressed in a navy, nurses uniform with a bronze name badge.

Nurse Lewis stood to the side of them and Mike thought that she probably didn't even make five feet, as she stood there in her black lace-up brogues. She certainly didn't look strong enough to deal with trouble minded adults and looked more fitting as a nursery nurse at kindergarten.

"We would like to ask you about Rachel's next steps," said Mike, wondering if the sister would invite her to sit down or was she going to simply leave her standing like she had been summoned to trial. "What is the procedure for reintroducing patients back into society independently?" Mike continued, wanting to know what processes were in place.

"Do they go into shared accommodation that has a degree of supervisory care?" Paul interjected, reminding Sister Bernadette that he was still in the room.

"Yes," said Nurse Lewis, nervously. "She moved into Keeper's Lodge, which comprises twelve units, partly self-contained but also have a degree of shared facilities, such as the communal kitchen and lounge, so that the occupants don't feel isolated and can make friends. There is a caretaker or warden, for want of a better description, who resides on-site and each patient is monitored by their assigned nurse on a weekly basis, until such time that they are deemed fit for independent living."

"And how is this independent living achieved?" Mike asked, wondering how this could be financed.

"Well, we assist them with sourcing employment, Sergeant," said Nurse Lewis in a slightly louder voice, indicating that there was more to her demeanour than at first perceived. "Our duty of care goes beyond these four walls, right up until we are satisfied that they have everything required both financially, emotionally and mentally to carry on with their lives independently."

"So there will be a detailed timeline of Rachel's ongoing movements?" Paul quizzed, wondering why on earth Sister Bernadette had kept this under wraps.

"We do have a partial timeline, Sergeant, but Rachel was extremely independent by the end of her time with us and moved out of Keeper's Lodge without notice. At this stage of their care if there are no obvious signs of decline in a former patient's health, no concerns of self-harm, etc. then we can be relinquished of responsibility and basically she was signed off."

"And at this stage of her care, did you not think that this was a possible sign that all was not well?" Mike asked, thinking that surely to disappear into thin air was not demonstrating stable thinking.

"This is an extremely grey area, Sergeant. I was on leave attending to a personal family crisis and was away from my duties for a three month period. Her temporary care worker became unwell and a series of locum care workers were assigned. Sadly her absence was not picked up until my return."

"Was this matter reported to the police?" Paul asked, standing up momentarily before retaking his seat. He crossed his legs and tried to get comfortable on a chair that felt as hard as a church pew and then asked the question again. "Was this matter reported?" he quizzed, wondering why they were both slow to respond.

"Sergeant, we took the approach that, as there was no evidence whatsoever that Rachel's mental state had declined, we signed her off our books," Nurse Lewis confirmed.

"A little unethical, wouldn't you say, Sister?" said Mike, turning to face her, realising exactly why she had been coy at providing any further information of Rachel's next steps.

"A rather big failing, I would say," said Paul, deciding to stand after all. Signing off a young girl in your care without even knowing if she was safe and well, who had a history of mental health issues. Not exactly outstanding CQC," he added, remembering Mel's comment from earlier.

"Sergeant, Rachel at no time during her care here demonstrated any type of identity disorder that you describe, neither was there any reference to such in her transfer notes. We based our care, and that of her ongoing care, on the information we had to hand. Now, if you will excuse us, we have important work to do here that requires our full attention," she said, reopening the door.

"Before we leave here today, Sister, I have one last question for you. Did a Nurse Julie Somers visit Rachel during her stay here?" Mike asked curiously. He found it odd that if Julie Somers had been continuing with her treatment then why did they have no history on what went before.

"Julie Somers? I've never heard of a Julie Somers, Inspector. What practice was she associated with?"

"She was Rachel's psychiatrist dating back to the start of her rehabilitation. She was based at Holden City General within their psychiatric unit. Our records imply that Nurse Somers continued her sessions with Rachel up until her sabbatical," said Mike.

"Well, I can assure you, Inspector, she did not visit this institution. If she had then I'm sure our records would not have been so fragmented."

Mike nodded, looking across at Paul.

"Did Rachel have any other visitors during her time here?" Paul suddenly interjected, wondering if anyone else had influenced her disappearance.

"None whatsoever, Inspector. Our records indicate that Rachel had no family. There is some reference to a sister but I have no information on her or whether this information is factual. Sadly, Rachel was alone in the world and she offered no information to indicate otherwise," answered Sister Bernadette.

"I see," said Paul, looking across at Karen Lewis.

"Miss Lewis, during your sessions with Rachel, did she mention any names to you of associates, such as someone we knew she held dear to her heart called Helena? Or was there any mention of a Linda or perhaps a Roberta or an Anika?" Paul quizzed, feeling it extremely strange that if they were holding any type of psychiatric sessions with Rachel, these names most definitely would have come up.

"I'm sorry, Inspector, but we had very little to go when she came to us from Casio Grange, but what I can say is that Rachel was extremely private and not very forthcoming with any history. Basically she seemed to have buried her past completely."

"Sadly, Nurse Lewis, Rachel Blossom's identity disorder appears to have outwitted you all and her former institution. She has managed to manipulate all the nursing staff that attended her into thinking that she is of sound mind. Frighteningly, it is possible that her most dangerous and domineering personality ego is the dominant one, and this will most likely lead to disaster."

"Why are you so certain, Inspector, that we have been outwitted and that she is a danger?"

"Nurse Lewis, with the utmost respect to you, Rachel had the most severe level of dissociative identity disorder, deemed untreatable, and yet she is now wandering around in the community unsupervised. I think that speaks for itself."

Paul looked across at Mike and shook his head and then stared up at the ceiling.

"Sister, we will require the address of Keeper's Lodge and please do expect to hear from us again," said Mike, finally bringing a close to the meeting, through sheer frustration.

Sister Bernadette nodded to Nurse Lewis. "Give them what they need and show them out please," she said, in a voice that firmly suggested that the show was over. She closed the door with a loud bang and headed off down the corridor.

Five

Mel sat staring at her computer until the writing blurred into a haze and then decided to shut up shop. She closed her laptop and pulled at the lead of her headphones allowing them to drop onto her desk. She just couldn't concentrate any longer. She was desperate to know how Mike and Paul were getting on at Danbury Manor and it was almost time to pick up Jack from nursery.

She would just have to wait until later to hear all the news but if she was honest she was stalling on going home. She just didn't want to be alone in the house with Jack, as Niko's release was beginning to unnerve her more than she would like to admit. Perhaps she could take Jack out to tea this evening, she considered, and then dismissed it as ludicrous. What was she going to do, take him out for a burger every evening and wander around the shops until Mike got home? No, she had to trust in the system. Niko was out on licence, GPS tagged and if he was to cross the line the police would know in seconds.

She looked across at the station clock and sighed. Come on get it together, girl, she said to herself, as she reached down for her handbag, wedged under her desk. It's time to switch into mummy mode and there's a gorgeous little boy waiting for you, she reconfirmed, as the thought of Jack's smiling face suddenly came into vision. She gave herself a shake as she rummaged for her keys and then decided on a quick pee, before departure.

Jack was helping Henry into his jacket as Mel walked into the classroom. She smiled as Henry then tried to help Jack with his zip. They were so cute with one another always helping the other achieve. "Hi Mel," said Liz, strolling into the classroom with a beam that lit up her whole face, "and how are my two favourite boys this afternoon? she said, addressing Jack and Henry with a big sweeping hug. Jack giggled and then decided to hide behind his mum's legs, popping back out every few seconds to check Henry was still there.

"Hi Liz, you look extra cheerful, if that's possible," Mel added, smiling up at her friend.

"Rob's home tonight, so I'm in a bit of a rush," she said, looking over her shoulder to check Miss East was out of sight before zipping up Henry's Jacket. She then giggled at the sight of both little boys standing there zipped up in their jackets like it was a winter's day. "We really are going to have to work on this jacket thing aren't we?" she said, looking at Henry's red face. "You're going to boil in the jacket!" She smiled at Mel, "I will attempt to entice him out of it before popping him into the car," she added, before turning to leave with a wave.

"Bye Jack," said Henry, waving frantically at his best friend.

Jack waved back enthusiastically and then rushed over to the window to watch him walk across the car park. He then observed the fact that his mummy was removing his jacket. "Mummy, take off," Jack suddenly announced, pulling at the zip of his jacket and jumping up and down.

Mel smiled knowing that he wanted it removed to be like Henry and assisted him out of his jacket. "Come on, little fella, let's get you home."

She pulled into the drive ten minutes later and attempted to unload a very noisy little boy onto the lawn. "I want Dhillon," he squealed, as Mel tried to release him from his car seat, enabling him to race up the driveway at record speed. She watched on bemused as Jack swept Dhillon the dinosaur from the sofa and started flying him around the room like an aeroplane and then pulled the patio doors to one side. She toppled slightly dodging out of Jack's way as he wriggled through her legs with his small cars, tipping them one by one over the ledge of the door and onto the patio slabs. "Boy you are a very busy little bee this afternoon," she said, smiling watching him switch between pursuits seamlessly.

It was a gorgeous afternoon and the sun was now high in the sky making their tiny garden feel like a godsend. Mel felt so blessed that they now had a grown up house with a garden for Jack to enjoy as she moved outside to watch Jack play. She sat down at the garden table directly outside the patio door and held her face up into the sunshine, enjoying the feel of the rays against her skin. She closed her eyes and then opened them quickly as she realised that the garden gate was slightly ajar. Weird she thought, standing up quickly to secure the bolt. They always kept it firmly locked to keep Jack safe and it was never ever open as it was a strict rule they had applied between them. She suddenly felt unnerved wondering if someone had been in the garden and then pondered if they had remembered to lock the patio door before heading out that morning. They were always in such a rush and now she couldn't remember if she had just unlocked it subconsciously before sliding the door to one side and going into the garden.

She tried to retrace her steps, trying to recall her actions, but seriously couldn't. She must have just unlocked it, she decided. They were police officers after all, she said, thinking that dementia was well and truly setting in. Nope she was sure she locked it this morning before heading out. Perhaps Mike forgot to lock the gate when he put the bin out earlier.

She headed back inside and contemplated what to make for Jack's tea, before settling on cheesy pasta. She put a cup of pasta on to boil and then stared at the newly named urn on the window ledge. "You are not going to haunt me," she suddenly shouted, making Jack look up from his game. Jack looked back down at his cars, wondering why his mum had suddenly called out and then he decided to ask for juice.

"Mummy, juice please," he said, standing up and walking across to her to pull at the leg of her trousers.

Mel tipped some apple juice into his beaker and handed it to him, while giving his forehead a gentle stroke and smiling at his cheeky little grin. "Your tea is almost ready," she said, dragging his little table out to the centre of the room and placing his chair into the correct position. "Do you want your hippo DVD on?" she asked, knowing that was his usual favourite to watch while eating. Jack nodded, moving his car collection up onto his table and started whizzing them off one by one onto the floor.

Mel grated some cheese and melted it into the freshly cooked pasta and then topped it with some sliced cherry tomatoes and cucumber pre-empting Jack's next request. He loved cherry tomatoes and saw them as a treat and Mel encouraged this knowing that in time this treat would be replaced by sweets. She knelt down next to him, as she placed the plate of food down onto his little table and then stared back across at the urn.

She had to get the thought of that evil man out of her mind. He was now invading her cherished time with her son, stealing precious moments and he had already had enough of her life, he wasn't getting any more.

Mike arrived home in time to read Jack a story after bath time and assisted with the bedtime routine. "What a day," he recalled to Mel, as they made their way back downstairs to the kitchen diner.

"You're telling me," said Mel, interested to know what had happened at Danbury Manor but also to find out whether Mike had forgotten to lock the garden gate. "Mike, when you put the bin out this morning, can you remember pulling the bolt across the gate? Only it was open when we came in this afternoon."

"I'm sure I did," he said, recalling the events from that morning.

"Yes definitely," he confirmed, while opening the fridge to see what he could nibble on. "I remember thinking how stiff the bolt was," he said confidently.

"Well it was open, Mike, and the gate was slightly ajar when we stepped out into the garden this afternoon.

"Odd," he said, hoping that he wasn't recalling information from the previous day.

He knew what Mel was thinking and tried to back track from being overly confident. "Actually, I think I may be recalling the stiff bolt from the other day," he said, not wanting to alarm his wife to the fact that they might have had an intruder. He knew for certain that she would assume it to be Niko and she was already on edge. "I will make sure I'm more diligent," he said, trying to reassure his wife that it was him.

Mel breathed a sigh of relief and then followed it with the fact that he needed to be more careful for Jack's safety and wellbeing. Mike closed the fridge door and turned towards the kitchen sink, staring out across at the gate. He was certain he had locked it that morning but there was no way he was going to alarm his wife, not with Niko being out on licence, she was nervous enough as it was. "How's your bite wound?" Mel queried, noticing traces of blood had seeped through the swab plaster.

"Sore," said Mike, wincing from the memory.

"Your arm doesn't look too clever, either," she added, thinking they needed to keep a close check on it as the scratches looked weepy.

"So what happened at Danbury Manor?" Mel quizzed, eager to hear all about what Mike had unearthed.

"Well you're not going to believe where Danbury Manor is," said Mike, now opening the freezer, wondering what on earth they were going to eat for dinner.

"Go on," said Mel, knowing that she wasn't likely to get much information if she didn't sort out his rumbling belly.

"You know the small stately home at the back of Westbury Fields Park, well that's it."

"You're kidding," said Mel, moving Mike to one side, so she could retrieve the cod from the second shelf, before switching on the oven.

"Cod, chips and peas." she announced, holding up the oven chips to confirm to Mike that she was on this.

"No, I'm not kidding, and what's more it's run by nuns," he said, closing the cutlery drawer and praying that they had remembered to put the dishwasher on last night.

"Nuns!" said Mel, watching Mike lay the table with cutlery direct from the dishwasher. She tossed some chips, together with the cod onto a baking tray and popped them in the oven and sat down on the sofa. "So it's a convent style psychiatric home run by nuns," said Mel, conjuring up some vivid childhood memories from the strict convent school she attended as a small child. She had hated it there, as the nuns were so strict that she cried every single morning until her mother gave way and transferred her to the local state run school.

She sat motionless, with her thoughts now on her late parents who died not long after in a car crash, leaving Mel and her brother Pete without a single relative, orphans of the state. "Not so sure I like the idea of nuns running a home for people with troubled minds," she said, bringing her thoughts back on track. "You need plenty of patience and from my memory the sister I knew used to have me quaking in my boots."

"Well, I'm sure they're not all like that," said Mike, tipping some frozen peas into a pot. "Anyway, Sister Bernadette was in fact quite a stern character, not giving much away, which made the interview quite a challenge. She was so dismissive, giving us minimal information and basically showing us the door. However, with the threat of a warrant and a thorough search of the home by a team of investigators, we finally got to speak with Rachel's care worker, a nurse called Karen Lewis. Funny little thing she was, timid and mouse-like but I suspect she was a bit of a whippet underneath. You always have to watch the little one's," he said, giving Mel a nudge.

Mel laughed at Mike's interpretation and then pushed for further information. "So what did she tell you?" Mel quizzed, thinking that Mike was getting more and more like Paul, never getting to the point without setting the scene.

"Well, it would appear that Rachel or one of her other alter egos managed to manipulate and convince the medical team that she was of sound mind. They had no previous notes to work with and based their care on the evidence provided by Casio Grange. Apparently there was nothing to suggest that Rachel was suffering from a mental disorder, so they were treating her for mild depression. Their evaluation was made up from the six months she lived at Casio Grange, together with the six months at Danbury Manor. Rachel managed to keep the charade going and was finally transferred to a place called Keeper's Lodge. From what Nurse Lewis described it is some sort of halfway house, where they live in partly self-contained accommodation but with some shared facilities, with a warden on-site.

"Karen Lewis explained that the patients receive assistance with finding employment so that they can eventually live independently."

"So where is she working then, I assume they provided this information?" said Mel, thinking that this was way too easy and that if Rachel had been found Mike would have been shouting this from the rooftops, as soon as he came through the front door.

"Well that's where she fell off the grid. Apparently checked out without notice while Nurse Lewis was on leave. A series of temporary locum nurses lost sight of this and it wasn't brought to light for a further three months."

"So did the home simply write her off then?" Mel asked, giving the chips a shuffle, before returning them to the oven.

"Yes, I guess they decided they had played their part in her rehabilitation and basically heard no alarm bells and simply closed the case."

"Do you know when that was exactly?" said Mel, reaching into the cupboard to retrieve the ketchup and salt.

"Best part of a year from the timeline described," said Mike, opening the oven again to check if his dinner was ever going to be served. Mel passed him the oven gloves and then placed two plates on the table. She watched as Mike tipped the contents of the baking tray onto the plates and then spooned some peas onto each.

"What about Julie Somers' visits, Mike? I just don't get how this could have happened. Surely her notes would have been cross referenced with theirs and the gaps filled. Especially in light of the fact that they had nothing to work with."

"Apparently they've never heard of Julie Somers," said Mike, his thoughts now turning to Casio Grange. "But I don't get it, we know she continued her visits. That was Julie Somers' downfall, what tipped her over the edge."

"Well my guess is Casio Grange is either as far as she got or something is very very wrong here. So what's your next step then, Keeper's Lodge?" said Mel, wondering where this lodge place was.

"Yep, going there with Paul first thing," he said, tucking into his dinner enthusiastically.

"Where is it?" said Mel, thinking she had never heard of it before.

"On the outskirts of Ramblers Hill," said Mike, reaching for the ketchup. "In the middle of nowhere."

"Sounds a bit creepy to me," said Mel, conjuring up the image of a houseful of moderately rehabilitated individuals stuck out in the middle of nowhere.

"Yeah you wouldn't want to be knocking on that house for assistance in the middle of the night if you ran out of petrol," said Mike, laughing, making Mel shiver.

"Have you called ahead or are you going to take them by surprise?" Mel quizzed, wondering what angle he was taking.

"Nope, we are going to turn up unannounced," he said, wondering what tomorrow would bring. "Definitely needs to be in daylight hours," said Mike, adding another layer of creepiness to his story while teasing Mel.

"Probably best to wait until the fog has lifted, at least," said Mel, joining in with his sinister account of Keeper's Lodge, sitting up high on the hill in the middle of the night surrounded by mystery and intrigue.

"Yeah does make you look at it in that light, doesn't it," he said, suddenly feeling quite spooked himself.

"Odd name, isn't it?" said Mel, "makes you think it's somewhere you can never leave," she added, shivering all of a sudden.

"Well it does now that you've dressed it up that way," said Mike, wondering if he now fancied going there in the morning. "Perhaps I'll sign it over to Jim and Dave," he said, giving her another nudge.

"Yeah like that's going to happen," said Mel, laughing again, knowing full well that Mike wouldn't be able to let go of the reins on this one.

She turned and looked out of the patio doors again, across at the gate. "You know, I'm not totally convinced we locked the patio door this morning either," said Mel, changing the subject back to the possible intruder topic.

"What makes you think that?" said Mike, licking his lips and rubbing his stomach with contentment.

"Because I remember sliding the door to one side and walking out but I don't remember releasing the latch," she said, trying to recall her steps.

"You probably just did it subconsciously," said Mike, standing up to load the dishwasher. "Hey," he said, turning around to give his wife a reassuring cuddle, "don't go getting all paranoid, sweetheart, or you'll drive yourself…" he stopped and considered his next words.

"Insane?" said Mel laughing again, finishing his sentence. "Well don't go treading on eggshells around me then. I'm not ready to join the nuns just yet," she said, thinking that she just heard Jack stir. "I'll go," she said, tossing the tea towel onto the side before heading up to the third level of their three-storey townhouse.

Mike turned and looked at the gate again through the window. He was damn sure he had locked it securely that morning because he had really struggled with the bolt. Tomorrow he would try to remember to fit a second one further down with a key, he decided.

Six

Mike looked across at Inspector Dhillon's empty office, baffled. Where was he? He was certain he was due back yesterday but he didn't show, neither did Karen his PA.

Inspector Dhillon was always punctual and hated lateness or non-attendance with a vengeance, and they had all experienced his legendary grillings at one point or another. He had spent the last month in the Caribbean, which again was most unlike him, to take leave for more than a week at a time.

The usual bustling office was exceptionally quiet this morning and with the absence of Billy and Ben, who retired two weeks earlier, things didn't feel the same.

"Morning," said Tina, strolling into the office without her usual cheery smile. She headed straight to Karen's desk and opened her top drawer and gave it a rummage.

"Morning, Tina," said Mike, bemused by this detour. "How's things?" Mike questioned, as she removed something small from the drawer and then moved across to her own desk.

"Not good," she said, slipping what now appeared to be a USB into her laptop.

"Have you heard from Dhillon?" said Mike, feeling compelled to get some sort of answer to this mystery.

"Yes, Karen called me last night around midnight. He's been taken unwell and was transferred to Holden City Hospital around seven yesterday evening."

"Transferred?" Mike queried, thinking it sounded like he had been moved from another hospital. He stood up and walked across to her desk. "What's going on Tina, spill? When did he return from the Caribbean?"

"Karen called last night to explain Inspector Dhillon's absence and hers. He's unwell and has been for sometime apparently. Karen said his health had been deteriorating slowly over a period of years and the stress of the job was a contributory factor. He was advised by his GP to take time out, hence the holiday but ten days into it, he collapsed. Some sort of thoracic aneurysm, which she described as fatty deposits blocking some of the arteries in his chest."

"A heart attack?" Mike questioned, sitting down in Karen's chair opposite. "Well she described it as a bulge or swelling for want of a better description in one of the arteries passing through his chest. I guess it cuts off the blood supply but I don't really know to be honest."

"Do they have it under control?" said Mike, trying to digest the information. "He's undergoing surgery this morning," said Tina, "so we will know more later but I expect it will be a long wait."

"For fuck's sake," said Mike, standing up. He had worked with Inspector Dhillon for over sixteen years and he never knew he had any type of adverse medical history or heart issues.

He slowly walked back to his desk and then turned to Tina. "What about his family, Tina? How's Sarah holding up, and the kids? They must be a mess. Jesus, Katie's only three," said Mike, thinking how the unexpected pregnancy had surprised them all a few years back and Sarah had described it as her menopause baby.

"In shock, obviously, but we are just going to have to wait this one out, Mike, before we know anything else. He should be out of surgery around four this afternoon. We will know more then." She headed out to the vending machine and then Mike could hear her briefing Bridget on the front desk.

He turned to face the window, staring into space. He just couldn't take it in. Was it a heart attack? What the fuck was this aneurysm?

"Hey you OK?" said Paul, removing his blazer and placing it on the back of his chair.

"Dhillon's had some form of heart attack," said Mike turning round to face him. "Well an aneurysm in one of the arteries in his chest and he's having surgery this morning," said Mike.

"What the fuck!" said Paul, sitting down and then turning to face his office. "But, I mean when did this happen?" Paul questioned, trying to absorb the information he'd just received.

"He collapsed ten days into his holiday and was flown home. Tina mentioned about him being transferred to Holden Central, so I assume he was taken somewhere else first."

"Is Karen in?" Paul asked, staring at her empty desk.

"No, she called Tina last night to explain, perhaps she will come in later," Mike said, standing up to retrieve some change from his jean pocket. "Coffee?" he said, edging away from the desk.

Paul nodded, as he turned to face Inspector Dhillon's empty office again. "Yes," he said quietly. Paul could hear Mike briefing Jim and Dave in the hallway and the new guy Jeff who had taken over Ben's role, which in turn led to lots more questions and then he heard Mel arrive.

"What's all that about?" Mel asked, addressing her question to Paul, after she had edged past them all in the reception area.

"Dhillon's had some sort of heart aneurysm, while on holiday. Apparently he collapsed and was flown home. He's having an op this morning," Paul said, still unable to take the information in.

Mel sat down in Mike's chair, totally dumbfounded. "We thought something was wrong yesterday when he didn't show but then we concluded we had just got his return date wrong," said Mel, listening to all the questions being thrown at Mike in the distance.

One by one they edged their way into the office, still asking questions, everyone talking at once, until everyone went quiet. Mike looked at Mel, as she rose from his chair and then he turned to face the others. "Business as usual guys, until we know more."

A tear slipped down Mel's cheek as she stared back at Mike. Despite Inspector Dhillon's direct approach, stern, almost arrogant demeanour, they were both extremely fond of him and held him in high regard. This was a sad day.

"Anything on Joe Treville yet?" said Mike, directing this question at Jim.

"A couple of alleged sightings, which turned out to be someone else fitting his description," replied Jim. "The little fucker's gone into hiding but we'll sniff him out," he added.

"I hope so, Jim, I really want to deliver some good news to Linda. His capture is paramount to her recovery." His thoughts then turned to her, wondering how her rehabilitation from that dreadful day was going. He was surprised that, with everything that went before, together with the day she was held hostage hadn't tipped her over the edge in terms of sanity.

Despite her years in a rehabilitation centre followed by assisted living, she had never once shown any signs of identity disorder like her sister. Yes, at the beginning when she was found wandering the streets of Gordon Square, she was an empty shell, not speaking, totally unreachable, but with the careful work carried out during her rehabilitation, restoring her faith in humanity and educating her, together with her own determination and strength of character she had made it through to the other side.

To suddenly have that all compromised by some sick twisted evil excuse for a human being, especially to then learn that he was the son of her original persecutor was totally incomprehensible. No, Mike was determined that they would find him, sniff him out from whatever rock he had crawled under and put him away for a very long time.

"Mel, make some enquiries at Hunters Estates please. I want to know how that panned out. It will be interesting to know how Tim Greyson's under-the-table negotiations at Arlington Terrace were received by Mr Franklin, the real owner.

"I suspect he now knows that his nephew sublet the place," he added and I also guess there will be a huge clean-up operation going on there.

Mel nodded and then gave Mike a grateful smile before rummaging through her papers for Tim Greyson's number. There were lots of unanswered questions relating to that property, and Dryden Walk for that matter, and she was pleased at having something else to fill her day other than typing up case notes from other uninteresting cases.

Mike looked back across at Jim and Dave who were busy wrapping up stuff relating to a jewellery heist case they had been working tirelessly on. They were due in court that morning for a preliminary hearing, which basically would set the date for the forthcoming trial, and Mike knew they were up to their necks in gathering all the evidence on Liam Masters and his gangster brothers, so that they would go down without question.

He also knew that while they were concentrating on that, Joe Treville could fall off the radar indefinitely.

"Jeff, how's everything going with you, you settling in OK?" he questioned.

Jeff nodded and walked across to Mike's desk. "Quiet at the moment but I'm sure that will all change shortly when my new partner Alan arrives," he said, confidently.

"Yes, he will be joining us on Monday, transferring from CID Vice,

South Wales," Mike added, filling in the gaps. Mike knew Alan well and had worked with him on vice cases before and was really pleased that he was now joining their unit, taking over from Billy.

Mike looked over at Tina who appeared to be transferring notes from the USB, a job Karen had set her. "Tina, how's your day looking?" he questioned, wondering what her day had in store. "As I thought, if you're not too hectic, you could team up with Jeff today and perhaps take the strain off Jim and Dave."

Tina smiled, pleased to have been singled out from her usual desk-based role. "Thanks, Mike, that would be great, I love getting involved in cases outside the unit."

Jim passed the Joe Treville file across to Tina and proceeded to fill her and Jeff in as to where they were at.

Mike looked around the office, everyone had a job to do and now they needed to do theirs.

"Paul, Keeper's Lodge?" he suggested, knowing that this was their next port of call.

Paul grabbed his blazer from the back of his chair in acknowledgement. "Definitely," he stated, eager to find out more about this creepy sounding place.

Seven

"It's a really strange place to have a halfway house of sorts," said Paul, staring out the car window, as Mike meandered his way round the country lanes heading deeper and deeper into the mountain range. "You would have thought that if you were trying to integrate troubled souls back into society you would want to base it within a town environment," Paul added, his attention drawn to the black clouds that were fast approaching in the distance.

"It's actually fairly close to the town of Ramchester," Mike advised, revealing the fact that he had actually looked it up the previous evening before heading to bed. "But I agree it's probably not ideal in terms of geographical convenience on a day-to-day basis. I guess they must ferry the residents into town daily for them to hold down any sort of job," he added.

"Yes, but that doesn't actually make them self-sufficient does it, when they are supposed to be demonstrating independence and they are transported into town like they are on a school bus," Paul continued. "Weird if you ask me!"

"I guess you can look at it from several angles," said Mike, reaching out to close the driver's side window to shield him from the wind. "The peace and tranquillity of a woodland setting will go a long way to sooth all those troubled souls but must be creepy as hell at night," he added thinking back to the website photos he viewed the evening before of a Scandinavian-style lodge set deep in the heart of the forest, surrounded by cabins. "And by the look of the sky and the wind getting up I'm guessing we are in for a storm," he said, looking down at his satnav to check they weren't going off course as the road forked off in two different directions.

"Not surprising after the hot weather we are experiencing," said Paul, thinking that the seasons were well and truly off kilter with global warming. "How much further?" he said, worried they were really heading off the beaten track.

"Five minutes," said Mike, thinking they had probably chosen the worst day to travel deep into the mountains as he flicked the wipers on.

"Look there's a signpost," said Paul, confirming that the satnav had actually chosen the correct route as they steered off to the left onto what was now a bumpy gravel drive leading up to a small set of stable-style gates. There was a short post staked into the earth that was leaning to one side which housed an old-fashioned intercom square box. Presumably, by the position of the post, it had been hit by a car at some time or other. Mike reluctantly opened his window once more to reach out for the button, soaking his sleeve as the heavens did their utmost to deliver as much rain as possible at that precise moment.

The intercom hissed and crackled as the sound of someone's voice came in out of range. "Did you get that?" said Mike, turning to Paul with a smirk.

"Sets the scene, doesn't it," said Paul, knowing what Mike was implying. Mike pressed the button again after realising that the gates were not electric, wondering if they should just proceed or wait.

"I guess we're letting ourselves in," said Mike, after a period of silence wishing he didn't have to disembark the vehicle in the middle of a storm.

"Well, either that or we wait it out," said Paul, wondering if perhaps they should hold back for a bit.

"Hey look, there's someone coming," said Mike, pointing to a figure approaching in a black hooded raincoat.

"Can I help?" said an old chap, as he gave the intercom post a kick. "Bloody thing, never works," he said, turning to face them.

"DS Brugge and DS Osman from Holden CID," said Mike holding

up his badge for him to view. "We would like to see whoever's in charge here please," he requested, wiping his face from rain that was now coming into the driver's side window.

The man took two steps backwards as if taken by surprise and then turned to face the direction from which he had come. "Do you have an appointment?" he asked, wiping his face with a cloth retrieved from his pocket.

"I'm afraid not," said Mike, hoping that this was not going to be as far as they got.

"I see," said the man making his way over to the gates, looking deep in thought. He released the catch and swung one of the gates to one side. "Make your way up to the lodge," he directed, as he reached for the second gate. "I'll catch you up."

They continued along the gravel drive surrounded by woodland on either side until they came to a large clearing. "Over there," said Paul, pointing to what was presumably the lodge set high up on the side of the mountain range. It looked absolutely breathtaking, set amongst the most magnificent backdrop of forest land.

"Picture postcard isn't it," said Mike, thinking the photos from the website didn't do it justice.

"Yeah it is," said Paul, feeling that the image he had conjured up earlier was a far cry from this.

"Bet it's even more stunning on a sunny day," Mike continued, suddenly feeling the creepiness from earlier seep away.

"It kind of looked gloomier on the website somehow," said Mike, looking round for a suitable spot to park his van. "The pictures were obviously taken at dusk and not by the best photographer I would say." He pulled on the handbrake and looked over his shoulder for his leather jacket he had slung in the back a few days earlier.

"A lot of steps to tackle as well," said Paul, looking up towards the veranda that surrounded the entire facade of the structure from the angle they were viewing from. The old guy from earlier was beckoning them over from the bottom step in the pouring rain.

"Well, it's all right for him in his windbreaker mac," said Mike, pulling on his jacket and exiting the vehicle.

"Well at least you're not in a summer blazer," said Paul, releasing the door and stepping out into the storm. They raced across the gravel drive towards the staircase and followed the old man up the steps and onto the covered veranda.

He retrieved the key from his inside pocket, and opened the door to usher them inside. Mike shrugged at Paul, thinking it odd that the door was locked considering it was mid-morning and this place was supposed to be encouraging independent living, which surely suggested residents were free to come and go as they pleased.

"Rather secure," said Mike, unable to keep his thoughts under wraps.

"Oh, every resident has their own key, Sergeant," he advised but we don't want any riff-raff letting themselves in and benefiting from our supplies. "I caught a tramp in here once helping himself to the contents of our communal refrigerator in the break out room. Nasty smelly chap sitting in front of the fire with his dirty boots up on one of the stools eating a birthday cake intended for one of the residents. Spoilt the entire celebration," he added.

Mike smiled inwardly imagining the whole scene where a group of partially recovered patients had assembled to sing happy birthday and were greeted by a smelly tramp eating their supper. Must have been mayhem as he pictured them chasing him out with a broom handle. "Is the manager available?" said Mike, trying his best to keep focused, as his eyes darted everywhere.

"Follow me," he said, gesturing once more the way forward as he led them along the dark oak corridor. He opened the door at the far end, which led into a cosy looking lounge area with a large open fireplace, very befitting a cabin-style lodge. It had a deep pile, red carpet and a range of cottage-style sofas and chairs in a pretty floral pattern. "Take a seat," he offered, pointing towards the nearest sofa. Mike and Paul sat down, expecting the old guy to fetch the person in charge but he sat down in the armchair opposite.

"I am the warden here," he explained. "All residents here are being assisted back out into the big wide world and just need that little bit of assistance to make that adjustment before they are discharged. All units are independent, styled like small apartments internally to mimic independent living so there's no actual manager as such. I am the warden, I live on-site and various nurses and care workers come in and out daily to monitor the residents. Most are seen weekly until their discharge."

"Your name?" said Mike, looking around the lounge, which presumably was a communal area for residents if they wished to socialise.

"Thomas Hamilton," he said, standing up. "Can I get you something to drink?" he offered, pointing to a small tea station just behind the adjacent sofa. "Coffee with extra sugar, please," said Mike, looking across at Paul.

"Same," said Paul, removing his wet blazer and placing it over the arm of the chair.

"So what brings you here?" said Thomas, as he assembled three coffees from a pre-prepared coffee urn.

"A patient called Rachel Blossom," said Paul, adjusting the crease in his sodden trousers. "Unfortunately she is now a missing person and her last residential address is Keeper's Lodge," he said, leading the questions.

"Ah yes, Rachel," he said acknowledging the fact that he knew her. "But that was quite some time ago," he said, looking up towards the ceiling as if he was recalling the timeline. "Frail little thing," he said, as he placed two coffees on the coffee table in front of them.

"But a lovely girl, always cheerful and exceptionally helpful," he added.

"Do you know when she checked out exactly, presumably you keep records?" Mike asked.

"Well, the nurses keep all the professional notes, you understand, I only keep a visitors' book, which, I hasten to add, I need you to sign today to record your visit. The storm has really thrown my level of thinking," he said, glancing at his watch and then out of the window towards the car park.

"Are you expecting someone?" said Mike, noticing him look at his watch a second time.

"No, I was just recalling the time, so that I could estimate your arrival time for my records," he said, confidently.

"I see," said Mike, stirring his coffee. "How long was it before you raised the alarm that Rachel was missing?" said Mike, wondering if they were going to get any reliable information from this old boy.

"Well I remember there were a series of locum care workers looking in on her because her full-time nurse was on leave, so sadly the alarm wasn't raised until sometime later."

"How much later?" said Mike, concluding that the old boy should have been retired years ago and was more of a caretaker than a warden.

"I'm not sure," he said, his voice now trembling, as his shaky hands tried to hold his cup still. "We have so many residents that come and go, I may not have noticed for a while," he said, looking down at the floor. "You tend to notice things more when things go wrong," he said, searching for an example. "Sometimes when you have a rowdy resident that causes mayhem, you tend to concentrate more on them to keep order. The quiet ones tend to keep themselves to themselves. I'm very sorry but it was a while before it suddenly occurred to me that I hadn't seen her around for a while, so I used my master key to check out her cabin when she didn't respond to my knocking. Her personal belongings were gone, which suggested to me she had checked out."

"Did you raise the alarm?" said Paul, wondering how quickly he reported this. "I did alert one of the nurses who came to check out another resident. My understanding is that because her belongings were gone, it was recorded as a conscious decision by the resident to check out, so it was not investigated."

"Mr Hamilton, how long ago was this?" Mike asked, hoping he could give some sort of indication of the timeline.

"I don't really know, perhaps a year, maybe less. I'm really sorry, I'm not sure. Am I in trouble?" he questioned, looking extremely concerned and drained of colour.

"I'm sure the responsibility lies with Danbury Manor, Mr Hamilton," said Mike, almost feeling sorry for the old boy, with his unruly silver beard and shabby beige cardigan. He was way past his sell by date for this type of role and Mike concluded that this was obviously his home and his next stop would probably be a care home for his own benefit.

"Please call me Thomas," he said softly, avoiding eye contact with Mike.

"Can we take a look around?" said Paul, curious what was on offer here.

"Possibly at one of the cabins as well," Mike added. "I assume Rachel's one has been reoccupied, possibly several times over by now?" he quizzed.

"It is actually vacant at the moment," said Thomas, rising to his feet. "Let me get the key."

They followed Thomas back out to the reception desk, where he retrieved a key from a locked cabinet under the oak-clad desk. "Unit twelve, he confirmed, holding up the key. Mike looked at Paul with a nod, indicating to Paul that it was strange that he immediately identified her cabin number without looking up her records, yet he was unable to recall a date of her departure. Something was adrift here.

"Thomas, presumably the lounge you took us to is not the communal one the residents use?" said Mike, wondering where everyone was.

"It is one of the lounges but no one really uses that one, so I use it myself," he advised. "The ladies tend to congregate in the lounge that faces south, the sun lounge they refer to it as. Much nicer aspect and leads out onto the veranda. Catches the sun all day," he added.

"Ladies?" said Paul, realising that all the residents were female.

"Are there no male residents here?" asked Paul, looking across at Mike.

"Interesting," said Mike, thinking that they needed to check out if Danbury Manor was an all-female institution as well. "Can we see the sun lounge as part of the tour?" said Mike, hearing the sound of some female voices coming from the room at the opposite end of the corridor.

"Well, let's start with her cabin?" said Thomas, suddenly looking nervous again, as he pulled on his mackintosh. "I don't want to alarm the ladies, but if we have time."

Paul pulled on his sodden blazer, which seemed totally pointless, as they followed Thomas back out onto the wooden staircase, leading down to the gravel drive and then back out into the forest in the pouring rain.

"So the cabins are separate from the lodge?" Mike questioned, thinking it must be quite scary for the residents to have to ramble through the forest to reach their cabins, especially at night. There was no indication on the website that the cabins were separated from the main lodge by forest land, it gave the illusion that they were just outside.

"Ah, it's just a short walk, Inspector. It's all private land, less than a minute's stroll, and not forgetting that we are surrounded by electric fencing installed to keep the local farmer's cattle at bay but it also serves towards the ladies safety with regard to intruders. Most of the ladies seem to congregate in small groups, safety in numbers, I guess, but anyone feeling nervous is escorted by my good self," he confirmed, turning to look over his shoulder at Mike and then wiping his wet face with the same cloth as earlier. "Plus it's very well lit," he reassured, with a sweeping gesture.

The forest soon opened up again into another wide open clearing, which had been gravelled in the same way as outside the main lodge. Five cabins proudly stood, set approximately ten metres apart in a circular sweep, amongst the forest backdrop.

"Wow this is quite something," said Paul, thinking that it looked more fitting as holiday lets than a halfway house dwelling.

"Yes, the complex was originally designed as a vacation retreat, each unit having complete independence from its neighbour. Which is why the cabins have been designed with the front doors all facing in a separate direction for privacy purposes."

"It's truly breathtaking," said Mike, wishing he was seeing it all in the sunshine where he could appreciate the setting in its full glory, as opposed to the pouring rain. He noted that each cabin had a small wooden table with bench seating just outside the front door, enabling the occupants to enjoy the benefits of outdoor dining during the summer months. Yes, it was definitely designed as a holiday retreat originally, there was no doubt about that.

"How many units are there?" Paul asked, wondering if the five in front of them were shared.

"Twelve units in total," said Thomas, as he continued to lead them once more into the forest.

Again, about forty seconds later they stepped out into another clearing where seven cabins were dotted into the mountain side, looking down over the town of Ramchester. Thousands of homes and businesses stood side by side in the distance making it look truly show-stopping, especially the nearby chapel with its grand steeple standing out like a candle on top of a cake. "I bet that looks quite magical at night," said Paul, imagining all the twinkling lights from peoples homes.

"Which one was Rachel's?" said Mike, turning his gaze away from the town below.

"Cabin twelve," Thomas confirmed, pointing to the one right at the edge of the clearing.

The cabin was in complete contrast to the communal lodge, offering modern bright airy living. It had a picture window giving a birds-eye view of the forest landscape and breathtaking views of Ramchester. It also had a small door leading out onto the veranda, indicating that these lodges were far superior to their counterparts. The room was equipped with a small modern chrome kitchen area to one side, separating the lounge area by a small breakfast bar, complete with two bar stools. There was a separate bedroom with an en suite, and the whole cabin looked extremely comfortable.

"They seem well equipped," said Paul, opening a kitchen cupboard that revealed a selection of utensils any homeowner would be proud of.

"How long does a resident usually stay for?" said Mike, thinking that the setting was too beautiful to leave.

"Depends," said Thomas, pulling the blind down on the bedroom window. "On what?" Mike continued to quiz.

"Well, how quickly they become independent I guess, some are here longer than others."

"Are all the lodges designed for two," said Mike, staring at the double bed. "No, some are larger with an extra bedroom, designed for families originally," said Thomas, hoping the questions would soon come to a close.

"Can we see the sun lounge, Thomas?" Mike asked, eager to meet some of the residents. Mike could see that this question was troubling Thomas, so he pushed on with his request. "Thomas, you seem a little reluctant for us to view this room, why is that?"

"I just don't want to alarm the ladies," he said, ushering them forwards so that he could secure the cabin door.

"Thomas, I'm sure if these ladies are almost ready to be integrated back into society, seeing two gentlemen won't alarm them. It's not as if we are in uniform, which I would then understand may give them some concerns."

"I guess so," said Thomas, placing the key in his trouser pocket.

He reluctantly led them back through the forest towards the main lodge, in silence, stopping at the foot of the stairs leading up. He turned and looked back at them, breathed a sigh and then headed back up the wet stairs slowly. He unlocked the front door and stepped back inside removing his mackintosh as he went. He slung it over the reception desk chair and then led them both down the corridor towards the sun lounge where he stopped outside the door. Again he paused and then popped his head around the door, then re-emerged looking somewhat relieved. "Ah most of the ladies have moved on to other pursuits," he claimed, opening the door wider for them to pass through.

This room was indeed bright and Mike could see why it was referred to as the sun lounge. It had been painted yellow and was filled with wicker furniture and resembled a conservatory. Large windows graced the entire wall, revealing the luscious woodland outside and a set of double doors led out onto the veranda. Mike could see why this room attracted all the residents, especially if it caught the sun all day. A beautiful setting to recuperate in.

There were two women sitting on a sofa at the far end of the lounge, facing towards the double doors away from them chatting and one reading in the far corner with her feet up on a stool. The rest of the room was devoid of company and Mike knew he had missed the opportunity of seeing more of the residents. He had wanted to perhaps strike up a conversation with some of them and maybe garner some clues but it was quite evident that Thomas was keeping them at arm's length, as he attempted to usher them back out the sun lounge door.

"Is there anything else I can help you with today, gentleman," he asked, as he led them towards the front door.

"Yes, how many residents do you have here at the moment?" Mike quizzed, turning round as he heard another female voice in the distance.

"Ah we are quite low on numbers at the moment," Thomas answered. "Nine at present but we do have a new lady arriving tomorrow, who has been assigned to cabin twelve," he confirmed.

"Thomas, do you drive the ladies into town each day so that they can hold down employment?" said Mike, curious as to how this was conducted.

"No, a minibus comes Monday to Friday at eight thirty in the morning to take them into town."

"And who drives this minibus?" said Paul, curious as to which cab firm they used.

"A guy called Brent," said Thomas, opening the front door.

"Does he work for the lodge or is it a contract with a local cab firm?" Paul continued.

"I have absolutely no idea," said Thomas, gesturing towards the stairs. "All I know is that he has been coming here for years and the ladies seem to like him." He looked across at the visitors' book resting on the top of the reception desk and nodded to Paul, indicating that he would like them to register their visit. Paul smiled, recalling their earlier conversation and then quickly added their visit to the records.

"Thomas, I take it you retain all historical visitors' records?" he said, replacing the pen in the holder.

"Yes," said Thomas, turning his gaze away so that he didn't meet his eye.

"And if we needed access to these records would they be made available to us?" he continued to question.

Again Thomas quietly said, "Yes." Refusing to meet his gaze.

"Do the nurses and care workers register on arrival, Thomas, or is this visitors' book strictly for guests of patients and other types of visitors," he added.

"Yes, everyone signs in and out," he confirmed.

"Do you know Nurse Julie Somers, from Holden Central?" Paul continued to question.

"No, I don't think so. The name doesn't mean anything to me."

Mike looked across at Paul and then turned to face Thomas. "Well, thank you for your time, you have been very helpful," he said, offering his hand and then shaking it firmly. Paul nodded, extending his hand and then headed out the door. Mike turned at the top of the stairs. "Thomas, who owns Keeper's Lodge? Is it part of Danbury Manor or is it independent?" he quizzed.

Thomas looked at them silently, looking as if he didn't want to answer this question. "I'm not really sure," he said, looking down at his feet.

"Thomas, are you telling me you don't know who your employer is, or who pays your wages for that matter. I find it a little hard to believe that you don't know where your pay cheque comes from?"

said Mike, staring across at Paul. "Well I guess we will be looking that one up as well," he added.

They stepped off the veranda and back out into the rain. "I think Mr Thomas Hamilton knows a little bit more than what he's letting on," said Mike, as they headed back to his van.

Eight

It was 3:55pm when they walked back into the station after deciding to stop for burgers at 'Jack's Joint'. The case was getting more and more mysterious and they wanted to thrash it out over lunch, laying everything they had on the table for debate.

"Our next move is to find out who owns Keeper's Lodge and establish if it's part of something else or independent?" said Mike, retrieving Paul's coffee from the vending machine and passing it to him. "It's total bollocks that he doesn't know who his employer is," he said, pushing another coin into the slot. He pressed the button for extra sugar and turned to face Paul. "You know the thing that's niggling away at me is the fact that the place is too fancy for the NHS, so it's either private sector, or independently owned and if it's independently owned what the fuck is going on there? I just can't believe that a group of patients recovering from serious mental illness are being nursed and integrated back into society legitimately in such fancy surroundings. Who is financing this and what is their gain?"

He looked across at Mel who was totally oblivious to his arrival as he took his seat at his desk. She was typing audio and seemed totally absorbed until she suddenly ripped the earphones from her ears and slung them across the desk. She placed her head in her hands and sighed and then looked up across at Mike's desk. "Oh you're back!," she said, wondering how long he had been sitting there.

"You OK?" he asked, turning to see if Paul was out of ear shot. He turned back to face Mel, after confirming that Paul was now chatting with Tina and walked across to her. "You OK?" he asked again, looking up at the clock. "It's almost four o'clock," said Mike, thinking Mel would normally be heading out the door to collect Jack by now.

"Jeez, I don't know where the afternoon has gone," she said, grabbing her blazer from the back of her chair and rising to her feet. "It's been a really interesting day what with my visit to Hunters Estates," said Mel but I'm totally behind with all this shit," she said pointing to the pile of files on her desk, "and to be honest I'm finding it hard to switch back to all this boring typing when I'm involved in something much more exciting," she said, reaching for her bag.

"Well, so long as that's all it is," said Mike, relieved that it wasn't the Niko shit getting to her.

Mel gave him a peck on the cheek and headed towards the door. "Catch you later," she said, giving him her best smile before heading out the door.

It wasn't just the typing that was getting to her, it was the creepy feeling she had that things weren't right. She had put her hand in the urn to retrieve the parole letter that morning and noticed it had been folded. She had rolled up the paper before popping it into the vase, she knew she had and it had played on her mind all day. Her logical side told her that Mike had realised that she had put it in there and had read it and put it back folded but her sinister side told her that it was unlikely that he would have considered the vase as a possible hiding place and this bugged her.

Obviously she could solve this mystery by simply asking him but she had decided to save this conversation until later, as she really didn't want to discuss Niko at work, it was both private and intimate. No, this was something to be discussed at home within their own four walls, not in front of the whole bloody office.

Also why would Mike go searching for the letter? It would be so out of character for him to go poking around. He was such a straightforward, honest-talking man. He would either assume she had put it away or had simply decided to throw it out. She certainly couldn't see Mike opening all the drawers and cupboards, then tipping up vases in search of it but someone had.

She pulled into the nursery car park just as Mrs East was opening the door. She parked next to Liz's car and joined the queue of parents, grandparents and carers eagerly waiting to see their offspring. Jack, as usual, was standing with Henry holding his hand. They were both wearing dinosaur t-shirts with matching blue rucksacks slung over their shoulders and were thankfully devoid of any kind of jacket. Mel smiled at him, her heart melting and then looked across at Liz. "Looks like we've solved the jacket dilemma," she said jovially, bending down to Jack's level to retrieve the painting he was holding that was almost as big as him.

"Yes, thank heavens," Liz said, smiling. "Henry was as red as a beetroot by the time we reached home the other day. He had almost reached boiling point."

Mel laughed, pleased that they had managed to get past that problem and then gave her attention to Jack's painting. "My, what do we have here Jack?" she said, studying the colourful painting with interest.

"It's a snake," said Jack, proudly, beaming from ear to ear.

"Yes it's a lovely curly snake," said Mel, her heart melting again as she looked at how many colours Jack had chosen to use. "Do you know what? I think it's a rainbow snake," she offered, holding it up high to view it.

Jack smiled, "rainy bow," he said trying to copy what his mummy had said.

"Liz, how's it going with Rob? I've been meaning to ask but it's just been so hectic.

"Really good, thanks. I'm so grateful that he's home and Henry's loving every second of it. We both are."

"Ah, I'm so pleased for you, we really must make a date for the four of us to get together for drinks," said Mel, as they made their way back through the car park.

"Yeah, that would be really nice, I would love that."

"OK, let's compare diaries for a Saturday night and set a date before the end of the week."

Liz lifted Henry up into his car seat, while he waved furiously at Jack. "See you tomorrow, Mel," she said, opening the driver's side door.

"Yeah, see you tomorrow." Mel looked down at Jack who was still admiring his painting. "OK, little fella, let's get you and rainy bow home, shall we," she said, scooping him up.

They pulled onto the drive just before 4:30pm after singing five continuous rounds of 'I'm a little tractor'. Mel opened the door and climbed out of the car and stared up at her house. This is a happy house, she said to herself inwardly, as she admired their new home. Our beautiful three-storey town house. It had taken a lot of hard work to get this house, the family home she had always dreamed of and she wanted to feel safe there and there was one thing she knew for certain, she wasn't going to let that scumbag spoil it for her. She sighed and then walked round to Jack's side to release him from the car seat and swung him around in the air. Mel laughed, hearing her son squeal with laughter. "Come on, let's see what we can make a very special little boy for his tea," she said, heading towards the front door.

She helped Jack attach his painting to the notice board, which Mike had installed specially for Jack's pieces of art and watched as he stood back and admired it. "Rainy bow, rainy bow," he chanted, as his attention was then drawn to his little car set, which he whizzed across the floor. Mel flicked the switch on the oven and then opened the fridge door, pondering the contents of her fridge. She really needed to shop but it was so difficult trying to fit it all in. She picked up a pack of sausages, checked they were still in date and made the decision to do an online shop after she had settled Jack for the night.

Bangers and mash was going to be the dish of the evening, she decided, as she pulled a half used bag of spuds from the bottom drawer. Simple and quick and they could all have the same, she thought as she rummaged through the cutlery drawer in search of the potato peeler. She stared across at the urn and then debated how she was going to raise the topic with Mike that evening. She didn't want him to think she was being paranoid, especially after the gate incident the other evening. No she would gently weave it into the conversation somehow, without making it look like it was troubling her, she decided.

She set to work peeling the spuds and put them to one side to wash. It was probably one of her favourite dinners, if she was honest. A proper winter warmer on a hot summer's day, she said to herself with a giggle. She watched as Jack whizzed his cars out into the hallway and then decided to have a pee while he was out there. She stood up with her knickers round her ankles and laughed as Jack whizzed his car into the cloakroom. She hadn't had a pee in private for the last year or so, or a bath for that matter. She washed her hands and stared into the mirror and then she turned to face the toilet. The seat had been up when she walked in there, she was sure of it. She dried her hands and wandered back into the kitchen going over her morning routine in her head. She had waved Mike off with Jack standing at the front door and then she had helped Jack into his trainers. She had nipped into the toilet just before leaving the house, as she specifically remembered having what she describes as a security wee, before leaving home. It was something she always did and she always put the toilet seat down without fail.

Someone had been in again, she was sure of it. Someone had been in their house. She picked up the saucepan of potatoes with shaky hands and rinsed them under the tap and then she placed them on the back cooker ring and switched it on. No don't be stupid she said to herself, retrieving the scissors from the drawer. There's probably a logical explanation, perhaps Mike had popped home during the day for something, or maybe she was remembering that routine from the previous day. She cut the string of sausages, tossed them into a baking tin and slung them in the oven.

No, she was losing her grip on things and she really needed to take hold. What the fuck was she going to say to Mike at dinner that night. "Hi honey, by the way did you read my private letter that I had stored in the vase on the windowsill, which by the way I have renamed the urn. Oh and I think someone came into our house today and used our toilet while we were out." No, she would be heading in the same direction as Julie Somers if she started that nonsense.

She stared across at Jack who was totally oblivious and happily playing with his cars and then she turned to face the patio door. Don't do this, she said to herself in a whisper, don't do this. Don't let that man take any more of your life. A tear trickled down her cheek, as she turned to face the freezer. She bent down to open the door and pulled open the middle drawer and then she sobbed quietly behind the breakfast bar.

"What are you doing, Mummy?" said Jack, peeping round at her kneeling down on the floor, holding a bag of frozen peas.

"Oh, I was just picking up the peas that I had dropped on the floor. Nothing for you to worry about," she said quickly standing up. She wiped her tears with the back of her hand and looked down at Jack who was standing there with a little car in each hand.

"Are you sad?" said Jack, watching his mummy reach for a tissue.

"No, Mummy's fine, sweetheart," she said, trying to reassure him with a big smile.

She looked down at his little troubled face and stared across at the urn. She had to get a grip, she couldn't let this affect Jack. She had to pull herself together.

She watched on as Jack returned to his car game and then tried to rehearse in her head what she would say to Mike about the letter. She would at least tackle that topic, which would reduce some of the worry. One thing at a time, she contemplated, as she gave the sausages a shake before returning them to the oven.

She was just about to dish up Jack's when she heard the key in the front door. Great, Mike was home early for once, which meant they could now all eat dinner together.

"And how are my two favourite people?" he said, stepping into the breakfast diner with a big beam.

"Daddy," said Jack, heading full pelt towards him and hugging his legs, the only thing he could reach. Mike bent down and kissed the top of his head and then looked across at Mel smiling.

"Well this is a lovely greeting," he said, while waiting for Jack to release his little grip.

He scooped him up and gave him a twirl in the air and walked across to the breakfast bar. "That smells delicious," he said sniffing the air for Jack's benefit, making him giggle, as he watched Mel retrieve two extra plates from the cupboard.

"How come you're so early?" she said, pleased that they could have a family dinner, which they seldom achieved on a weeknight. Plus she now felt safe.

"Ah, decided to throw in the towel today. Both Paul and I decided that more family time was needed. I think hearing what happened to Dhillon has brought home to all of us how special family time is and we need to make more time for it."

Mel smiled, grateful that he was home but also knowing that Mike really believed what he was saying. Trouble was the job always got in the way, so she needed to treasure these stolen moments.

She dished up the two extra plates and they all sat around the family table, using Jack's booster seat so that he could reach. "I've told Liz that we would have drinks with her and Rob one Saturday evening, in the not-too-distant future," said Mel deciding to keep the conversation light while Jack was still up, and save the more colourful conversation until later.

"Yeah, sure," said Mike, leaning across to cut up Jack's sausages into tiny pieces. He knew that Liz had become an important friend to Mel and he wanted to encourage the friendship, as he knew that Mel felt very vulnerable by herself at the moment.

They chatted briefly about Keeper's Lodge, saving the nitty gritty till later and attempted to keep the conversation on Jack, hearing about his day at nursery and discussing the rainy bow picture proudly displayed on the notice board. "Right," said Mike, standing up, rubbing his belly. "Let's get cleared up and I'll bathe Jack tonight," he said, giving Mel a peek on the cheek. "I want you to sit with your feet up," he told her, as he carried the plates across to the dishwasher.

"My, I am being spoilt," she said, lifting Jack down from the table. "You couldn't make it home by five thirty every evening, could you?" she said with a smile. She watched as Jack continued playing with his toys and joined Mike by the sink. "I love it when you're here, it really makes things complete," she said, rinsing the dish cloth under the tap. Mike smiled, thinking this type of talk was way too soppy for Mel. She was such a tough cookie and despite all that she had been through she wasn't overly open with her feelings, a trait inherited from her childhood, from being orphaned so young.

"Well, I will do my best to make it happen some of the time," he said, stroking the back of his wife's neck. He kissed it gently and then gave the signal to Jack that it was time for his bath.

Mike lifted Jack up onto each stair playfully, pretending that he was a pallet of bricks being hoisted up to the top of a skyscraper building that was being built and was the tallest one in the world. "We are nearly at the top, Jack, don't look down," he said jokingly. "Wow, Jack, we made it to the top," he said, playfully bringing him down onto the landing floor. Jack giggled as he was returned to his feet and then raced off into the bathroom.

Mike followed, filling the bath and searched for Jack's bubble bath amongst Mel's many potions. He sat on the toilet seat watching Jack play with his bath toys and then was completely taken off guard.

"Daddy, peas make Mummy cry," said Jack, as he dipped Dhillon the dinosaur under the water.

"Cry," said Mike, kneeling down beside the bath so that he could tune in better. "When was Mummy crying?" Mike asked, reaching for his bath sponge.

"She dropped the peas," said Jack, sadly, looking up into his daddy's eyes.

"I see," said Mike, gently sponging the water, so it cascaded down his back. "Well I had better go and cheer her up," he said, lifting Jack out of the bath and wrapping him in a fluffy white bunny rabbit towel. "But not before I've popped you into your pyjamas and read you a story," he said, glancing at his watch.

He carried Jack through to his bedroom wrapped in his towel and sat him on his little bed. Mike scrambled through the top drawer and held up a pair of dinosaur pyjamas for approval and Jack nodded in full agreement. "Is this the story book you are reading at the moment?" Mike questioned, seeing it perched on the edge of his chest of drawers.

"Yes," said Jack, running over to it so that he could show his daddy.

"Right, hop in," said Mike, holding the summer duvet up so that Jack could climb in. He looked at his son, his heart melting, as his little face lit up. He loved a bedtime story and he could often hear Mel doing all the different voices of the animals or characters in the book. He had a lot to live up to.

"No Daddy, no, not like that," he said, correcting Mike when he didn't make the noise of the alligator properly. "Mummy does it like this, 'roarrrrrrrrr'," he demonstrated, finishing with a bright red face. Mike laughed as he tried to repeat the growling bellow sound his little boy was making. Mel could hear this from downstairs and was giggling to herself, enjoying the pantomime from overhead.

"Well done," she said, clapping as Mike entered the room fifteen minutes later. "You've got the job," she said playfully.

"Well quite a talent you obviously have there, Mrs Brugge, because apparently you do it best," he told her, giving her a hug.

Mike flopped down on the sofa and reached for the remote and then decided to replace it back on the table. "Mel, come sit down for a moment," he said, gesturing for her to sit down beside him.

"Jack said he saw you crying today because you dropped the peas. What did he mean by that?" he said, opening the evening's debate.

"Oh Mike, I really didn't want him to see me upset. I'm so sorry about that," she said sitting down beside him. "I guess I got a bit overwhelmed while cooking dinner this evening. Mike, I want to ask you something but please don't think I'm paranoid, I just want to know if you took my parole board letter out of the urn, I mean vase," she said, correcting herself quickly.

"What do you mean?" Mike questioned, wondering what on earth his wife was on about. "What urn?" he quizzed, deciding to head across to the wine rack. He held up a bottle of Merlot without comment and Mel nodded.

"Yes please," she said, standing up to retrieve two glasses from the cabinet. She placed them on the table and watched as Mike poured and then sat back down on the sofa.

"The parole board letter regarding Niko's release," said Mel, accepting the wine offered, as Mike sat back down beside her. "As you know I stored it in the cupboard for a while, before I decided I couldn't stand staring at it every time I opened the cupboard door," she continued. "Well, I rolled it up and stuck it in the vase on the kitchen window ledge. Then I had this crazy thought about burning it and that the vase would then effectively be an urn, hypothetically of course," she added. "Anyway it's been in the urn for a few days now but I have to confess I've retrieved it a couple of times and popped it back but when I last did that the letter had been folded into four and I know for certain that I did not do that."

Mike took a sip of wine and then placed his glass down on the coffee table. He felt a little dumbfounded because he had no idea where his wife had put the letter and had hoped that she had just decided to throw it away.

"Mike, say something! Don't just sit there. Did you retrieve it from the urn?" Mel demanded in an agitated fashion, like she was interrogating a suspect in the interview room.

"Mel, take a breath, you probably did it subconsciously," he told her. "You've been under tremendous strain," he added.

"So, you're telling me you didn't retrieve the letter from the urn, I mean vase?" she questioned again.

"No," he said, regretting his actions, knowing that this would now become something really huge.

A tear rolled down her cheek, as she reached out for her wine with trembling hands. She steadied her glass with both hands and then took a deep breath. "Mike, I think someone's been in the house while we've been at work. I really think we left the patio door open the other day, you know, when the back gate was open," she reminded him.

"Mel, I told you I forgot to lock the gate. You're reading too much into this."

"I'm not, Mike, I know someone's been in here," she said, shakily.

"Look," said Mike, taking hold of her hand and giving it a squeeze. "Why would anyone come into our house and retrieve a letter from a vase? A letter that no one knew you had even put there, not even me," he said reassuringly.

"I know I rolled it up and slid it into the neck of the vase, Mike, I know I did."

"Yes, but we all do things subconsciously. Sometimes I wonder how on earth I made it to the station. I often pull into my parking space and I have no memory of the journey at all. We often do things in pilot mode. Everyday stuff that's commonplace. We do things in robotic mode because our brain can deal with those things subconsciously without much thought. Mel, look at me. Nobody has been in our house, I promise you," he said, looking directly into her eyes.

"Or used our toilet?" she said, sarcastically, rising to her feet. She poured herself another wine and held up the bottle.

Mike shook his head, holding up his half-full glass. "No thanks. What's that supposed to mean anyway?" he said, gesturing for her to come back to the sofa.

"Nothing," said Mel, wishing she hadn't mentioned that bit. "I'm just a bit cranky I guess. The parole thing has really gotten to me," she added, hoping that he wouldn't question her any further on the toilet topic.

"Mel, you've come so far. Please don't let this undo everything you have achieved. We have a great life together. We are so very lucky in so many respects. Just think how long we worked together, nursing one another through broken romances and life's tribulations, only to realise that we had been perfect for one another all along. We found one another and built a life together and then if things couldn't get any better we had Jack."

"I know all that, Mike. That's why I am so fearful of losing it all. You and Jack are my world. I now have a family, something I never thought I would have. With the exception of the early years that I have trouble recalling, it's just been a series of children's homes and broken relationships, you know that. I feel I'm losing my grip on everything and I'm frightened."

"Hey, I'm never ever gonna leave you. I'm going to be by your side always. You have no idea what you and Jack mean to me. This is a family unit that will stick together no matter what. Hey, look at me, Mrs Brugge, you are listening to me aren't you?" he said, lifting her chin up with his forefinger.

"Yes," said Mel, tears now freely flowing down her cheeks and onto her lap.

"I love you, Mike, so much," she said, staring into his eyes.

"And I love you too, more than you will ever know," he said, leaning forward to kiss her gently.

Nine

Mike looked up from his notes as Mel said her cheery good mornings to everyone in the office.

"Good morning, Mrs Brugge," he said playfully, as she took her seat at her desk. "How are you doing this morning?" he said, walking over to her with a glint in his eye. He had missed her at breakfast, as he had made his way into the office before she was even awake. The previous evening had been full of emotion and they had fallen asleep in one another's arms, each promising the other the world and truly meaning it.

"I'm OK," she said gently, looking over her shoulder to make sure no one was listening, "You?" she questioned, knowing he was referring to their night of passion and promises.

"I'm good," he said, smiling before walking back across to his desk.

"How did you get on yesterday with Hunters Estates?" he questioned, suddenly recalling the mission he had set for his wife the day before. "Did you get to speak with Tim Greyson?" said Mike, thinking that they hadn't covered that topic at all the evening before, due to Mel's anxieties.

"Oh, I spoke with him face to face," said Mel, taking advantage of the fact that this wouldn't be under the eye of Inspector Dhillon.

"Yeah, I guessed you would pay him a visit, rather than conduct it over the phone," said Mike, looking across at Paul.

"And?" said Paul tuning into the conversation, eager to see what Mel had ascertained.

"Well he's under notice," said Mel, walking across to their desks. "He was packing up his stuff, as I walked in. He was only in the office for a disciplinary hearing and had basically lost his case. He's not officially terminated until the end of the month but he is on garden leave, so to speak. He spoke to me while carrying his stuff out to his car. He told me that Mr Franklin, the owner, and his nephew Aaron Stephens were removing all their properties at Arlington Terrace and other sites away from Hunters, so basically, Tim Greyson had lost them the entire contract. The manager of Hunters was up in arms and was under pressure from his bosses."

"Did he say which estate agents the contract had been passed to?" said Mike, wondering if there would be any further leads on that part of the operation.

"No, but I did a drive past Arlington Terrace and the sign outside is Palmers, so it has been assigned to one of the bigger chains," said Mel. "Tim Greyson was effing and blinding about the whole thing. Let slip that this job was kind of his last chance as he had lost his previous position due to fraud. So, basically he's lost everything including his wife."

"Well, I guess that wraps up anything further being ascertained from the Arlington Terrace property," said Mike, wondering if Joe Treville alias Jason Topaz, would be renting from anyone else under an assumed name and new identity.

There were so many loose ends to this case that Mike was beginning to wonder what else could be thrown into the mix. He strolled through to the briefing room and stared at the case wall. Joe Treville's face sat painfully at the top overshadowing everything else. With his blonde hair and deep green eyes, he was a handsome guy and no doubt could possibly seduce anyone that took his fancy. The problem was that what he fancied was something sinister and painful. What turned him on was seeing someone else's agony, humiliating them and watching them suffer.

Mike shuddered as he moved his gaze down to the two sisters Rachel and Linda. Linda, a beautiful blonde woman, but if you looked closely you could see a haunted look deep within her eyes, like her soul had been removed. How he wished with all his heart that she would recover from this set-back. Rachel's picture was at least four to five years old, given to him by Linda but was probably not a true likeness as to what she looks like now. Her photo looked quite childlike, as though she was stuck in a time warp but the dark circles under her eyes looked quite creepy on such a young face.

He sighed as he looked at all the other photos linked to the case. Julie Somers was by far the most disturbing. He found it really hard to relate to this picture of Julie, as to him it represented Emma, a dark haired, frail malnourished, frightened young girl who had moved into Arlington Terrace to escape her best friend who had turned into a controlling bully. It bore no resemblance whatsoever to her former self, a well respected, highly educated psychiatrist working alongside Doctor Gyllensvan. This photo had been placed to the left-hand side along with Doctor Gyllensvan, as there were still some unanswered questions lodged deep within her psychotic mind that needed extracting.

His thoughts then turned to Thomas Hamilton at Keeper's Lodge. What wasn't he telling them and why was he so reluctant to let them speak to any of the residents there. He picked up his marker pen and added his name to the case board along with Sister Bernadette, Karen Lewis and Ivy Mason. He needed to know more about all of them and how they were linked. He also wanted to know about the new resident moving into Unit 12 at Keeper's Lodge. Where was she being transferred from and what was her back story. He replaced the maker pen in the tray at the bottom of the board and turned to leave. He took two steps and stopped and then decided to add the driver of the cab firm to the list. Who was this guy that arrived every day at Keeper's Lodge to ferry everyone into town and what was his name? He wrote the word cab driver with a question mark and then returned to his desk.

"Karen's in," said Paul, pointing to Dhillon's office. "Arrived a few minutes ago but hasn't said a word yet."

Mike looked across at Dhillon's office and then rose to his feet. "Well, let's see what I can unearth," he said, slinging his pen down on his desk. He tapped on the door and opened it gently before she had a chance to respond.

"Morning, Karen, can I have a quick word?" he said, stepping inside and closing the door firmly behind him.

"Yes, of course," said Karen perching on the edge of Inspector Dhillon's desk.

"Well it's more of an update I'm after really," said Mike, suddenly feeling intrusive, when he could clearly see she had been crying. "You OK?" he added, hoping that there hadn't been a decline in the governor's health after the operation. It had been a success but was obviously early days.

"Yes I'm fine, just still a little shaky," she said, giving her nose a gentle blow. "Just still can't believe it, I guess," she said, replacing the tissue in her pocket. "I obviously knew he had some health issues, which I had been sworn to secrecy," she said, looking down at her feet, as if she didn't feel worthy of looking him straight in the eye.

"Karen, we do all understand the position you were in. If he asked you to keep it under wraps then you were obviously in his confidence. But what we would like to know now is how he's doing?"

"Well it's total rest for the time being, so he won't be returning for some time, but I have a letter for you along with a message." She reached into her bag and passed him a hand-written note in the inspectors handwriting. "Mike, he wants you to run the unit in his absence until further notice," she said, closing her handbag and standing directly in front of him. "He said he has total faith in your ability to step up to the role and that from this moment forward you will be acting chief inspector."

Mike sat down in the chair immediately in front of Inspector Dhillon's desk. The chair he normally received instructions and occasional grillings from. The note basically repeated what Karen had just told him, which he then folded and looked across at her. "Understood," he said, rising to his feet. "Karen, he's going to be OK, isn't he?" said Mike, looking her in the eye.

"I hope so, Mike, but it's not going to be a quick fix so be prepared for a long ride."

Mike nodded and pushed the note into this jean pocket. "Thanks Karen." Mike opened the door, stepping back to allow Karen to exit first and then he walked slowly across to his desk.

He looked around to check everyone was present and then he made an announcement. "Guys, I would like to speak with you all in the briefing room please." He watched on as everyone made their way in and then he followed closing the door behind him. "Karen has updated me on Inspector Dhillon's progress and, while we all know the operation was a success, he will now need time to recuperate back to full strength. In the meantime he has asked me to cover for him in his absence."

Paul nodded in full agreement, knowing full well that Mike was his next in line. Everyone nodded and muttered their words of acknowledgement and then waited for further information.

Mike turned to face the briefing wall pointing out the additional names he had just added to the board to which he now needed photos.

"Yesterday Paul and I took a trip out to Keeper's Lodge, which I have to say may not be what it seems. From the website it is described as the final steps before integrating mental health patients back to independent living. The setting is absolutely idyllic and resembles that of a holiday retreat and not what one would expect to see fitting the description. We interviewed the warden, Thomas Hamilton, who did explain that the dwelling was originally built as a luxury retreat but what we need to establish is why it changed direction. Someone bought it out and now it serves as a halfway house, which provides the final leg of the journey for patients that have suffered a breakdown of sorts.

"It's a strange setting for an establishment offering independent living, integrating patients back into society when its setting is so remote. Obviously the residents are supposedly holding down employment, proving that they are capable of independence, but because of its remote location a contract has been drawn up with, presumably, a cab company who transport the ladies into town daily."

"Ladies?" said Dave, tuning into this comment with interest.

"Yes, we have also established that Keeper's Lodge is an all-female institution," said Mike turning back to the case board.

"Paul and I also paid a visit to Danbury Manor, which is run by nuns, incidentally. We interviewed Sister Bernadette, who introduced herself as the person in charge there, who then went on to introduce us to Rachel's case worker Karen Lewis.

"So, what do we know?" said Mike, turning to face them all. "We know that after the fire at Victoria's Retreat, Rachel was transferred to Casio Grange. Through a series of blunders caused by a lack of case notes and inexperienced staff, her then case worker, Ivy Mason, deemed her fit for assisted living, and then encouraged the transfer to Danbury Manor. From there she was transferred to Keeper's Lodge. So, we ask ourselves what happened next? How could a young vulnerable girl with an extreme identity disorder manage to manipulate professionals into thinking she was fit to be integrated back into society? So I ask two questions. One, did Rachel really manipulate staff into thinking she was in fact of sound mind or two, is something sinister happening there to young vulnerable females?

"We also need to check where Joe Treville fits into all of this. We know that he has been following the rehabilitation of Linda and Rachel and in his sick twisted way of thinking wanted to punish them for the loss of his inheritance. According to his mother, Diane Treville, he holds them responsible. We need to find out if he is involved in any of this."

"But didn't he lose everything to the sisters in his father's trial?" said Jim, questioning Mike's suggestion.

"The Treville's lost most of the father's estate but Diane Treville was wealthy in her own right, so there is money there," said Mike. "Paul and I went over everything yesterday, while driving back from Keeper's Lodge and one of the things we debated was the fact that it's only an assumption made by us that Joe Treville thinks he drove Rachel insane, mistaking her identity with that of Julie Somers, alias Emma. We have assumed that he thought he had achieved his objective and then moved on to Linda. But we don't know that for sure."

"The case is completely wide open and may or may not be connected but we do know that Rachel is missing and we do know that Joe Treville has been following her for over seven years. Paul and I are going to continue with our investigation of Keeper's Lodge. Jim, Dave, I realise you are still tied up with the Masters trial but I want you to keep up to speed with this as well and follow any leads and jump on the case as soon as you are free. Jeff, Tina, see if you can establish if Danbury Manor and Casio Grange are both all-female institutions and, if so, what happened to all the male residents from Victoria's Retreat? I want a complete track of all residents, where they went and where they are now and who their case workers were. Let's see if there's any type of pattern.

"Mel, find out what you can about Ivy Mason and Karen Lewis. Where did they work before, is there a connection?"

Mel nodded, pleased to have been assigned something other than typing. "And extract their photos from the Casio Grange and Danbury Manor website and add them to the case board please. Also, do the same for Thomas Hamilton. I need to see faces," he said, turning around to face the board, "and do some digging on him. OK, that's it, everyone, for now," said Mike bringing the briefing to a close. He looked over at Karen and smiled. Karen nodded and smiled sadly at Mike and then slowly left the room.

Mike watched as everyone except Paul followed and then turned to face him. "OK, lets see who this guy Brent is and whether he's from a legitimate cab firm or privately hired. Also, where does he take the residents every day? Let's see what type of jobs they hold down," he said, thinking there was so much to do.

He left Paul studying the case board and went in search of Karen who was standing in front of the vending machine staring. "Let me help you with that," he said, reaching into his pocket for coins. "Hot chocolate?" he suggested, knowing that it was a firm favourite of Karen's. Karen nodded and accepted the offer as she leaned back against the wall.

"Mike, I feel totally lost without the inspector," she said, accepting the hot chocolate with shaky hands. "I'm not sure where to start or what to do next," she said, suddenly feeling completely redundant.

"I totally get that," said Mike, acknowledging her situation. Karen had been the inspectors PA for so long and her secretarial skills were without question exceptional. "But you are part of this team and I now need you to cover a lot of the desk-based work within the unit. I've assigned Mel and Tina a lot of additional duties, so there are all the usual case notes to cover and keep on top of, so please chip in and help Mel and Tina out in that area, to free them up," he said, setting the scene. "Alan, Jeff's new partner has been delayed and won't be with us for a few weeks, so it's all hands on deck. Then I will be throwing lots of stuff at you as we go along," he said, trying to ensure she didn't lose momentum. He really needed her desk-based administration skills to kick in now that he had shuffled up some of the team's job roles.

Karen nodded, pleased that once more she felt useful and then went on to assure Mike that she would do her best to keep the admin side of things up to speed. Mike gestured for her to head back to her desk and then he leaned against the wall.

Jeez, he had been in charge for less than half hour and he had already reassigned the team. There was no way he was going to move into Dhillon's office, he needed to stay firmly at his own desk, opposite Paul where he could keep an eye on the action and be in the thick of things. He turned and headed back into the room.

Ten

Mel stared at the four additional pictures she had placed on the case board and then restructured the position of each to how they connected to the other. The case board was now full of extra information garnered by the team but they still didn't know if Joe Treville was related to any of it or whether his involvement ended when he took Linda hostage, the day he disappeared into thin air.

She had been digging into the history of Ivy Mason, which, due to her young age was very limited. Her picture did nothing to enhance Mel's opinion of her, likening her to a high school student, as opposed to a qualified psychiatrist fit to make life-changing decisions about patient's lives. She stared at her dental braces and pigtail braids and then shook her head in disbelief. She then studied Karen Lewis's profile thinking she too looked too frail and meek to hold such an influential role. There was no substance behind these two females, nothing at all to suggest that they had the knowledge and strength to determine paths for peoples futures.

Sister Bernadette, in contrast, jumped off the case board with almost throttling hands. You definitely wouldn't want to get on the wrong side of her with her stern expression and heavily wrinkled skin and droopy eyes. She not only looked positively ancient but she looked terrifying. No, she was definitely not someone you would want visiting your bedside in the middle of the night if you were unwell or needed comforting. What an odd looking crew of people looking after such troubled souls, Mel thought, as she sat down on a chair as she continued to stare at all the photos.

She looked at Thomas Hamilton, who looked like he had done his best to scrub up for this website mugshot, but still managed to look like he was a homeless soul. Where did you come from Mr Hamilton, what is your backstory and how did you come to be the warden at Keeper's Lodge? She had been digging into Karen Lewis and Ivy Mason's past and was surprised to see very little history. They both had similar qualifications certified against their profile and appeared to have graduated at different times but through the same channels. She noticed they had both trained using an Open University degree course but in different years. There were at least five years separating them from their studies but did they know one another? She desperately wanted to know if there was a connection. Casio Grange appeared, according to the records located, to be Ivy Mason's first role as there was nothing on record anywhere prior to this. Karen Lewis had been employed at Danbury Manor for the last ten years but there was very fragmented history prior to that. She suspected that Sister Bernadette's history would go back to at least BC. She smiled to herself inwardly at her mocking and then looked at Sister Bernadette's photo again pondering her hair colouring underneath her veil. Maybe she didn't have any hair, she considered. Perhaps it had departed along with her manners, she decided, remembering how rude and dismissive she was with Mike when he had visited the home.

Her thoughts then turned to yesterday afternoon, when she had noticed yet another unexplained issue that had kept her awake the entire night. She was preparing Jack's tea when she noticed Dhillon the dinosaur was outside on the garden table, right in the centre, standing upright like it had been placed there. It had really startled her. I mean, how the hell did it get there? She hadn't even opened the patio doors yet, as they had only been home ten minutes and Jack was watching a DVD. She knew for certain they hadn't been in the garden that morning before nursery as they never had time for garden pursuits prior to nursery, especially with her strict routine. He would never have gone to bed without his favourite toy, that was totally out of the question. She had raised it with Mike later that evening but he had persuaded her with his logical thinking that it had possibly been left out there from the previous day, but Mel thought differently. She knew her son would never go to bed without it and he would never have placed it in the middle of the table where he couldn't reach, and neither of them had.

This was eating away at her and she was now finding it really difficult to keep focused on her role. How fucking frustrating. Mike had switched things around to make her job more interesting because he knew her desk-based role was driving her mad and now she was distracted so that she couldn't give it her best shot. She looked down at her feet and then stamped them on the floor. She had to pull herself together before she was either demoted or handed over to the great Doctor Gyllensvan, she thought cynically. She was really beginning to feel herself unravel and now she was beginning to doubt her own judgement. "Why did they let that man out on parole?" she suddenly screamed out loudly, before quickly looking around to check no one had heard her. She placed her head in her hands and sobbed quietly.

Mike stepped back from the doorway so that he remained out of sight. He had witnessed Mel's outburst but had just managed to dodge out of view as she had looked up. He reacted out of instinct and then doubted his own judgement. Should he have gone in and comforted her or was it best that she had that moment to herself to reflect? He just didn't know and it was eating away at him. He was becoming seriously worried about her recent level of thinking. Every night for the last week she had mentioned something that was out of place or not quite left in the place she had remembered it to be and it was alarming him.

He had witnessed her neurotic behaviour and constant questioning and now he was really worried after witnessing this outburst. He had switched her role to make it more interesting to distract her from her paranoia, hoping it would keep her focused but she was clearly not managing. He wanted to suggest to her that she saw Stephanie, the force counsellor, or revisit her counsellor who had painstakingly seen her through her rape ordeal and had monitored her ongoing progress for several years afterwards. He knew Mel trusted her but it was linked to something so painful that it might reverse her progress if she revisited the person she related to her previous torture.

What the fuck was he going to do? Mel was unravelling because Niko had been released and there was nothing he could do to reverse that decision. He stood staring up at the ceiling and then he turned and walked across to Karen's desk.

"Karen, I have a job for you," he announced quietly, making sure no one was in earshot. He gestured for her to follow him to interview room two, after checking it was empty and then closed the door firmly. "Karen I have a job for you," he repeated, "which I want you to run with the utmost discretion. I know from the level of secrecy you applied to Dhillon's health issues that I can totally rely on your integrity and professional approach to the job I have for you…"

Karen looked across at him curiously, wondering what he had in store. She crossed her legs and clasped her hands poised ready to receive the secret information Mike had decided to cloak her with.

"What is it?" she asked, after Mike paused, wondering where to begin.

"OK, so where do I start?" he said, before taking a seat behind the interview desk. He looked up to the ceiling and put his hands behind his head and then he drew breath.

"Niko, the animal that raped Mel seven years ago is out on parole," he said, unable to believe that he had let those unspeakable words come out of his mouth. "He is out on licence, tagged obviously, but he is out nonetheless." He took another breath and closed his eyes and then he opened them looking straight at her.

"Oh my God," said Karen, not knowing what else to say. "How is

Mel? Sorry that's a stupid bloody question, she must be in pieces," she said crossing and uncrossing her legs. "Mike I don't know what to say." She looked down at the floor, unable to tolerate Mike's eyes burning into her. "How can I help? Is that what you've brought me in here for?" she asked nervously.

"Yes," said Mike, realising that he was making her nervous. "I want you to run some checks on him for me. I know it is unethical, but find out where he's living and what his bail restrictions are, down to the letter. Let me know who his parole officer is and anything else you can find out which will reassure me that Niko is…" he paused and then sighed before continuing. "To reassure me that Niko is nowhere near us," he said, clenching his fists and then clicking his knuckles.

"What's going on Mike?" said Karen, realising that Mike was behaving oddly. She knew he would know how bail restrictions work and that the moment Niko crossed the line he would be intercepted and back inside before his feet could touch the ground.

Mike let out another deep breath. "Mel is convinced someone has been in our house, more than once," he carefully added, ensuring he didn't give too much away. "She's probably just being paranoid because she knows he's out but I know it's making her feel unsafe."

"But surely even you know that it's impossible for it to be Niko because he will be unable to breach bail, as his tag alarm would go off and police would intercept him in minutes," she said, puzzled as to where this was going.

"I know that, Karen, but there have been numerous incidents and I think I may need to get Mel some professional help with this, as, like you say, it's almost certainly paranoia. But I also know Mel better than anyone and I have to rule out anything else otherwise it feels like I'm betraying her and I just can't do that," he said standing up and turning to face the wall. "I owe it to her to check," he said, staring up at the ceiling.

He stood staring at the ceiling for what seemed like ages before he turned and said, "All the things that she has noticed are quite small and, to be honest, under normal circumstances, would go unnoticed but Mel is constantly noticing that things are not as she left them. The thing is she has convinced herself that Niko has been in our house. Obviously that does seem illogical seeing as he's tagged but there is a particular incident that she can't get past and now it's getting out of control.

"What incident?" said Karen, curious as to what could have possibly happened to convince Mel that Niko was stalking her.

Mike unclenched his fists, sat back down, and stared directly at Karen. "When Niko received parole, in line with normal protocol, Mel was notified by letter of his release. The letter detailed the conditions prevailing upon him, so that she was reassured of her anonymity and safety. Mel received this letter like it was from death row. She basically feels sentenced to a life of never ever feeling safe again. Anyway this letter is a constant reminder, which until recently she refused to put away or dispose of. However, one day Mel rolled it up and popped it into the vase on the kitchen window ledge in an effort to bring a close to the haunting, for want of a better expression. Sadly, she occasionally retrieves the letter to reread it, I guess because she just can't get past the fact that he's out.

"The last time she retrieved it, it had been folded into four and placed back in the vase. She is convinced she didn't do that, as it was always rolled up and now the whole sorry saga has turned into a nightmare."

"But, Mike, that ludicrous, she obviously folded it subconsciously. We all do things like that. I mean how would he get into your house, let alone the fact that he's tagged and then, and I guess this is the biggest obstacle to explain, how would he know the letter was in the vase, or for that matter would he even know there was a letter, let alone break in to try to find it? Mike, this doesn't make logical sense, surely you can see that?"

"Of course I can see that, for God's sake," said Mike, banging his fist on the table. He placed his hand on his head. "I'm sorry, Karen,

I didn't mean to snap at you," he said, suddenly feeling overwhelmed by his outburst. "Please accept my apology, it's not you I'm cross with, it's just the ludicrousness of it all."

Karen nodded, knowing that Mike seldom lost his temper but nonetheless chose her next words carefully. "Mike, the release of Niko is bound to unsettle her. Any of us would feel the same," said Karen, feeling a little nervous as to where to go from here.

"Karen, I think Mel is suffering from anxiety caused by Niko's release and I would like her to see a counsellor, possibly Stephanie, but I want to approach that with Mel very cautiously and with the utmost privacy. However, if I don't check Niko out I know Mel will feel betrayed, so please just do this one thing so I can at least lay that to rest," said Mike, wondering if Karen was the best person for the job after all.

"Yes of course I will, Mike, but get her to speak with someone," said Karen, rising to her feet. Mike nodded, suddenly wishing he had just checked Niko out himself instead of bringing in an outside person to this extremely private and sensitive situation.

"Karen, please keep this conversation strictly between us," Mike reinforced as she headed to the door.

Karen nodded, "Of course, goes without question," she said, reassuringly.

Mike sat there staring at the wall wishing he hadn't brought in an outside person to this truly delicate situation. Mel would probably see that as a betrayal and now he suddenly felt really nervous. He looked up at the ceiling and then felt like he wanted to shout out loud, just like Mel had earlier. Maybe they both needed counselling, he concluded.

He sighed, drew breath and then headed back to his desk, just in time to hear the end of Paul's telephone conversation.

"Go on," said Mike, eager for Paul to enlighten him with the latest development. He turned quickly to check that Mel was back at her desk and then turned his attention to Paul.

"Well, I've contacted all the cab companies in the immediate vicinity of Keeper's Lodge and none of them have a person on their books called Brent. "So," he said, taking a breath, "my guess is that Brent is employed by the lodge itself."

"I think it would be really interesting to see where this Brent takes them each day and check out what businesses are employing these troubled souls. Then after he's made the drop, let's see where he goes next," said Mike, knowing for certain that there was no way he was staying put within the confines of the station in his inspector capacity, sitting in Inspector Lawrence Dhillon's office, waiting for news to be brought to him. No, he would deputise on the wing, he decided, he was going out.

Paul smiled, knowing exactly what Mike was thinking. He would run the show without doubt but he wasn't missing out on any of the action. "Right, in the meantime, let's see what we can find out about the ownership of Keeper's Lodge."

Eleven

It was 8:05am when they finally veered off to the left and headed up the bumpy gravel drive which led to the stable gates of Keeper's Lodge. They were checking out the mysterious driver, Brent, eager to establish what the hell was going on here.

Mike smiled inwardly to himself thinking how bizarre the whole saga was that he 'Acting Chief Inspector Mike Brugge' was staking out a potential villain, like it was a dodgy drug deal, when in reality he should be sitting in Dhillon's comfortable office, waiting for his team to bring the news to him.

He reached for the flask of coffee that Paul's Wife, Jane, had prepared for them earlier that morning and then turned to face Paul. "Looks like it's going to be a nice day," he said, thinking back to their last visit in the torrential rain.

"Yeah it already feels muggy," said Paul, opening the window to let in some air.

Mike had chosen a fairly good spot to park, where they could see the entrance gates, but sufficiently shielded enough from view. He glanced at his watch hoping that they hadn't missed Brent's pickup and then settled down to wait. He was fairly confident that the pickup would be around 8:30ish seeing as the town was around twenty minutes drive away. That was assuming that the residents started work at 9am. However, the whole stake-out was based on approximations and nothing was guaranteed.

"How's Jane doing?" said Mike, wondering how things were going.

"Ah, she's just blooming," said Paul, his face suddenly blushing from his choice of words. "Pregnancy suits her," he added, "and after such a long wait why wouldn't she be?" he decided to add.

"That's good to hear," said Mike, looking down at his watch again. "I hope we've got the timings right here," he said. They had left really early that morning and the drive into the mountains had been much more pleasurable than the time before but they had needed to stop for petrol and that delayed things somewhat.

"Well let's hope they didn't leave at 8am," said Paul, knowing what Mike was thinking. That was the time they had been originally aiming for but they hadn't quite achieved.

"Well, it is what it is," said Mike, sipping the steaming hot coffee and feeling grateful that Jane had been kind enough to prepare it for them. He looked at his watch again and then stared into his wing mirror willing Brent to appear.

"OK, he's here," said Mike, as a silver minibus came into view and then passed by without noticing them. They watched on as Brent got off the bus, opened the gates and then headed up to the lodge. He was much younger than Mike had first envisaged but then, thinking back to Thomas Hamilton's comment about the ladies liking him, it wasn't really surprising. He had jet black hair and a physique like a bodybuilder with bulging biceps. Not your typical cab driver that was for sure.

"Wonder how long it takes to round up a herd of troubled females," said Paul, conjuring up the image of a sheepdog trying to contain some sort of order. Mike smiled at his analogy and then thought of how long he usually waited for Mel to get ready if they were going out and that was a single female.

"Ah, I expect Mr Hamilton has them all lined up ready to board," said Mike, suddenly wondering about the new girl that was scheduled to take over Unit 12. "Would be interesting to establish where the new resident is from," said Mike sharing his thoughts.

"She was going to take over Rachel's cabin, if you remember."

Paul nodded, agreeing it was something to explore.

"Right, they're coming back," said Paul, suddenly sinking in his seat out of view. Mike smiled, thinking that it was really weird how the mind played tricks on you. It was like when you drove under a bridge and you suddenly ducked your head. It was an uncontrollable instinct but totally pointless, just like Paul's unconscious action. "Don't know why I did that," said Paul, sitting up straight and feeling foolish all of a sudden.

"We all do it," said Mike, thinking that the mind was a strange and complex thing, especially where Mel was concerned at the moment.

Mike waited until they were further down the path almost out of view before he restarted the engine and then pulled away cautiously. They arrived in Ramchester around twenty-two minutes later and parked across the street from Brent. The town was bustling with people starting their day and a queue had formed outside the local coffee shop called 'On the Run', positioned right on the corner outside the station.

"My guess is that he will do the rounds of various businesses around the town, dropping the residents off at different locations," said Mike, watching a young chap take a bite out of a sausage roll as he walked across the crossing, making him lick his lips. Boy how he loved a hot sausage roll.

"Hey, there all getting out, Mike," said Paul, bringing Mike's attention back on track. "Well, five have got out but I can't see anyone else on the bus from here, can you?"

"No, I can't," said Mike, thinking this seemed really strange.

Mike suddenly felt really torn. What would be more beneficial, finding out where the women went or following Brent to his next post.

"Mike, they're heading into the station, we're going to lose them."

"Right, get out and follow them, Paul, and ring me when you find out where they're heading. I will come and get you. I'm going to follow Brent before we lose him," Mike instructed, restarting the engine. He pulled away before Paul even had the chance to close the door properly and then he was gone hot on Brent's heels.

Paul stood staring at the station opposite and then quickened his pace before the women boarded a train without him. Where the fuck were they heading?

Mike followed Brent's minibus deep into the heart of Ramchester and then was totally taken by surprise when the minibus pulled onto the drive of a very fancy residential home on Beverley Drive, which had to be worth in excess of three million.

He reached for his mobile and dialled Mel's number. "Mel, run me an address check in Ramchester will you?" he said, stretching to see the number etched into the sign at the foot of the drive. "Twenty-two Beverley Drive, I'm outside it now and I think it might be the driver's house, the chap who ferries the residents from Keeper's Lodge into town every day."

"OK, hold fire," said Mel, entering the details into the database. "Brent Carter is the registered owner, since 2006, owned outright by the looks of things, no mortgage or other financial liabilities attached to it."

"No 'Mrs Carter' listed, I take it," said Mike, curious as to whether this chap was a family man.

"Nope, solely owned," said Mel, checking the details laid before her.

"OK thanks, see you later."

Mike pondered his next move and then decided to give Paul a call. "How are you getting on?" Mike quizzed, hoping that Paul had managed to board the train on time.

"Well, three of the women disembarked at Fishery Rise, so I had to make the split decision to either jump ship or follow the remaining two. Anyway, I decided on the former, which led me to a day centre out by the harbour and I've just been served a cup of coffee by one of them wearing a name badge identifying herself as Marianne. It's a place that assists homeless people or people with limited means. You know like a drop-in centre type of establishment where people go to get a hot meal or just have someone to talk to. These women are working in the canteen, waiting tables, etc. The next stop on the line is Market Town and then Holden, so Lord knows where the other two got off. How are you doing?" said Paul, wondering if Mike had had any success.

"Well, I followed Brent back to his residence. He lives in Beverley Drive, an extremely upmarket area, not what I was expecting. But I now have a last name for this guy, so we can at least run some checks on him. He's called Brent Carter, so let's see what we can find out about him. What's the name of the day centre?" Mike quizzed, attempting to enter the details of Fishery Rise into his satnav.

"St Clement's," said Paul, wishing he would hurry up as a smelly tramp chose to sit opposite him at his table.

"On my way."

He picked Paul up just after 10am, after purchasing two steaming hot sausage rolls fresh out of the oven from the bakery by the station. "Seems funny that I can't seem to manage a stake-out without a sausage roll," said Mike amused by this fact.

"Indeed," said Paul trying to capture the pastry flakes in the napkin that he had neatly laid across his lap. "Goes hand in hand, I would say," he said, releasing the door catch to get out of the vehicle, so that his next course could be a ciggie.

"So, at least we have the name of one of the places that the residents go to each day," said Paul reaching into his pocket for his lighter. We can now find out what their arrangement is with Keeper's Lodge and whether they have any other drop-in centres in Market Town or Holden," he said, taking a drag of his cigarette. "I'm guessing the other women would be heading to similar places," he added quickly.

"Yeah, I want to find out what this Brent guy's connection is. Why would a wealthy chap drive daily to a halfway house to ferry recovering patients to and from town. It just doesn't make sense," said Mike, thinking that there was something very unethical or sinister going on here.

"Mel's running some checks on Keeper's Lodge and the infamous Thomas Hamilton for us this morning, so let's head back and put everything out for debate."

They arrived back at the station just as Mel was ending a call. She replaced her headset in the cradle and turned to face them. "Well, how did it go?" she asked, wondering if they had managed to garner any information from their early-morning stake-out.

"Bit of a mixed bag really," said Mike, placing his coffee down on his desk. He looked across at Tina and Jeff to see if they had anything to add and then decided to call a briefing.

They filed into the briefing room armed with their morning's findings and waited eagerly for Mike to start the debate.

"Right, let's see what we've got so we all know where we are at. Tina, anything from your end with regard to Cassio Grange and Danbury Manor?" Mike quizzed.

"Well there is definitely a connection of sorts between the two homes," said Tina, looking up from her notes. "The information is extremely vague, however, compiled from various sources but until we obtain a warrant to check these findings against patient lists to see who passed through their hands, nothing is conclusive. The whole process is hindered by the fact that all the records from Victoria's Retreat were destroyed by the fire and the assignment notes are held between both institutions, which, until we get the warrant, is a handicap. Obviously some would have been farmed out elsewhere. However, Karen Lewis's name comes up in records from both homes, so that is a definite connection."

"That's very interesting," said Mike, turning round to face the case board. "So she presumably knows Ivy Mason!"

"Well it's possible but, having said that, I'm sure in their profession they probably know lots of colleagues from other institutions," said Tina, wishing she had more to offer.

"Find out if she ever worked at Victoria's Retreat?" said Mike, thinking there was more to this little whippet than meets the eye.

"I have been looking into both of their medical training qualifications," said Mel, bringing her findings to the forefront. I can't find anything before 2016 for this Karen Lewis, it's like she drops off the radar at that point. Just suddenly appears at Danbury Manor as a psychiatrist and takes up her appointed role. She has a degree of sorts and followed a similar training path to Ivy Mason via the Open University, which again doesn't give us many references to work with… I also think there is a big difference between what is required to be a certified psychiatrist and a counsellor."

"Are you implying that we need to delve into these qualifications and see if they have been fudged in any way?" said Tina.

"Well, we could have counsellors here posing as psychiatrists. Something doesn't sit right with me," said Mel, moving in to take a better look at Karen Lewis and Ivy Mason.

"OK," said Mike, looking at Mel and then across at Tina. "Follow up on whether it is possible to do psychiatry totally online because

I'm not convinced. Postgraduate learning definitely, as people have to constantly refresh their knowledge but I want to know how these women qualified and from where."

"Jeff, anything yet on the ownership of these two homes?" said Mike, hoping that he had unearthed something.

"Both are registered independently but I've yet to delve beyond that," said Jeff, knowing he needed to investigate further.

"Keep digging," said Mike, turning to look at Paul. "Well, we have found out that the driver who chaperones the the women daily into Ramchester is called Brent Carter. I followed his route today and after dropping them at the station he then returned home. Brent lives on Beverley Drive, in a mansion in an extremely wealthy area. What is this guy's involvement here, I ask? It seems bizarre that this wealthy guy takes time out of his daily routine to ferry recovering mentally ill patients to a drop-in centre where they serve beverages and hot meals to down and outs. Paul followed some of them to a place called St. Clement's down near the harbour, which is the place I am referring to. Anything on Thomas Hamilton yet?" Mike quizzed, looking at Mel by the case board with a marker pen in her hand. Mel shook her head. "Yet to be investigated," she said, turning back to the board. "I'll get on that this afternoon."

Mike watched as Mel added all the additional information to the case board and then he dismissed everyone from the room.

"How are you doing?" he asked, removing the marker pen from her hand and turning her round so he could look at her directly.

"I'm OK" she said, picking the marker pen back up and turning back to the board. She really didn't want to be reminded of anything to do with Niko. She wanted to concentrate on the case, nothing else but the case.

Mike smiled, kissed her on the back of the head and then slowly walked out of the room. He was really struggling to know what to do for the best.

"Hey," said Mike as he walked back into the main office. "So how did the trial go this morning?" he said, addressing this question to Jim and Dave who were now back at their desk.

"We got them," said Dave, patting himself on the back.

"Going away for at least twenty years apiece," said Jim, holding up his coffee like it was champagne.

"Good job, guys, well done. Right, I need you both back on the Joe Treville case, as that's falling by the wayside. Find that man and bring his head to me on a plate."

Twelve

"It's so hot today. Who would have thought it would be this beautiful in May?" said Mel, shielding her eyes from the sun and then waving her hands in front of her face, mimicking a fan.

"Yes I keep meaning to pick up a little paddling pool for Henry," said Liz, thinking what fun he would have with that.

"Yeah, that's a really good idea," said Mel, pulling her phone from her pocket to check them out.

They had taken the boys straight to the park after nursery so that they would benefit from the barmy weather and could run off steam. However, they had decided to hunt for ladybirds instead of playing on the swings and were kneeling down beside a log watching with interest. It had really amused Mel how passionate Jack had been telling her about the story Mrs East had read to them that afternoon and now seemed to think he could have one as a pet.

"Look," said Jack pointing to one they had found. Both boys were squealing with excitement as they watched it scurry across the log.

"Ah, it's probably running back to its mummy," said Mel, trying to discourage her son from asking to take it home. "It's really important that we only watch and that we don't disturb him," she said, "so that he can stay with his family," Jack nodded smiling up at her, and then told Henry not to touch.

Mel glanced back at her phone and continued to scroll through the various assortment of paddling pools and then made the impulsive decision to purchase one forthwith. "OK, should arrive tomorrow," she announced, pleased with her spontaneous purchase. "I'll set it up after nursery tomorrow if you fancy coming back."

"Great," said Liz, as Henry pulled at her hand encouraging her towards the swings. She was secretly pleased that Mel had been so impulsive as money was a little tight and, in truth, it would have probably had to wait until the end of the month.

"You coming back for a cuppa?" Mel asked, as she pushed Jack back and forth.

"Ah not today, Mel, I want to get back to Rob. I need to make the most of the time while he's here but tomorrow would be great and I know Henry will love the pool."

The rest of the afternoon passed by quickly and Mel felt really relieved as she made her way back down the stairs. Jack had fallen asleep before she had even finished his evening story and so far she hadn't noticed anything out of the ordinary. Perhaps she had been over thinking things, she pondered, thinking that Mike was right, she needed to stop looking for things and reading too much into them.

She switched on the kettle and then glanced at her watch, willing Mike to appear. She hoped he wouldn't be too long now that she was sitting there by herself. No, she needed to keep busy and keep her mind off Niko, she decided, standing back up. She should really put the bins out, a job Mike normally did but it looked like he had been held up and she didn't want anything else detracting from their evening.

She had made a spaghetti bolognaise earlier and just needed to boil some pasta. She desperately wanted the evening to be just right and was going to pull out all the stops. She knew that she was wearing Mike down with her continuous accusations that things weren't as she left them and she really wanted this to stop. Tonight there was going to be no talk of Niko, none whatsoever.

She slid the patio door to one side and stepped out into the garden and then headed off round the side of the house to retrieve the bins. She looked at all three, debating which two needed dragging round the front and then unhooked the catch on the top of the side gate. The bin was extremely heavy and by the time she had dragged it towards the street, she was completely out of breath. God, how did they accumulate so much rubbish, she pondered, heading back up the path for the recycling. She had just passed through the gate when she heard someone whistling in the distance.

She froze on the spot, a cold shiver running through her entire body. Her instinct made her turn and there he was across the street, leaning against a neighbour's car smiling across at her. There was no doubt about it, it was him. She could see the black leather jacket and his mop of jet black hair. It was him, he was back for more, she wasn't safe, the system had failed her.

She dropped to the floor trying to catch her breath, gasping for air. Her chest felt tight and she just couldn't breath. Her legs wouldn't work and she couldn't move or stand, as she desperately tried to move forwards on her knees. God, her body was failing her, she couldn't move a muscle she felt paralysed with fear. "Help," she called out but there was no sound coming from her mouth. She was calling in her head over and over "Help me someone, help me," but as her lips mouthed the words she knew her desperate cries couldn't be heard.

She tried to stretch out to steady herself against the wall of the house but she just couldn't reach. It felt miles away despite it being right by her side. The brickwork kept coming in and out of focus and then somehow merged with Niko's face laughing. She tried to breathe but she couldn't, she was suffocating and there was no one to help her, no one. Her chest was pounding so loudly that it was drowning out the sound of the sickening tune, which was playing over and over in her head. Her mind was now really muddled as she felt his hands tighten around her throat. Was she on the top of her staircase? She must be, as she could feel the top of the stairs in her stocking feet. Panic and extreme fear engulfed her entire body as though it was squeezing the life out of her. He was going to push her down the stairs, she knew he was. Oh my God I'm going to die.

"Jack, I need to get to Jack," she mouthed before the darkness descended over her and her body lay lifeless on the ground.

"Mel, I'm here," said Mike, stroking her brow, with shaky hands, a tear trickling down his cheek. "Is she going to be all right?" he questioned, turning to face the paramedic who was adjusting the electrodes wired into an ECG monitor.

"Yes, her vitals have settled considerably," he said, reading the report that was spilling out of the machine. "There is no evidence of a heart attack, so everything points to a panic attack," he confirmed, adjusting the drip that had been placed into a vein on the top of Mel's right hand.

"Can you tell us what might have led to this?" he questioned, reaching for his clipboard. "Does she have a history of panic attacks?"

"No, not really, although she is a little anxious at the moment," Mike answered, trying to downplay the fact that he was terrified Mel was losing her grip on reality. "I found her in the side alley when I came home from work," said Mike, trying to retrace his steps. "I didn't see the side gate open at first when I pulled onto the drive and headed straight on into the house. I assumed she was upstairs and called out to her. When she didn't answer I went up but she wasn't there but Jack was fast asleep in his bed. I instinctively knew something was wrong and headed up to the third floor but she wasn't there either. I kept calling her but nothing. When I went back down I noticed the patio door was open but she wasn't in the garden either, so I started to panic and then that's when I noticed the bins had been moved at the top of the side alley and then I found her lying on the floor at the side of the house. She had obviously been putting out the bins but I don't know what caused her to pass out," he said, looking down at her.

"Are you going to take her to hospital?" said Mike, thinking that he needed to arrange a sitter for Jack, who was oblivious to any of this.

"Well, she's been unconscious for a while, which does concern me," said the paramedic, looking at his watch. "It may of course be shock, as there is no evidence of trauma to the head but until we can discuss this with her to find out what happened, we are working on assumptions but, like I said, her vitals are now within an acceptable range."

He looked across at his colleague for collaboration and then made the decision to monitor her for a little longer. "I suggest you make arrangements for your son, just in case," the paramedic suggested.

"Hey, Leanne," said Mike, pacing back and forth in the garden. "I know this is last minute but I was hoping you might be free to look after Jack for a bit. Mel's been taken unwell and we may be heading to the hospital for some observations but I don't really want to disturb Jack," he said, painting the scene with as little information as possible.

"Is she OK?" Leanne questioned, sounding worried.

"I think she's been working too hard, to be honest, and has totally overdone it. She had a bit of a turn and the paramedics would like to monitor her for a while, possibly twenty-four hours." Mike looked across at the door as one of the paramedics gave the nod they were definitely taking her in.

"I will be right over," said Leanne, hanging up without any further explanation needed.

Mike watched on feeling totally redundant as he observed them transferring Mel from the sofa onto a stretcher trolley, wrapped in a red blanket. He felt immediately transported back in time to the night he had found her battered and bruised viciously attacked and left for dead by Niko, her violent rapist.

Had he failed her again? he questioned, discounting her fears and assuming them to be paranoia. He couldn't let her down again, he just couldn't he thought, looking at her limp body being carried out to the ambulance.

He sat on the sofa with his head in his hands, wondering how long they were likely to be at the hospital and what this would mean to Jack in the morning when he woke up without his mummy. Then he stared across at the patio doors. What happened here tonight? What could have possibly taken place to cause Mel to pass out in the side alley?

He stood up as Leanne came flying through the front door. "Mike, you go," she said, looking back out the front door towards the ambulance. "Jack will be fine, I will make sure he's fine," said Leanne, giving him the signal that she had this and was in control.

"Thanks, Leanne, I will keep you posted," he said, heading out onto the drive with a look of gratitude written all over his face.

The ambulance doors closed and headed off to Holden City Hospital, like they had seven years ago and all Mike could do was hold her hand and pray.

"She's stirring," said Mike, alerting the paramedic, who was writing his notes ready to hand to the hospital crew. Mel's eyes had suddenly darted open and her body was now trembling involuntarily.

"Mel, you're safe," said Mike reassuringly, stroking her brow. Mel looked up at Mike and then started to take in her surroundings. "Am I in an ambulance?" she questioned, trying to sit up.

"Yes, we are on the way to the hospital," said Mike, trying to explain where she was.

"Did he rape me?" she questioned, trying to pull back the red blanket, so that she could check her clothing was in place. "Did he rape me?" she repeated again.

"Mel, you passed out in the side alley, while putting out the bins," he explained, trying to piece the event together for her, so that she could recall the incident.

"But I saw him, Mike. He was across the street, leaning against a car." Mike looked at Mel, trying to comprehend what she was saying. "It was him, Mike, I know it was him in his leather jacket and jet black hair. He was whistling that same creepy tune, you know the one I told you I heard as he left the apartment, all those years ago."

"Mel, look at me," Mike asked, trying to divert her gaze away from the ECG machine. "You have had some sort of panic attack brought on by stress," he said, trying to reassure her that she hadn't been raped. "The creepy tune was possibly all part and parcel of the episode and you thought you heard the same tune."

"I saw him, Mike, I saw him. Why won't you believe me?" she suddenly screamed at the top of her voice.

"I believe that you thought you saw him, Mel. The mind plays strange tricks on us when we are stressed and anxious."

"For fuck's, Mike, he was outside our house," she said, suddenly lowering her voice. "You don't believe me do you?" she questioned, trying to rip the drip out of her hand.

"Mel, calm down, you're going to hurt yourself," he said, watching the paramedic try to re-engage the line.

"What are you putting into me?" she screamed.

"It's a light sedative," said the paramedic applying a syringe into the line on the back of her hand.

"Don't let them drug me, Mike, I know what I saw," she said, tears now streaming down her face.

"It's very light, just to relax you a little," the paramedic reassured her.

"It was him, Mike, I know it was him," she said, closing her eyes.

Mike looked up at the ambulance ceiling and sighed in disbelief. What was happening to Mel? Was she having a breakdown? He just didn't know but everything pointed to it.

They arrived at the hospital with Mel drifting in and out of consciousness shouting out Niko's name every so often. Mike's head was all over the place as he glanced at his watch, not knowing which way to turn. It was 8:45pm and instead of having a romantic evening with his beautiful wife, he was watching her being stretchered into hospital, wrapped in a red blanket like she was insane being carried into an asylum. This couldn't be happening.

He followed the ambulance crew into the hospital and listened as they verbally transferred notes to the receiving crew, giving her vitals and on the spot information necessary for her ongoing treatment, together with written notes and ECG recordings.

The A & E department was overflowing with emergency cases, most needing immediate lifesaving treatment. Mel was moved into a cubicle for assessment where a nurse retook Mel's vitals and transferred all the information onto a clipboard, which she placed firmly at the foot of the bed.

"A doctor will be along shortly," the nurse confirmed, as she pulled a curtain across the front of the cubicle.

Mike looked across at his wife, unable to believe what was happening. He needed to look after her and he wasn't going to leave her side until he knew she felt safe.

He looked down at his phone and scrolled for Karen's number. He needed to make that call, he needed to make absolutely certain that Niko had nothing to do with this episode this evening.

"Hey, Karen," he said, stepping out from behind the curtain and moving away from the cubicle so that he couldn't be overheard by Mel. "Karen, I need you to run some immediate checks on Niko's whereabouts this evening. Mel claims to have seen him near our house today and I need to rule out that possibility," he said firmly, and then, wondering to himself if she had made a start on the task he had set her earlier.

"OK, I'm straight on it," she confirmed, promising to get back to him as soon as she had anything.

Mike let out a deep breath and then decided he needed a coffee. Well, he needed a whisky if he was honest but a coffee would do for now. He popped his head back round the curtain to ensure Mel was still asleep and then followed the arrows towards reception in search of a vending machine. He rummaged in his jeans pocket for some coins and then he spun round to face the reception doors. God, it was like deja vu creeping over him then. He had suddenly recalled the vision of Jim and Dave coming through the doors when Mel had been attacked all those years ago. He gave himself a shake, inserted a coin into the slot and pressed the button for extra sugar. This was going to be a long night.

He slowly walked back towards Mel and then quickened his pace, suddenly panicking that she might wake up while he wasn't there. He had already made a promise that he wouldn't leave her side and yet he had wandered off in search of coffee. He just couldn't think straight and wasn't making the best decisions. He returned as Mel was murmuring and rolling her head back and forth and shouting out Niko's name every now and again. He sat down next to the bed and waited for the doctor to come and confirm that his wife was not going mad.

He looked down at his phone willing it to ring and then jumped out of his skin when it did. "Hey Karen," he said, stepping out from behind the curtain. "What have you got for me?"

"Mike, Niko hasn't left his flat all day. His tag has confirmed he's been stationary."

"OK, thanks, Karen, that's good to hear. Have you had the chance to run any other checks yet, like I asked?" he said, suddenly feeling impatient and wanting answers.

"Yes, but the information is limited, Mike, he hasn't breached any of the conditions. Whoever Mel thought she saw, it wasn't him. She either saw someone similar and it was mistaken identity or she imagined the whole episode. Like I said, Mike, the mind plays funny tricks on us when under stress."

"Yeah it does," he said, collaborating that fact. "Thanks, Karen, goodnight."

He pulled back the curtain and stepped back inside. He repositioned the chair and reached for his coffee. God, it was disgusting and now it wasn't even hot. He replaced it on the side cabinet.

"Who were you talking to?" Mel questioned, staring him straight in the eye. Mike jumped, totally not expecting Mel to be awake, let alone to have tuned into the conversation he was having.

"I was," he coughed and cleared his throat, "I was just checking out Niko's tag restrictions, Mel, to ensure he hadn't breached any of his conditions," he said, suddenly feeling really uneasy.

"And," said Mel, attempting to sit up.

"He hasn't left his flat all day. I've just had it confirmed," said Mike, reaching out for her hand.

"But I saw him, I know I did."

"Mel, you have been under tremendous strain and to be honest I think we all need a break away from all this," he said, wondering where to start. A tear rolled down her face, which she wiped away angrily and then turned to face the doctor as he appeared from behind the curtain.

"Good Evening," he said, collecting the clipboard from the end of the bed, before moving in closer. "I'm Doctor Crowley," he offered, before extending his hand out to them both.

"So you have had a bit of a turn, I see from your notes here, and have experienced a panic attack," he said, reading through the comments made by the ambulance crew. "Can you explain to me what it was that brought on this episode," he asked, placing the clipboard down on the bed, while retrieving a small torch from the top pocket of his white coat.

He shone it into her eyes and then felt around her temples, before replacing it in his pocket.

"I've been a little on edge recently," Mel replied, looking directly at Mike. "I guess I've been overdoing it," she added, in an attempt to make light of the matter. She looked across at Mike with a stare that he immediately deciphered as a warning signal that if he divulged anything too invasive she would shoot him down in pieces.

"I guess everything just suddenly became a bit much and I passed out," she said, hoping that he would be satisfied with the whistle-stop tour of her recent health issues.

"I see," said the doctor, picking up the clipboard again to check that the paramedic attending her didn't identify anything more sinister. "It says here that you were found unconscious in the side alley of your home," the doctor continued to question.

"Yes, I was putting out the bins, possibly a task too many after an exceptionally busy day," she added, while continuing to stare at Mike.

"It also states here that you displayed signs of distress in the ambulance and that in order to calm you down a sedative was administered, as you were trying to forcefully remove the line from your hand," he said, looking over the top of his small rimmed glasses.

"Look, Doctor Crowley, I know you're only doing your job but I can assure you that the reason for my outburst was because I was disoriented. It's not everyday you wake up in an ambulance with a drip in your arm," she reasoned, while attempting to sit up, adjusting her pillows.

"Let me help you with that," Mike offered, jumping up and glaring at her, while shielding his face from view.

"Well, I can't see any evidence of physical trauma and your vitals are all within an acceptable range," he said, turning to face Mike for reassurance. Mike nodded in agreement, like he was being handcuffed and gagged and then collaborated her version with a smile.

"We will monitor you for another hour or so and then I can see no reason why you can't be discharged," he said, returning the clipboard to the foot of the bed.

Mike shook the doctor's hand, confirming that he would keep a close eye on her and then he pulled the curtain back with a forceful sweep after he excited the cubicle.

"I know, I know," said Mel, with her hands in the air, pre-empting what Mike was about to say.

"How could you do that, Mel, when you know how serious this is?" he yelled, unable to believe that she had been signed off like she had grazed her knee.

"Because I'm not staying in this godforsaken place any longer than I have to," she snapped, looking at the floor to see if she had any shoes.

Mike sat down beside her and took a deep breath and then followed it with another. "Mel, this is serious. What do you think would have happened if I hadn't come in when I did. What if Jack had woken up while you were in the side alley and couldn't find you. He would have been frightened out of his tiny mind and may have even wandered out onto the street. It just doesn't bear thinking about," he said, in an effort to make Mel realise what was at stake.

"He wouldn't have got past the stair gate," said Mel, tears running down her cheeks.

"Mel, you know what I'm saying. This could have happened while he was awake and downstairs with you," he said, passing her a tissue.

"I know, I'm so sorry, Mike, but I did see him, I swear I did," she said, her tears now free flowing, so that she was choking and gasping between sobs.

"We need to get you some help with this. Niko's release has hit you much harder than we all thought and you need to talk this through with a counsellor," Mike offered. Then, trying to reason with her maternal side added, "For Jack's sake as well as your own." He wrapped his arms around her and held her.

"I'm not mad, Mike. Don't go packing me off to one of those homes like the ones we are investigating," she said, feeling really alarmed. "And don't make out I'm unfit to look after Jack," she added, suddenly feeling really angry.

"Mel, I would never do that, you are a great mum. I just want you to be well and I want to get you the help I think you need. Why don't you have a chat with Stephanie, instead of bringing in any outsiders. Let's do this with her, where we have a little more control."

Mel nodded, drying her tears. "OK but I'm coming home and I'm still coming to work," she said, laying down the ground rules.

"I think we need to address how we manage our day-to day stuff until you get a handle on this. I don't think you should go home to an empty house at the moment. I will organise for Jane or Leanne to pick up Jack from nursery for the time being."

"But how will that work?" Mel questioned, suddenly feeling the panic set in all over again.

"We will commute to and from the office together and I will adjust my hours until we get past this," he offered, trying to work it all out in his head. But tomorrow we will both stay at home, so that you can rest. Hey, we will get through this, I promise," he said leaning forward to kiss her on the forehead.

Thirteen

"Paul, I need to talk to you privately about something extremely delicate and personal."

"What is it?" Paul asked, switching his mobile across to the other ear. "It's Mel, she's not been feeling too great recently. Niko has been released on licence and the strain of it all has shaken her up. Let's just say she's in a bit of a delicate place at the moment, for want of a better expression. Anyway, I want to take the day-to-day strain off her a bit, which is where you come in."

Paul listened intently while Mike did his best to convey the situation without giving anything too sensitive away and then he discussed it with Jane later that evening. A new timetable was put in place and a brand new routine was set in motion, allowing Mel the space to be able to come to terms with Niko's release.

"I'm really grateful for your and Jane's help with Jack," Mike offered, as he indicated to turn into the gravel drive leading up to Keeper's Lodge.

"It's really no trouble," said Paul, knowing that Mike didn't want to discuss the matter in detail. "Jane's really enjoying having something new to concentrate on, other than her usual chores. She's actually found it quite boring being at home after being made redundant but there's no point in her pursuing a new career path this side of the baby's arrival and to be totally honest she's enjoying every second of it. All those maternal hormones kicking in," he said jovially.

Mike smiled as he reached out the window towards the intercom, "Well all the same it's truly a great help to us and very much appreciated," said Mike, pressing the button a second time. They waited a few more minutes and then decided to let themselves in.

"I'll open it," said Paul exiting the vehicle, before Mike could disagree. Paul jumped back in, leaving the gates open and Mike continued his way along the gravel drive.

"Yeah, it would be good to catch them off guard," said Mike, hoping that in doing so, they would unearth more than Thomas Hamilton's account of things. He parked his van in the same space as before and then decided to move it out of view at the far end, where it was less obvious.

"What's with the cloak and dagger approach?" said Paul, amused by Mike's sudden change of direction.

"Well, if we are going to take them by surprise, let's not make our arrival obvious, as this way we can buy ourselves more time," said Mike, stepping out of the vehicle and looking towards the cabins.

"Like it," said Paul, closing the van door quietly. "What do you have in mind?"

"Cabin 12, for a start," said Mike, stepping into the forest in the same direction as Thomas had led them the other day. "I want to meet the occupant of cabin 12 and, providing she is in of course, this is the most likely way of achieving it."

Paul smiled, knowing what Mike was like, charging in all guns blazing. "It really is remote," said Paul, taking in the forest surroundings and picturing it at night. "I still find the whole setup really bizarre, if you ask me."

Mike held up his hand and gestured to Paul to stop and then turned and mouthed the words, "someone's coming."

"Well what do you expect me to do scramble up a tree like a squirrel?" he said, in a whisper. Mike grinned and then signalled for them to move forwards again as the cabin door closed with a bang.

It suddenly reopened and a heavily pregnant woman stepped out right in front of them. "Oh, I'm sorry to startle you," said Mike, trying to prevent her gasp from turning into a scream but we are looking for cabin 12," he said making the whole scene seem very above board and normal. She pointed towards the backdrop of forest to the cabin at the highest peak and then turned and fled back inside her cabin.

"Did you see the size of her?" said Mike, continuing before she raised the alarm.

"Yeah, ready to drop, I would say," said Paul thinking about the petite bump his wife Jane had at the moment.

"Bit odd though, isn't it?" said Paul, thinking that a woman in her condition was the last thing he had envisaged coming across.

"Yes, a question for Mr Hamilton later," said Mike, stopping outside cabin 12.

"Can I help you gentleman?" said Thomas Hamilton, stepping out from the shadows.

"Yes," said Mike, freezing, feeling like he had been busted by his parents, trying to sneak out when he was grounded. "We were hoping to be able to speak with the occupant of cabin 12," he stated in a calm voice, wondering if Mel or Tina had managed to secure a warrant on the place yet.

"Well, I suggest you come up to the main lodge," he said gravely, waving his arm in the air, indicating that they should follow him. "And sign in using our normal checking in process," he added. "I don't want you frightening any of the residents, wandering around in the forest unannounced," he said, angrily.

Mike suddenly felt foolish, what was he thinking? Such a rookie mistake to make. "Ah, apologies, Mr Hamilton, we did try to alert you to our arrival at the gate but the intercom system appears to be malfunctioning again," he added, trying to justify their presence.

"Nevertheless, Sergeant, our reception is at the main lodge and like I said I don't want you unnerving any of the ladies," he said, stopping at the foot of the stairs.

They followed him up the staircase, gesticulating to one another like two naughty school boys and then waited while he unlocked the front door. "Please sign in," he said sternly pointing to the visitors' book. They signed in in silence and then followed Mr Hamilton through to the same lounge as before. "Take a seat," he instructed, pointing to the nearest sofa to the door. There were no pleasantries or coffee offerings attached to this visit. Mr Hamilton seemed really pissed.

"Like I said, Mr Hamilton, apologies for not booking in immediately on arrival," said Mike, in an attempt to break the ice. "But your non-response at the gate suggested to us that you were either absent from your post or engaged somewhere else with your duties," said Mike, determined to proceed further with his visit.

"Mr Hamilton, I must say I was surprised to see one of the young ladies is pregnant, almost full term, I would say!" he continued.

"Yes Mary-Rose is expecting and the due date is almost upon us," he said, sitting down and clasping his hands.

"Is this the first pregnancy the home has had to deal with?" said Paul, wondering if this was an isolated case.

"It's happened once before, many years ago, so it is very rare."

"Must be quite hard to manage what with all the extra maternity care they require, let alone the burden on their fractured souls," said Paul, wondering how to describe a person who was recovering from mental health issues.

"Well, like I said to you before, Sergeant, these ladies are free to come and go as they please. They are adults and are entitled to conduct relationships, just like anybody else. While we do try to discourage male interest, in an attempt not to add any other emotional issues to their disturbed minds, we cannot enforce celibacy, you understand."

Mike nodded, agreeing that this would be a heavy burden on not only the individual but on the home and the ongoing care of the resident. "In circumstances such as this, Mr Hamilton, what ongoing support will that young lady receive from this institution? My guess is that you are now duty bound to provide some sort of ongoing assistance," Mike questioned.

"Mary-Rose will move on to a mother and baby unit, Sergeant, where she will be given the support required, which will serve the best outcome for both mother and child."

"Sergeant, what is your interest in the new resident of Unit 12?" said Thomas, curious as to the purpose of their second visit. "I thought your interest here was with Rachel Blossom, to which I have already advised we have no further information."

"Mr Hamilton, we are investigating her disappearance which is the ongoing purpose of this investigation. However, to aid our search it would be really useful to follow some of the patients root paths both before and after their stay here. We are trying to look for similarities and patterns," said Mike, hoping he hadn't given too much away.

"What institution did the new resident come from?" Paul quizzed, hoping that they wouldn't lose Mr Hamilton's input at this point.

"Danbury Manor, I believe," he said looking up to the ceiling to recall the information. "Yes, that's right, Danbury Manor."

"What is her name?" asked Mike, realising that he had no idea who she was. "Fiona Willis," said Thomas recalling this information instantly.

"Where is she now?" said Paul, curious as to whether she had actually been in the cabin when they approached it.

"Well she will either be in her cabin or perhaps the sun lounge, I don't track them, this is not a prison."

"So she won't be at work today then?" said Mike, wondering if this would provoke a reaction.

"No, Miss Willis is very new to us and hasn't yet been appointed to a role in one of the many companies that support us with our project."

"Mr Hamilton, you mentioned to us during our last visit that you had limited knowledge of the driver who transports the residents to and from town. Is it the same driver every day or are there several drivers?" Paul quizzed, wondering how many Brent Carters they might be looking for.

"Same driver everyday," Thomas confirmed, "but he never comes up to the lodge, so I have no involvement with him. "Now unless there is anything else, I need to get on with my duties," he said standing up.

"Mr Hamilton, what hospital will Mary-Rose go to to have her baby and what mother and baby unit will she transfer to afterwards?" he continued.

"Sergeant, this is a fairly isolated incident, so I have no information to offer you with regard to this. Her midwife and carer will have all the details on this I'm sure," he said, edging towards the door.

"Well, if you could furnish us with the names of the midwife and carer, together with their contact details we would be most grateful," said Mike, staying firmly in his seat.

"Sergeant, why are you so interested in Fiona Willis and Mary-Rose?" he quizzed, opening the lounge door.

"Like I said, Mr Hamilton, we are investigating the disappearance of Rachel Blossom, and any leads, patterns or similarities need to be explored, so with that in mind perhaps you would be so kind as to locate Miss Willis, so that we can have a chat."

Thomas stood rooted to the spot, staring into space. "Mr Hamilton, why are you so reluctant to help us with our enquiries?" Paul asked, crossing his legs and making himself comfortable, as if to say he wasn't moving until he had achieved his objective.

"It's not so much reluctance, Sergeant, it's just I feel like we are under unnecessary scrutiny and seeing as we provide such a valuable contribution, helping them take that final step towards independence, I feel somewhat unjustly persecuted. I guess I'm just making a stand," he said, turning towards the door again. Wait here,

I will see what I can do."

"I actually feel really uncomfortable now," said Paul, turning to face Mike. "You know, seeing as he phrased it like that, but something's not right here."

"Well perhaps he's just not part of it. You know they have placed him here to watch over the residents but that's his total involvement," said Mike, standing up to walk across to the window. He pulled back the curtain to view the surroundings from the side elevation and then turned to face Paul. "There's another gravel drive leading towards the rear of the plot," said Mike, walking towards the window at the far end of the room. "It would be interesting to find out where that leads," he said, turning round when he heard voices approaching from the hallway.

Thomas re-entered the room accompanied by a frail looking girl who looked somewhere between eighteen and twenty. She had long mousy hair, tied back in a ponytail and was wearing an old-fashioned floral dress. "This is Fiona," said Thomas, introducing her to the proceedings. "Like I said, Fiona is new to us and is just settling in," he added.

"Good afternoon, Fiona," said Mike, walking towards her with his hand extended ready to shake hands. He stalled halfway across the room, when he noticed her recoil and place her hands behind her back and then turn her head so that she couldn't see him.

"I'm DS Brugge and this is my partner DS Osman from Holden CID," Mike continued, suddenly feeling really uneasy. "There is nothing for you to be alarmed or concerned about, we would just like to ask you a few questions," he said, as he retook his seat near Paul. "You are probably wondering why we have singled you out from all the other residents, but it's merely because you are new here and have transferred from Danbury Manor. Similar circumstances to a young woman we are trying to locate. Please sit down," he offered, pointing to the sofa opposite. She looked across at Thomas, who nodded, and then sat down to order. "Fiona, do you know a young girl called Rachel Blossom?" Mike asked, eager to have this question answered. "She used to reside at Danbury Manor, the same as you prior to coming here."

Fiona sat staring at the floor, her hands clasped on her lap. She looked as nervous as hell and was now twisting them like she was wringing them out. "Fiona, have your paths crossed at any time during your stay there?" Mike continued.

"I don't think so," she suddenly said, almost in a whisper.

"Please, take a look at this picture," said Paul, standing up to pass her a photo. "It's a little out of date, possibly four or five years but it may jog your memory. Fiona, please look at the photo and see if you recognise this woman," Paul asked again. Fiona glanced at it briefly and then shook her head.

"Fiona, how long were you resident at Danbury Manor?" said Paul, retaking his seat. He placed the picture back in his inside pocket and waited for his question to be answered. "Fiona, do you remember how long you were at Danbury Manor?" Paul repeated.

"I'm not sure," she answered quietly, staring down at her brown lace-up shoes.

"Did you reside anywhere else prior to Danbury Manor or did you only reside there?" Mike asked curiously.

"I can't remember," said Fiona, avoiding his gaze. "It was a long time ago," she said, starting to tremble.

"I think that's possibly enough now, gentleman," said Thomas, suddenly looking really protective towards his ward.

"Just a few more questions, Mr Hamilton, so that we can get a clearer picture," said Mike, making sure that they didn't lose their only connection at this point. "Fiona, if it was a long time ago, then that suggests you have been at Danbury Manor for quite some time, possibly several years. Can you remember who your nurse was during your stay there?" Mike continued to prob. "You must remember who your nurse was, Fiona?"

"I think her name was Ivy Lewis," she stuttered, wringing her hands so tight, they were now deathly white. "No, that's not right," she said, staring upwards trying to recall. "I'm sorry I can't remember," she said tearfully.

"It's OK, Fiona, you're doing really well. Do you think you might have stayed at Cassio Grange before that?" Mike quickly slipped in, before Thomas brought a close to the whole proceedings. Mike looked across at Paul, who nodded in acknowledgement that they had both picked up on the fact that Fiona had managed to merge both Ivy Mason and Karen Lewis's names together, suggesting that she knew them both.

"I can't remember," she said again, "I might have done."

"OK, Sergeant, I really think that's enough for today," said Thomas, finally bringing a close to the questions.

Mike frowned, agitated that his questioning was halted, just when they were making progress. "Well, thank you for your time today, Fiona," he said, standing up to shake her hand. He withdrew it quickly, remembering his earlier mistake and then smiled as he watched her scurry from the room.

"Thomas, please furnish us with the details of the midwife assigned to Mary-Rose before we leave here today," said Mike, making absolutely certain that this did not fall off the radar.

Fourteen

"We really need to get hold of that warrant," said Mike, turning his van around so that they could exit Keeper's Lodge. "I just don't understand why it's taking so long," he continued, catching sight of the lodge in his wing mirror as they continued down the gravel drive. He desperately wanted to explore the other path at the rear of the building but decided without the warrant it would hinder the progress they had already made.

"Paul, find out what the hold up is," he requested, feeling more and more pissed off as they continued down the drive. Mike listened as Paul entered into a conversation with Tina and then ended his call with a sigh. "Nope, Tina has chased it again this morning but the person she spoke with couldn't actually find the original request, so Tina has had to start the process again," he said, feeling really miffed by the delay.

"That all seems a bit hit and miss to me," said Mike, thinking they didn't usually experience delays with warrant requests, which is for the most part instantaneous. He was reluctant to do the visit today without it but after chasing it himself earlier and speaking to a young clerk who seemed to have no idea what she was doing had decided to tackle the infamous Mr Hamilton again with his hands tied behind his back.

"Yeah, almost feels like there is someone purposefully meddling with our inquiry," said Paul, echoing Mike's thoughts.

They drove back to the station in silence, each lost in their own thoughts. Mike was really beginning to struggle with the fatigue attached to his intermittent sleep pattern, which was now plaguing him night after night. He had tossed and turned the entire night worrying about Mel and what this would mean to their family unit if Mel continued to decline.

He was worried sick that she would have a complete breakdown, which would not only affect Jack, one of his primary concerns, but he just couldn't cope with the love of his life suffering the way she was. It was also impacting her new role that he was trying to carve for her, now that he had some power to influence the day-to-day running of the team. While this may be lower down the list of priorities it was still a major concern. He knew how much Mel hated her current role and that this was having an effect on her happiness, and adding some extra responsibilities to her role to make it more interesting seemed key to her continued happiness working at the unit. It was the link to making her work-life work in harmony with their family life and now with Niko's release the whole fucking thing was caving in on them.

It had taken years for Mel to sufficiently recover from the aftermath of her rape. Years of counselling trying to come to terms with what happened. He had cradled her in his arms, night after night, trying to reassure her that he would keep her safe from harm and that nothing like that would ever happen to her again. They had painstakingly worked through the torment together and then with the arrival of Jack their world was complete, transformed beyond their wildest dreams. Mike had felt certain that if he jazzed up her work life and added some baubles and tinsel, Mel's daily routine would be as perfect as he could make it.

But every time he thought about that sick twisted bastard, he felt like he wanted to squeeze the life out of him, and now, somehow, despite Karen confirming that he hadn't breached his bail terms, he seemed to be taking over Mel's world like a tumour overtaking her body, out of control and she was now losing the battle. He was a fucking termite infesting their world and he was going to stamp him out and obliterate him, of that he was certain.

He thought about his beautiful wife and how much he loved her with all his heart. Seeing her unravel again was complete torture and he just couldn't let it happen, he wouldn't let it happen, full stop.

"Hey," said Paul, giving him a nudge. "You OK?"

"Yeah, why?" said Mike, giving himself a shake.

"Just the way you are gripping the steering wheel and the look on your face," said Paul, thinking that it looked like Mike was about to rip it from its column. "Yeah, just a lot on my mind," said Mike, pulling into the station car park. He pulled on the handbrake and let out a sigh and then rotated his head making his neck crack. He reluctantly opened the door and stepped out of the van watching Paul light up a cigarette. Boy could he do with one of those right now, he mused, breathing in the smoke that was wafting over the van.

He strode towards the station steps, leaving Paul to enjoy his smoke and headed off inside in search of Mel. The new arrangement meant that Mel was always in company and never by herself. She was surrounded by her colleagues at all times and Mike had made her promise never to leave the station by herself. They would travel to and from the station together, so that Mel felt safe and secure at all times.

He stopped at the vending machine after nodding at Bridget as he passed through reception and then smiled inwardly as he made his selection. He could hear Mel chatting with Tina reasonably cheerfully, which suddenly made him feel a little better. They would get through this together, as always, he knew they would.

He smiled through the double doors at Mel holding up his coffee, indicating that it was on offer if she desired. She shook her head, implying that she was OK and then strolled towards her husband returning his smile. "How did it go at the lodge?" Mel asked, eager to catch up on all that was on offer. She was desperately trying to keep her mind focused on the job and hoped that Mike came bearing gifts.

"Well, we were, as you can imagine, hindered by not having a warrant, which is really beginning to piss me off," he said, feeling somewhat aggravated that they were right back at the beginning with their application. "Tina informed us that our application was not on the system, so she has had to apply all over again."

"Really?" said Mel, looking somewhat perplexed. "Mike, I applied for that myself. I put in the application and I have a reference number," she said, thinking something wasn't right. "Who did Tina speak to, do you know?" she quizzed, walking across to her desk. "Look I have it here," she said, turning her laptop around to face him.

"Paul made the call but she told him that she had to make the application again," he said, sitting down behind his desk.

"Where is Tina?" he asked, thinking she was here a minute ago.

"Ladies, probably," said Mel, looking at her empty desk. They waited for her to return and then grilled her about her conversation.

"What did they actually say?" Mel quizzed, showing Tina the reference number.

"Well, they just said there was no record of our application, so I processed it again. The clerk was a bit dizzy, if I'm honest," she added.

"Very convenient," said Mike, starting to feel that everything was against them. "Keep on it, Tina, and I want to know the minute it's in."

"You seem very agitated. What happened at the lodge?" Mel asked, staring directly at him.

"Well, we tried to approach unannounced, without checking in," he said, pulling open his desk drawer to rummage for a sugar sachet. "We didn't want to give them the heads up, hoping that we would get a better idea of what was going on there but we were busted," he said with a smirk. Mel laughed, picturing them getting caught creeping around. "Anyway we headed straight for the cabins before that happened, hoping to meet some of the residents but before we could, Mr Hamilton appeared out of the shadows and intercepted us."

"I see," said Mel, sitting down on the edge of Mike's desk, to hear the full story.

"We did, however, see one of the residents, who stepped out of her cabin and then scurried back in again," said Mike, turning to face the window. "And?" said Mel, eager to hear what happened next.

"She was heavily pregnant and, as it turns out, the baby is due in the next week or so," said Mike, turning around to face her.

"You're kidding," said Mel, standing up and then sitting down again.

"Yeah, surprised the hell out of us, but appears to be an isolated case. Thomas Hamilton made it quite clear that the residents could come and go as they pleased and that there was no curfew as such. He went to great lengths to emphasise that while they discouraged male interest, so as to not complicate their final steps and hinder their progress, it was not something they could enforce."

"Yes, I guess they are adults and one step away from independence. So much harder to monitor than when they were in a secure home with no outside influence," Mel added, thinking it through.

"He did say it had happened once before, many years ago but that this was a rare occurrence."

"What will happen to her? I mean she is just about to make the leap back into society and managing her own emotions will be hard enough, let alone a small baby's needs. Just think of all the hormones floating around. Suppose she gets postnatal depression?" Mel continued to speculate.

"I did ask what support she would receive and apparently she will be transferred to a mother and baby unit," Mike confirmed. "We also spoke to Fiona Willis, the girl who moved into Unit 12, which was the cabin originally assigned to Rachel. She was a funny little thing. Meek and mild, barely spoke and sat trembling like she was being interrogated. We did unearth that she had been transferred from Danbury Manor but what was more interesting, she said she knew Ivy Lewis."

"What," said Mel, thinking Mike had got this wrong.

"Yes, she managed to merge Ivy Mason's name with Karen Lewis's, so she knew them both by the look of things. Which also means she may have stayed at Casio Grange the same as Rachel. There is a pattern emerging here, Mel, so check through all the records as far as you can get. I want a warrant and access to records of all three homes," he said, turning round to face the window.

He turned round again suddenly, catching hold of Mel's hand. "Share the load with Tina, obviously," he said, wanting to ensure she knew he was looking out for her.

"Yes of course I will. Stop worrying, Mike, I like keeping busy, you know that."

He watched as she returned to her desk and then looked across at Paul who was engaged in a conversation with Jeff and Tina. He was filling them in with this morning's findings and he smiled inwardly when he heard Tina gasp when she learned that they had run into a heavily pregnant woman at the lodge.

His thoughts then turned to Joe Treville, wondering where he was hiding, and then he headed into the briefing room to see if Jim and Dave had added anything else to the case board.

He stood in front of the board, staring at Joe's picture and then reached for his phone. He scrolled for Dave's number and then sat patiently while it continued to ring. He was just about to give up when Dave answered, sounding completely out of breath.

"You OK?" Mike asked, thinking that he sounded like he had just run a marathon.

"Yes, we are over at Arberlour Drive, outside Linda's flat," he said panting.

"Go on," said Mike, eager to hear what they had unearthed.

"Well, we are trying to retrace Joe Treville's steps from the moment he left Linda's flat when you disturbed him. However, as you know there is no surveillance on the outskirts of town but we have picked him up on some camera footage getting on the 96 bus on the Ridge Way, heading in the direction of the hospital. It was around twenty minutes after you found Linda, if our timings are correct but we are certain it was him."

"Where did he get off?" Mike quizzed.

"Well, that's where we are stomped at the moment," said Dave, sounding really pissed off. "We have no footage of him getting off the bus, it's like he vanished into thin air."

"That suggests that he stayed on until he reached the outskirts of town on the other side," said Mike, wondering where they were heading with this.

"No, I said the bus was heading in the direction of the hospital but it actually terminated at the bus terminal by Lucy's Diner, where the final three passengers disembarked. We've run through the footage three times at the station this morning, Mike, joining everything we got from various sources. He didn't get off but he definitely got on. That's why we are at Arberlour Drive now. We've done the bus journey, retracing his steps and we are now back at Linda's flat."

Mike paused wondering when or if Linda would return there, or whether the experience was way too painful to even consider it. "Go on," said Mike, starting to feel a little impatient.

"There are two possible routes he could have taken to get to the stop where he boarded the bus. We took the most obvious route earlier today but there is another path he could have taken, assuming he left the block via the fire escape at the rear of the building. We are running through this as if we were him, so that we can make the decisions he may have made. Mike, I will call you later when I have more."

Mike hung up curious where they were heading but he had complete trust in Jim and Dave's skills at sniffing out missing people. He knew they would be climbing inside Joe Treville's head by analysing everything from the crime scene itself until they had him in their grasp. Anyway he had to trust in their judgement what other clues were there…? None whatsoever.

He pondered momentarily on the fact that he was sighted boarding the 96 bus and then decided to view the footage himself. He made his way round to the surveillance room after alerting Mel and then rummaged through the case files on the shelving.

"What ya got?" said Mel following him into the room.

"Joe Treville has been sighted boarding a bus twenty minutes after holding Linda hostage," said Mike, looking at the cassette tape that Dave had labelled 'Joe Treville–bus journey' compiled from traffic/law enforcement cameras, together with some bus company footage. "Dave just gave me the tip off. They are at Arberlour Drive now retracing Joe Treville's potential route. Trouble is he was seen boarding the bus but then basically disappeared."

"What, he didn't get off?" Mel queried, sitting down next to him to view the footage.

Mike slipped the tape into the receiver enabling them to view Joe Treville's final steps before falling off the radar. They watched him run across the road and board the bus with seconds to spare, causing the driver to reopen the doors. He was wearing jeans and a white t-shirt and there was no doubt that it was him. They watched the journey pieced together by Jim and Dave observing passengers getting on and off at various stops along the way, until the bus finally pulled in at the terminal opposite Lucy's Diner where three passengers disembarked. "Where the fuck did he go?" said Mike, replaying the footage from the beginning again.

He pulled the tape from the machine after watching it through a third time and then replaced it in the cassette box. "The guys like a chameleon," said Mike, thinking how he had managed to elude them at Arlington Terrace. "How does he do this?" said Mike, pulling at his hair and turning to face Mel.

"Well, he definitely boarded the bus, Mike, there is no doubt about that. Maybe he stayed on board out of the driver's sight, on the upper deck hiding behind the seats or something. The driver probably glanced in the upstairs mirror briefly and perhaps exited the driver's cab unaware he was still on board," said Mel, trying to come up with a logical explanation.

Mike pondered Mel's suggestion, concluding that it was possible for Joe Treville to have then made the return journey without being noticed, jumping ship at any point later on that day.

Mike wound the footage on carefully, ensuring he hadn't missed anything as he scrolled until he was at the point where the bus left the terminal again thirty minutes later.

Once more they scrutinised the footage willing Joe Treville to step off the bus at some point along the way until the footage suddenly went fuzzy and then ended. "We need to run through the rest of the traffic camera footage," said Mike, standing up to stretch his legs, feeling agitated that the lads had stopped at that point.

"Where the fuck did he go," yelled Mike, banging his fist down on the desk and making Mel jump.

"Mike, there are some points along the route he could have got off which are not on the enforcement cameras. Small sections of roads which are out of view, etc."

"Yes, but the bus would have to physically stop and open the doors and legally they are not supposed to do that unless it's an emergency," said Mike, thinking it was unlikely.

"Well, perhaps he threatened the driver," said Mel, retrieving the tape from the machine. "Now that we know he boarded the bus, we should interview the driver," Mel added. "Perhaps it was reported."

"Anyway it's time we headed to Jane's," said Mel, looking at the clock on the wall. It's four thirty already," she added, thinking that she desperately wanted to see her son's smiling face. "Let's ask Tina or Jeff to go through the rest of the traffic enforcement and bus company footage to see what they can uncover in case my first hunch is right," she suggested.

Mike nodded, knowing that he was getting drawn in again. He wanted that creep almost as much as he wanted Niko and he could feel it taking over him again. "Yeah you're right, hand it straight over to them."

He sighed, stood up and smiled at Mel. He needed to be careful and know when to draw the line. But deep down he knew he wasn't going to rest until he had brought an end to them both. He wanted them dead.

Fifteen

"It's hard to believe that we are a week further down the line and we are still no further forward with that bloody warrant," Mike yelled. "Tina, where are we at? Surely to God you're not going to tell me again today there is no record of our application."

"I've got it, Mike, it's just this minute come through," she said, waving it in the air, after collecting it from the printer.

Mike sprung to his feet snatching it from her hand like it was a jackpot winning lottery ticket and then gave the paper a kiss. "Hallelujah," he yelled, kissing it again.

They had made numerous applications and were finally advised that the system had broken down and the application was now being dealt with manually. "System broke down my arse," said Mike, thinking how they managed this before everything went electronic. "That's the problem with technology, everything comes to a standstill when the system says no."

They had been desperate to turn over the place at Keeper's Lodge and delve deep into the archives and every member of the team was feeling Mike's frustration. It had come to the forefront the evening before when Brent Carter had been sighted, escorting two pregnant women into town.

They had been hot on his heels all week, taking turns to follow his movements but the findings over the last twenty-four hours had raised serious alarm bells.

Mike and Paul had managed to strike up a conversation of sorts with one of the women called Marianne when they had decided to pay a visit to St Clement's, the day centre on Fishery Rise, the day before. This visit really raised the bar when, after speaking with the woman, it became apparent that she was possibly on drugs.

"I just don't understand it," Paul had commented, after leaving the centre. "That girl is on something, I'm sure of it. Did you see her glazed eyes and her face was expressionless? I mean she could hardly string two words together, it was like extracting teeth, trying to engage with her."

"To me it was like she had been brainwashed and everything she did was mechanical, her actions, her one-word answers, everything."

"The woman working behind the counter seemed to be in the same state, just prerehearsed, one-word answers and was wandering around in a trance," said Mike.

Mike had declared, when news of the pregnant women had been reported by Jeff that same evening, that if the warrant wasn't in by the following morning, then he would be passing it to his superior for urgent intervention.

But now he had it in his grasp and they were going in all guns blazing.

Four units were deployed at 9:15am to Keeper's Lodge and the findings were harrowing beyond belief.

"Mr Hamilton, we have a warrant to search the premises of Keeper's Lodge," Mike announced, holding up the warrant so that there was no doubt about it, they were coming in.

"Stand aside, please," Mike said, stepping into the reception area where a blabbering Mr Hamilton was doing his best to shield the doorway.

"What's the matter with you people, why do you keep bothering us," he screamed, stepping back as the officers filed in.

"Mr Hamilton, one of my officers will escort you to round up the residents so that we don't cause them any unnecessary alarm. Please assemble them in the sun lounge, as quickly as possible."

"Unnecessary alarm," he said, swinging his arms in the air and then clapping them together like a symbol. "Of course this is going to alarm them when they catch sight of you lot, rounding them up like bloody football hooligans. These women are frail, recovering from ordeals beyond your comprehension and this is totally unfounded."

"Mr Hamilton this is not a riot. Please assemble the residents in the sun lounge, as requested, otherwise we will have to carry out this task ourselves. The choice is yours." Mike, advised, trying to keep his cool. He had waited too bloody long to get in here and he wasn't going to let a cantankerous old warden prevent him from doing his job.

Mike nodded at Jeff and Tina to accompany the old boy out to the cabins to round up the residents, and then instructed two officers to check the upstairs rooms, together with the rest of the lodge. "Right," he said, walking out onto the veranda and addressing the two additional teams. "Block all entrances until further notice, no one leaves until I say so."

"OK, Paul, let's do this," he said, striding down the hallway. "I think we are about to uncover something really ugly."

They stepped into the sun lounge unannounced, startling some of the women that were sitting close to the door.

"Good afternoon, ladies," he said, stepping into the room. "My name is Sergeant Brugge from…" He stopped mid-sentence unable to believe what he was seeing and then turned to face Paul completely dumbfounded. "By God, it's way worse and I could have possibly imagined," he said, watching Paul's expression change to a look of sheer horror.

He gathered himself, gave himself a shake and then continued with his broken sentence. "My name is Sergeant Brugge and this is Sergeant Osman from Holden CID," he said, wondering where the fuck he was going to start. "Mr Hamilton has just gone to assemble the rest of the residents and he will be joining us shortly. I think perhaps it would be best to wait until the rest of you are here, so I can address you all together," he said, turning to face Paul.

Never in his wildest dreams, did he expect to see at least fourteen expectant mothers set before him. What the hell was happening here and why did the numbers exceed the twelve residents declared previously?

He turned to face Paul with an expression of sheer disbelief and then looked over at the doorway as Thomas Hamilton escorted three more women from the cabins into the room. Peter, one of the uniformed crew, led in four more from the upstairs dormitory, three of whom did not appear to be pregnant or were in their first trimester.

Mike immediately recognised Marianne from the St Clement's drop-in centre, together with two other women that were serving there yesterday. Twenty-one women, nineteen of whom were, without doubt, expecting, stood lined up like soldiers, staring directly in front of them, expressionless and completely still. Why were they standing in lines like they were prisoners of war? He watched totally blown away as Marianne took her place at the end of the line.

Why hadn't they noticed when they had visited before and managed to wangle their way into the sun lounge? Mike tried to recall their visit and then remembered they were sitting down at the end of the lounge, so their condition would have been disguised. It also occurred to Mike that seeing as it was a weekday, there could be more victims working in town that could sadly increase the number further.

"My God, look at them, Paul, they are all dressed the same in floral maternity frocks and brown lace-up shoes."

Paul was standing there with his mouth open, speechless, unable to absorb what he was seeing. He leaned against the arm of the sofa, as if he had been knocked off his feet and then he stuttered his way through his next sentence. "Mike, it's a baby farm," he said, likening it to the Victorian practices from the last century. "My God, what have we stumbled across."

He looked at them with their glazed expressions, standing motionless, dressed in identical dresses, making it look like a uniform from the Victorian era. The only difference being the colour of the printed flowers on their paisley dresses, possibly representing the trimester they were in.

Mike turned to face Thomas Hamilton, and then towards the women, completely flabbergasted as to where to start. How could he address the women, when each and every one of them had suffered a mental breakdown of sort at some time or other and had possibly been brainwashed. They may not even understand what was happening to them, passing through the system on a conveyor belt, confused and exploited.

"Ladies, please make yourselves comfortable and I will be back with you shortly," he said, gesturing towards the many sofas and armchairs. "Mr Hamilton, I would like to talk to you outside in reception," he suddenly announced. There was no way he could address the women until he had an accurate grasp of the circumstances set before him. He looked at Paul and nodded towards the door, giving him the signal to exit. He needed to ask questions and the only person who was likely to have any answers was Thomas Hamilton, warden of Keeper's Lodge.

"Mr Hamilton, I am arresting you on suspicion of abusing your position while caring for vulnerable wards in your care," he said, sitting down on the bench immediately opposite the reception desk. He could feel his legs trembling beneath him, the wind completely knocked out of his sails. It was hard to categorise the offence until they knew more but it was blatantly obvious that these women were not here of their own free will visiting a fertility clinic. "Paul, read him his rights and hand him over," Mike ordered, giving himself a shake. He had made the split second decision to deal with him under caution at the station, where everything could be recorded and documented. When he had fully digested the entire menu of events.

"You've got it all wrong," yelled Thomas Hamilton, waving his fist in the air. "I'm just the warden here, employed to watch over the residents. I mind my own business, ask no questions and that's my total involvement," he screamed, as two police officers handcuffed him, while Paul continued to read him his rights between his pleas of innocence.

"We will interview you further at the station," Mike confirmed standing up to continue the search.

"Mike, one of the women has gone into labour and her waters have broken," Tina informed, poking her head out the sunroom door. "I've called for an ambulance as her contractions are quite rapid but she's really confused and I can tell she's not sure what's happening to her."

"For fuck's safe," said Mike, under his breath, thinking this was all they needed.

It wasn't long before the place was crawling with police reinforcements, two doctors, three nurses and a midwife. It was complete pandemonium and if it wasn't so serious, you would think it was an adult pantomime and that the line up of women were about to burst into a chorus line.

"Paul, this is bigger than we could have ever envisaged," he said, wondering about the logistics of transporting twenty-plus pregnant women into care. "There are so many possibilities attached to this. Have these women been assaulted, artificially inseminated? Who has conducted such an atrocity to all these mentally unstable patients?"

"Yeah, the list of questions is so extensive," said Paul, stepping back to make way for the stretcher bed that was being wheeled past them in the corridor. We also have to consider how long this practice has been running," he added, walking out of the reception door. We could be talking years and what about all the infants?" he said, making his way down the veranda stairs. He pulled his cigarette box from his blazer pocket and gave them a shake, before retrieving one from the pack. "I thought I had seen most things but this wins hands down," he said, watching the ambulance door close, muffling the groans of a seriously confused and frightened young woman about to give birth. He patted his pockets in search of his lighter and then leaned back against the wall. "I'm not really sure what I was expecting to find here, if I'm truthful, but this is way beyond anything I had envisaged."

.

Mike let out a deep sigh as he took in the sight of all the flashing blue lights circling the driveway. "We need to turn the whole place over," he said, recalling the pathway at the rear of the building. "Do you think there is a delivery suite on-site?" Mike suddenly asked, wondering if there was a birthing room somewhere in the forest. "I mean you can hardly keep turning up at the hospital with pregnant women all dressed like they come from some sort of prairie," said Mike, thinking they resembled a cult where men had more than one wife.

"Well, they're basically being treated like cattle," said Paul wondering if they had been tagged in any way. He stamped out his cigarette and turned to face the veranda staircase. "Let's go and find out," he said, taking the stairs two at a time.

Mike could hear nurses and medics attempting to extract information from some of the residents, as they painstakingly checked out everyone's vitals. It was complete anarchy as some of the women rebelled, not comprehending that they were in fact being saved from the devil himself. Cries of despair could be heard all around the lodge ranging from hysteria to gentle whimpering, as the women reacted with different levels of understanding.

"Jeez, this is really chilling," said Paul wincing, when he heard one of the women cry out like she was being tortured and then run from the sun lounge. Mike stopped halfway up the staircase, watching helplessly as a paramedic tried to reason with a young woman who could barely speak English.

"Mike, there's a dormitory down here," said Paul, opening the door at the far end of the corridor. "Eight beds in total," he said, stepping into the room and counting as his eyes swept around the room. It was fairly sparse in comparison to the rest of the lodge and it looked like someone had attempted to fit in as many beds as possible, including a camp bed, under the window.

"They're definitely maxing out on space here," said Paul, thinking that it didn't look very comfortable compared to the lavish cabins.

He looked at the name above the nearest bed to the door and observed it was Marianne Foster, the young woman that had served them at the drop-in centre. "It doesn't look like this is where the pregnant women are held," he said pointing to the name printed in bold above the headboard. "I expect this is where they stay when they are not pregnant," said Paul, looking across at the next name plaque. "This dorm is for the women that go out to work,

which enables them to keep up the charade of running a reputable home. What a cover up."

"Yep, they are possibly rotating the women making it appear that they are building a foundation on which they can eventually become independent, when all the time they are being mistreated, basically enslaved," Mike added. "I wonder how many rounds they do before becoming surplus to requirements," Paul questioned, pondering the women's long-term fate.

He looked at each bed, which was set alongside a small bedside cabinet, and then stepped forward so he could open the drawer. He walked across to open another before declaring his findings. "Mike, their personal effects basically consist of a bible, toothbrush and a comb," he said pulling open another drawer. He reached down into the cupboard underneath where an identical dress to the ones they had witnessed earlier was neatly folded along with some underwear. "That's it, Mike, they get one change of clothes, this is all their worldly goods."

They made their way along the corridor taking in the sight of each room as they went. Some rooms had twin beds, some had bunks but none of them had anything personal or special that might bring comfort to someone. These women had been stripped of anything that went before and were now on a conveyor belt to hell.

"Well they are not all living in the lap of luxury, as was conveyed to us with the lavish cabins," said Paul, thinking they looked desperately deprived.

"Perhaps they earn their soft furnishings depending on how fertile they are," Mike concluded, after seeing a makeshift bed on the floor. "Whoever sleeps there must be positively sterile," he said wondering what her fate might be if her womb couldn't bear fruit.

"Does make you wonder who stays in the cabins?" said Paul, thinking that perhaps some of them were reserved for staff.

"Well, well, well," said Mike, walking into a room that was presumably Thomas Hamilton's quarters. "Resembles a gentleman's club, don't you think?" said Mike staring at the leather studded chesterfield sofa, taking centre stage in the room. There was a matching green leather wingback chair positioned by the window, overlooking the forest grounds, and the room was surrounded in oak cladding with bookshelves floor to ceiling.

"Guess he gets to see all the comings and goings from here," said Paul, sitting down in the chair and taking in the extensive view. He looked down at the circular coffee table, which was laden with magazines and leather bound books.

"Looks like he's been here for centuries," said Mike, taking in the amount of paperwork stacked on the selves, covered with dust.

To the right-hand side of the window was a stack of old newspapers most of which had turned a yellowy brown colour and the smell of damp and musty furnishings filled the air. "Mike, this newspaper dates back to 1984, which seems rather bizarre seeing as the lodge itself is fairly new."

"Well it's not that new," said Mike, walking across to the window. "It's at least twenty-five years old, according to the land registry."

"Why would he bring old newspapers with him?" Paul questioned, pulling one from the stack so he could see what he was preserving.

"I expect they contain articles relevant to this arrangement," said Mike, pulling a few from the pile. "I'll get some of them taken back to the station for analysis," he added, throwing them down on the coffee table.

"Paul, I want to see where that path leads," said Mike, starting to feel impatient again. "I'll get the lads to strip this room of anything relevant for analysis but I want to head round the back." He took one last look around the room and followed Paul down the back staircase.

"Mike, I don't think Rachel left this establishment of her own free will, as described. Do you think she was among the women in the sun lounge earlier? I mean we would hardly recognise her now would we, it's been years!" he said, wondering what she might look like now.

"The thought had crossed my mind," said Mike, stepping out onto the veranda and taking in some breaths of fresh air. "If her fate was anything like these women then it doesn't bear thinking about," he said, wondering how on earth you could impregnate a woman with a history of mental health disorder.

"I dread to think what we are going to uncover," said Mike, taking the lead.

"Well let's hope it's not a nursery," said Paul, bending down to tie his shoe lace, before following Mike round to the rear of the building.

They edged their way through a thicket of trees, emerging as if they had been tracking through the forest for hours. They both felt weighed down with sheer disbelief not only with what they had just left behind but by what might be behind the double doors of the small square building immediately in front of them.

Mike acknowledged the young police constable that was standing guard at the right-hand side of the doors, observing the yellow and white police enforcement tape that was already set in place shielding the scene. The young constable nodded at Mike and then stuttered a few words nervously, making Mike sympathise at how nerve-racking this situation must be as he watched him shuffle from one foot to the other. The innocence of not yet having experienced shocking scenes that even more experienced officers found hard to witness, but not having the experience to be able to leave the job at the door at night and switch off. He didn't doubt for one second that there was a high possibility that this young chap would at some stage during his career in the force need counselling by Stephanie, the force psychiatrist.

Mike took a deep breath as he pulled on the door handle, stepping forward into what could potentially be a nursery full of infants. "So what have we got?" said Mike, addressing a constable named Kevin who was making his way towards them.

"We have two operating theatres that look pretty terrifying," said Kevin, looking like the stuffing had been knocked out of him. "And through there," he said, pointing through a glass window, "there are some incubators. Looks like some sort of baby intensive care unit to me," he added, suddenly excusing himself, as he quickly held his hand over his mouth and rushed from the building.

Mike took another deep breath as he reached out gingerly towards the first set of double doors. He could feel his heart racing, wondering what it was that made Kevin Monroe flee from the corridor before he spilled his guts out all over the floor.

"For fuck's sake," said Mike, as he took in the sight of the theatre that was without doubt set up as a delivery suite. The room looked as if it had been abandoned either mid-delivery or shortly afterwards from the volume of blood that had soaked into the white paper liners that had been draped over the birthing bed. The placenta was still there, resting on the end of the bed with the umbilical cord still attached to a pair of scissors. A trail of blood led across to a set of scales, where the baby had almost certainly been weighed by the blood-imprinted image left behind inside the white tray. Paul could feel his stomach wrenching and then he placed his hand over his mouth and turned away.

"You OK," said Mike, turning to face him, when he heard him reach.

"Yep," he said, composing himself and pulling a tissue from his pocket. "Bit queasy," he said, knowing that he would be seeing that vision again soon when his own wife gave birth. Thankfully under much happier circumstances.

The birthing bed was equipped with a set of stirrups that looked way too historical for the current era and looked more like a leather belt harness more suited to holding up a pair of trousers. The trolley next to the birthing station was laden with surgical instruments that looked terrifying, and a set of forceps was lying on the floor at the foot of the bed, which appeared to have been discarded as though they had been thrown to one side in a hurry, splattered in blood. A foetal monitor to the right-hand side of the bed was still switched on with a graph hanging from its mouth piece and a sonography screen to the left was showing a pre-recorded image of a baby.

"Paul, look, there's a time and date on this graph," he said, ripping it from the monitor. "Good God, it's got today's date on it. Paul, they must have fled as they heard the sirens approaching the lodge as the reading was from nine fifteen this morning."

"Guess there must be another way out through the grounds," said Paul, turning his attention to the line of gas and air canisters lined up against the wall.

Mike stood staring at the image on the sonography screen and then squirmed when he caught sight of a suction probe that resembled something that you would unblock a drain with.

"Paul I'm going to look next door," he said, feeling like he needed to escape the carnage set before him. Paul nodded, taking in one last sweep of the room, before his eyes fixed firmly on the stirrup strap attached to an overhead hanging device, which looked like something from a torture chamber.

Next door was a second theatre, set up for caesarean sections and complicated deliveries with giant overhead lamps positioned at the far end of the operating table. A green fabric screen was set to one side, suggesting that they did offer some form of empathy towards the mother by shielding the surgery from view. This room looked scrubbed ready for action with surgical instruments set ready for use. Mike wondered if this had been prepared for the woman who went into labour earlier. If it was, she definitely had a lucky escape.

Mike's thoughts then turned to Kevin Monroe's comments earlier when he described a room with incubators. "Paul, I'm going to take a look at the neonatal unit," he said, suddenly wondering where all the babies were.

Paul turned to follow Mike out of the room and headed further down the corridor towards the room with a large viewing window. Mike stood staring through the window at the two incubators set up side by side at the far end of the room and let out a sigh of relief. Both units were switched off, out of use, thankfully.

"Mike there's another room with a viewing window, around here," said Paul, turning the corner at the end of the corridor. "This must be where they take the babies directly after birth," Paul stated, looking through the window at the row of transparent cribs with little pink and blue cellular blankets.

He moved inside and headed towards the back of the room where a baby station of supplies had been assembled, containing rows of milk formula bottles, together with newborn nappies and wipes. "Mike, there's only one size of nappy here," Paul commented, thinking that was really strange.

"Does suggest that the babies get moved on swiftly," said Mike.

"We obviously disturbed them mid-delivery," said Mike, thinking that the theatre scene made it look like the baby was ripped from its mothers womb in a hurry, with little compassion. "But it doesn't explain where the babies are now," he said, staring at the six empty cribs.

"We need to find the archives where they store all the patient records," Mike stated, looking at the two feeding chairs in the middle of the room. "We need answers," he said, heading towards the door. "I'm wondering if perhaps the orchestration of this practice is so seamless, they impregnate the girls in blocks, you know almost like a harvest."

Paul stared at Mike, contemplating his suggestion. "You know I think you might be right. It's a continual loop, which is why the babies aren't here. The last lot have already been moved on. Oh God, Mike, that means this new harvest, so to speak, is about to happen. That's why there was a delivery today and the other woman's waters broke this morning."

"I wonder how many other women are part of this trimester?" said Mike, pushing open the double doors and leaving the building. "Paul, we need to speak to the midwife and nurses and get them to examine these women and work out which ones are due shortly. They're all going to need immediate attention. By God, they probably don't even realise what's happening to them. They are on a conveyor belt and my guess is that someone has messed with their minds to assist with the robotic process so that they are compliant and not hysterical."

Paul closed his eyes, stopping in his tracks and then looked up at the sky. "Mike, they've been programmed, otherwise the emotional turmoil of having their babies wrenched from them would be impossible to manage," he said, picking up pace again.

They made their way back up into the lodge in search of the archives. The frenzied madness from earlier had heightened further and screams could be heard from all corners of the lodge. The women were being organised into groups, ready for departure.

"Nurse, can I just have a quick word," said Mike, beckoning her over to him. "We have ascertained that the women, although not proven yet, appear to have been impregnated in groups. It looks likely that some of these women's due date is upon us, one of them has gone into labour this morning. We have also discovered that someone gave birth here this morning but the mother and baby have already left the scene."

The nurse looked around at all the expectant mothers, with tears in her eyes. She was so young and even if she was 200 years old there would never be enough wisdom learned over the term to manage feelings of this magnitude.

"May I make a suggestion," said Paul, raising his hand, like he just remembered something. "The women's dresses are different colours, so it may well represent their trimester. The one who went into labour was wearing a dress with a green paisley pattern. Those two women standing over there are wearing the same colour and they look to me, to be full term. Start with them."

Mike gesticulated in agreement, thinking Paul had hit the nail on the head.

"Yes, if that turns out to be the case, organise for those women to be seen by the midwife immediately, so that they can be dealt with first," he instructed.

"Mike, we have another one here who is complaining of stomach cramps," said Tina, pointing to another woman in green.

"My God, they're popping out all over the place," said Mike, quietly to Paul.

"Tina, take her down to one of the ambulances," he instructed, noticing that four more had pulled up on the drive.

"Mike, what's the plan here?" said Jeff, looking a little shaky.

"The nurses are organising the women into groups now. All the women in green need to be assessed by a maternity unit immediately, so should be the first to leave," Mike stated.

He pulled at his hair looking around at all the other troubled pregnant souls. "We now need immediate support from all the local homes that deal with mental health," he said. Suddenly remembering the women that might be returning from town shortly with Brent Carter.

"Paul, Brent Carter will be returning with the other residents in about an hour," he said, looking at his watch.

"OK, I'll organise for him to be intercepted before he gets here," he responded. "We don't want him running for the hills."

"Right, let's continue our search for the archives, so we can garner some medical history on these women," Mike gestured, pointing to the stairs. There was nothing else on the ground level that suggested storage other than a small kitchen, which was now possibly part of the charade, making it look like a reputable home allowing the occupants to be self sufficient in a communal way. To the rear, according to Kevin, was a large kitchen/pantry and seating area, implying that the meals were managed in groups. This information also suggested the possibility of kitchen staff.

They continued their search of the upstairs quarters, noting two small bathrooms at each end of the corridor before striking lucky. "It's here," said Paul, stepping into a small office with an old-fashioned desk and chair set in front of a blackboard that reminded Paul of his school days. On the opposite side of the room was a row of filing cabinets, with draws labelled A-Z.

Mike stood in front of the cabinets, willing all the answers to be inside, and he attempted to open the first cabinet marked A-E. "They're locked," he said, staring at the combination code on the front of each drawer. He swiftly left the room and marched along towards the staircase and yelled down over the banister. "I need a crowbar up here," he shouted to one of his colleagues.

Mike stood back as the sergeant crowbarred all of the cabinets open, and then he returned to the first one. He wanted to start with Rachel Blossom, so he nervously flicked through all the files in the

B section until he shouted out.

"Paul. Rachel Blossom's file," he said, holding it up in the air as proof. He moved across to the desk and sat down in the chair opening the folder nervously. Paul stood behind him, reading the contents over his shoulder. "My God, it's her complete history since Casio Grange," said Paul, moving closer.

"For fuck's sake," Mike yelled, banging his fist down on the desk. "She gave birth three months ago to a little girl, weighing in at six pounds, three ounces," he said, passing the paper to Paul.

"What happened to the baby?" said Paul, reading swiftly through the sheet. "She was adopted five weeks later," said Mike, pulling at his hair. He passed another paper to Paul, who continued to read, hoping to find the answers.

"She went to a couple called Mr and Mrs Smith," said Mike, wondering if it was a bogus name to keep their anonymity.

"Are there any address details," said Paul, retrieving the paper from Mike.

"None whatsoever," said Mike, standing up from his chair. "But she sold for forty-three thousand dollars, which suggests they are based in the states," said Mike, moving across to the window.

"These babies are going out to childless couples in the states," said Mike, staring out across the grounds.

"Yeah, couples that are probably desperate for children and quite possibly have been convinced that the babies have come from single mums not able to look after them. You know like they did in the workhouses and convents years ago," said Paul, remembering all the harrowing stories where babies were ripped from their mother's arms without consent. "I expect through desperation, the parents have asked no questions and turned a blind eye," Paul added.

"But this is on a completely different level, Paul. Someone has messed with these women's minds and basically turned them into birthing robots," he said, reaching for another file.

"It doesn't bear thinking about how that was achieved," said Paul, taking another file out of a different drawer. "I mean have they done this with drugs suppressing them or do you think they might have been operated on?" said Paul, questioning the method. "We could have some lunatic wannabe doctor out there performing operations on these victims," he said, with a shiver.

He opened the file of a woman called Penelope Brown and sat down on the floor. He spread the papers out across the carpet, noting that she had been at the home for the last six years.

"Mike, this woman was transferred here in 2020 from Danbury Manor. She has no family as she was orphaned as a young girl and passed through a series of children's homes. She showed signs of paranoia in her late teens that evolved into various conditions such as bipolar with episodes of mania. By the time she was twenty-one she was transferred to Hatten Heath, a psychiatric unit for evaluation. Her past homes include Cassio Grange. Mike, her nurse was Ivy Mason for fuck's sake."

Paul pulled another file from the cabinet and spread it out across the floor. "It's similar again," he said, throwing it to one side. "No family, and the mother died in childbirth," he said, standing up to stretch his legs. "They're concentrating on mentally ill females that have no family. That way they can lose them in the system," said Paul, sitting down in the chair. No one is going to come looking for them.

"Rachel Blossom fitted the bill perfectly," said Mike, agreeing with Paul's overview. "We need to find out at what point along the chain of events she got intercepted."

"At the moment everything points to Casio Grange where we know Ivy Mason and Karen Lewis worked. But what if it goes back as far as Victoria's Retreat?" said Mike, throwing another possibility in the mix.

"Or," said Paul, opening another file, "was the fire just a lucky break for them, spilling out dozens of mentally ill patients into neighbouring institutions. It would have enabled them to replenish their stocks. Fuck, it must have been like the January sales," he added.

"Now, this is just a guess," said Mike, clenching his fists and then cracking his knuckles. "Suppose Ivy Mason or someone else managed to get hold of the information of all the female patients that had no family and orchestrated it so they filtered those across here?" he speculated, opening each file and casting it a side, as he went through them one by one. "Let's see how many started this journey from Victoria's Retreat and crossed through Casio Grange and Danbury Manor. If you think about it, this place offers the final steps, making it appear that patients have come out the other side as whole human beings, leaving their troubles behind and going out into the community. No one knows they're still here because the records show them passing through, holding down jobs and eventually leaving for independence."

"Mike, the cabinets over here start from A-Z again and there's another file for Rachel Blossom." He opened it up and stared in disbelief. "Mike, this cabinet contains files they must show to officials and regulators for their industry. All these files have been falsified, as the version of events Thomas Hamilton told us about Rachel is in here, just like he told us."

"That's exactly what this is," said Mike rummaging through the cabinet. "It's like having two sets of accounts where one is for the tax office." He turned to face Kevin who was now standing in the doorway. "Kevin, will you organise for everything in here to be boxed up and taken to the station," Mike instructed, rotating his head and cracking his neck. God, he felt so stiff. In fact he felt totally knackered.

He looked at his watch and then rose to his feet. "Paul it's nearly four o'clock," he said walking towards the door. "Let's wrap it up here for now." They made their way down the staircase into the aftermath of the earlier mayhem, which now appeared to be a lot calmer.

Most of the women had been transported out already, with the remaining few waiting to leave. Mike looked across at a woman with ginger curls leaning against the wall, noting how slim she was. He wondered how many children she had borne this institution and then stepped back startled when she suddenly stood up, did a quick curtsy and moved her hand out gesturing like she was addressing her audience. My God, where did she think she was?

Tina entered the room with a clipboard to round up the final few. "Maizy-Jayne Whitfield, Beverley Jones and Eileen Stephens, please come out to reception."

Sixteen

Brent Carter had been intercepted 200 metres from the lodge twenty minutes earlier and had put up real resistance. He had wrestled two of the officers to the ground and was finally handcuffed and taken away in a police wagon. He had four women on board his minibus bringing the total number of victims to twenty-five.

"Well I have to say," said Paul, pressing the button on the window to let in some air. "That's got to be one of the worst cases of multiple abuse I have ever come across." He thought about all the cases he had worked on over the years. "It's hard to get your head around," he said, knowing that they had to head back there again tomorrow to mop up.

There were still some areas of the lodge they needed to investigate and not all rooms had been scrutinised. The main priority was moving the women to safety and the task ahead was huge. Numerous homes had been contacted and prepped, ready to receive some of the victims but there was still a long way to go. Some had been taken to hospital for further checks and five were now at Holden Maternity Hospital preparing to give birth. Mike wondered, seeing as they were all going into labour on the same day whether they had been given something to induce labour.

Mike had deployed police units to Casio Grange and Danbury Manor, which meant that the entire team and supporting units were now working on the same case. This was the largest case Mike had ever been in charge of.

They pulled into the station car park at 5:55pm just as Ivy Mason, Karen Lewis and Sister Bernadette, were stepping out of a police vehicle. "This is going to be a long night," he announced, heading towards the steps.

Bridget was at the front desk booking everyone in and Mike could see Mel standing in the doorway opposite the vending machine. "Hey," he said walking towards her. "And how's my favourite girl?" he said, like she was five years old. Mel smiled, thinking it was rather sweet and then handed him a coin for the machine. "Thanks," he said, enjoying the fact that she knew him so well, as he turned to select a coffee.

"News has been coming in all day," said Mel, letting him know that she was fairly up to speed with things. "It must have been completely harrowing seeing all those pregnant women," said Mel, "especially as they are all unhinged," she added.

"Ah, it gets far worse than that," said Mike, sipping the steaming hot coffee. "They are walking around like robotic zombies," said Mike, making his way over to his desk. "So one of the most urgent things is to establish whether they are being suppressed by drugs or something more sinister," he said, wincing at the thought.

"What, like some sort of lobotomy?" Mel quizzed, wondering where he was heading.

"Well, if you think about it, drugs could interfere with the pregnancy and it's not like they care about the woman, the baby is the prize here. Mel, there are so many people to interview here this evening," he said, listing them one by one. Paul suggested on the way back here that you and Jack stay at theirs tonight." Mel let out a big sigh and sat down in Paul's chair. "It's for the best, Mel, and makes total sense."

Mel took a deep breath and then exhaled slowly. She knew he was right and after all Jane had already collected Jack earlier from the nursery and she couldn't go home alone. "But what about our stuff?" she quizzed, wondering about a change of clothes and nightwear.

"I'll get one of the lads to take you by the house to collect what you need," he said, feeling totally exhausted.

"OK," she said, agreeing with this logic. She knew Mike was really under pressure as acting chief inspector and she felt she had already put him through so much already. She also knew that he was likely to be at the station all night.

"I'll sort it," he said, standing up.

"Mike, Thomas Hamilton's in room two," Paul informed, as he walked into the office. He smiled at Mel and then turned, leaving Mike to say goodnight.

Mike felt like he was being pulled in all directions. He had made a promise to her that he would be by her side and he felt as though he was letting her down. Deep down, he knew that he had phrased it a little differently, modifying it to mean that she wouldn't be left alone but still her vulnerability was eating away at him.

He made arrangements with Bridget at the front desk to ensure she was escorted home to collect her belongings and then taken straight over to Jane's. He had made it quite clear that the officer was not to leave her unattended at any stage until she was safely delivered.

He made his way round to room two and stood momentarily outside the door. He took a deep breath and turned the handle, stepping into the room. Thomas Hamilton was sitting behind the interview desk looking extremely agitated and fit to burst. He jumped up immediately Mike entered, shouting all sorts of obscenities. "Sit down, Mr Hamilton," Mike instructed, irritated by his outburst.

Paul was sitting opposite him with the tape recorder set ready to record the interview. Mike sat down next to Paul and gave the nod for him to start the recording.

"This interview is being conducted at Holden Central Crime Investigation Department on Friday, 30th May 2026 at 6:30pm. Present in the room is Thomas Hamilton, Detective Sergeant Paul Osman and Acting Chief Inspector Mike Brugge," said Mike, following protocol.

"Today at approximately 9:30am Thomas Hamilton was apprehended at Keeper's Lodge, Ramchester, where he was arrested on suspicion of abusing his position of trust with regard to the wards in his care," said Mike, taking a deep breath.

"I was unjustly arrested," said Thomas rising from his seat again. "The whole bloody thing is ludicrous," he said waving his arms in the air. "You bloody lot charging in and upsetting all the ladies."

"Mr Hamilton, sit down," Mike instructed, gesturing towards the chair. "We would like to ask you some questions relating to the wellbeing and nature of the care you are providing these women, under the guise of a sanctuary providing the final step for patients recovering from mental illness."

Mike paused, looking Thomas straight in the eye. "Mr Hamilton, the home is described as 'An establishment assisting patients in becoming self-sufficient, paving the way for them so that they can hold down employment and assisting them with life skills, so that they can be independent.' Do you agree with that description?"

"Well, to a degree," said Thomas, pondering the description. "But it's more of a home for young ladies who have found themselves to be in the family way. These ladies have nowhere else to go. Some of these ladies are young and have been shunned by their families, bringing disgrace to the family name. Some simply have no family or friends to help or have perhaps left behind an abusive husband or partner," said Thomas, giving a completely different spin on things.

"They are vulnerable and frail and some are suffering from mild mental health issues or depression. We simply assist them in providing shelter and food during their pregnancy. We give medical support right through to the birth, where they are then passed on to a mother and baby unit. So I really don't understand why you have burst in like the army going into battle, rounding them up like prisoners of war, frightening these vulnerable ladies and causing chaos," he said, with a deep sigh.

Mike looked across at Paul, raising his eyebrows at Thomas Hamilton's perceived understanding of what the lodge's purpose was about.

"Mr Hamilton, or can I call you Thomas?" Paul questioned, seeking approval. Thomas nodded, clasping his hands and placing them on the table in front of him. "Thomas, how long have you worked at Keeper's Lodge?" he continued, starting the questioning again in a calm and professional manner.

Thomas looked up towards the ceiling, as if he was trying to pluck the information from above. "Around twenty-four years I would say," he said, finally settling on a number. "Give or take," he added.

"I see," said Paul, pulling his chair closer to the table. "And what is your position at the lodge?"

"I am the warden or caretaker, however you wish to identify me," said Thomas, staring him straight in the eye.

"Can you elaborate?" Paul continued, wanting a full understanding of his responsibilities.

"My role is to keep an eye on the residents in case they need anything. If they need any little jobs undertaken in their cabins. I take care of the grounds, minor repairs, security and I guess I'm also the gatekeeper," he said proudly listing his duties.

"Do you have a contract of employment?" Mike asked, wondering if they would get to see it.

"I don't have any paperwork," he said, twisting his hands nervously. "I was simply given the role, word of mouth," he said, with a shaky voice.

"So how did you come across the role?" Paul quizzed, curiously. "Where was it advertised?"

"It wasn't advertised," he said, his eyes darting around the room. "I was approached by a chap at a drop-in centre near Fishery Rise," he said, recalling the event. A place called St. Clement's. I was out of work, homeless and depended entirely on the charitable service they provide there. They had a soup kitchen and provided shelter back then, they still do but nowadays it's evolved somewhat. There is a cafeteria at the front of the centre open to paying customers, at charitable rates of course, where the funds are ploughed back into the centre to keep it going. It's entirely funded by the community with no government injection."

"So this chap who approached you, what did he say?" said Paul, feeling himself getting drawn into his version of events.

"He said there was a role going at a home that provided help to women in the family way that had nowhere else to go. He said it was a caretaker/warden role, like I described. The pay was fairly low but it came with accommodation and all my meals were included. I jumped at the chance," he said, still avoiding eye contact.

"Thomas, you said earlier that you didn't know the name of your employer," Mike quizzed, remembering his earlier comments.

"I just know he's called Peter but I've never actually met him," he said, starting to tremble. "Am I in trouble for not paying my taxes?" he said, his face growing redder.

"How do you receive payment, Thomas?" said Paul, inquisitively.

"Cash, it's delivered to me monthly by post, special delivery," said

Thomas, trembling. "Sergeant, the job was like a gift from heaven above," he said, looking up to the ceiling again. "I had been homeless for so long, hungry and desperate and I wasn't getting any younger. So I accepted the role. I never asked any questions and I kept myself to myself," he said, turning to face them both.

"Thomas, that does seem like a very feasible account of how this came about but surely you must have noticed that these women never left. Never went on to become independent, as described. Some must have been there for years. Didn't you think that was a little strange?" said Mike.

"Yes, it did make me question things at the beginning but my understanding was that some of these ladies were a little free with their assets, so to speak. You know, not learning from their mistakes. It is also my understanding that some of them were prostitutes, ladies of the night. So it wasn't surprising at all to see them keep circling around," he said, gesticulating a sweep with a shaky hand.

"I find that a little hard to believe, Thomas, that you didn't question the fact that some of these women had been resident for many years and constantly in the family way," said Mike, starting to feel like he was being played. "Why did you tell us the other day that the pregnant woman we saw was an isolated incident?" said Mike, seeing holes in his story everywhere.

"I really don't know what to say," said Thomas, starting to tremble violently. "I don't feel very well," he added, suddenly turning as white as a ghost. "I feel queasy," he added, holding his hand over his mouth. "Can we stop?"

"OK, Thomas we will adjourn for a break," Mike said, gesturing towards Paul to switch off the recorder.

"This interview is adjourned at 7:10pm," Mike stated for the purpose of the tape.

"I will get you some water," said Paul, walking towards the door.

Mike stopped and looked across at Thomas pondering his age. Did this chap simply turn a blind eye to what was really going on? He looked positively ancient sitting there trembling, his scruffy white beard, wild and animal like. He looked to be at least eighty or was it that his prior life on the streets with harsh conditions had had a detrimental effect on his health? Was the offer of lodgings and a hot meal daily too good to refuse for a man who was cold, hungry and desperate? Did he just look the other way?

"What did you make of that?" said Paul, as they walked up the corridor.

"Well, some of it seems feasible but you can't tell me he didn't notice that some of these women had been there for years and had multiple births," said Mike, trying to keep a grip on reality. "They're walking around like pregnant zombies for Christ's sake. There is the possibility of course that he simply turned a blind eye, though. The guy is positively ancient, was homeless, etc. like he stated, he looked on it like it was a gift from above. Does make you question his morals though," said Mike, stopping to select a coffee.

"Who's in room one?" Mike asked, as he walked out into reception.

"Tina and Jeff are interviewing Brent Carter in there at the moment," Bridget confirmed looking down at the log book "and Jim and Dave have got Sister Bernadette in room three."

"Thanks, Bridget, can you organise some water to be taken into room two, please," he requested, giving her a smile. Bridget smiled, happy to oblige. "Another late one for you?" Mike quizzed, as he fumbled through the log. "Nothing to go home to," she answered sadly. Mike gave her that knowing look, feeling her pain about how it felt when a child leaves home. She was struggling with her empty nest after her daughter had gone to university and he was struggling with the fact that his daughter, Laura, had emigrated to Chicago. It was a heartfelt wrench.

"Mike, it's ludicrous that he's trying to make us believe that he didn't know the other building was there. There is a hospital operating theatre, neonatal unit and nursery on-site and he's denying all knowledge," said Paul. "He's the fucking caretaker for Christ's sake."

They had been interviewing Thomas Hamilton for the last forty minutes and his version of events was slowly unravelling.

"Yeah, while it is obvious that this isn't his brainchild, he knew deep down that things weren't right but he possibly chose to look the other way. He's got one foot in the grave, Paul."

"Well one thing's for sure, when his time comes, he will be residing in hell," said Paul, anger seeping from his bones.

"How did it go with Brent Carter?" Mike asked, looking over at Jeff, as he walked into the office.

"Jeez," he said, walking towards them. "The guys a fucking nightmare. Claims to know nothing and is simply employed to drive the women into town and back again Monday to Friday," he said, stating the obvious. "There's flaws in everything he says of course. Holes everywhere."

"What about when you questioned him about how he came across the job, who employs him, etc?" said Paul, curious as to what the explanation was.

"It's been a forty minute interview of 'no comment'," said Jeff, looking a little embarrassed about the lack of information he could bring to the table.

Mike raised his eyebrows and turned back to Paul. "OK, let's move on to Ivy Mason," said Mike, standing up and stretching out his arms.

Seventeen

Mike and Paul were sitting at their desks, feeling totally exhausted. They had worked through until 2am, when they had finally thrown in the towel and headed home for some shut-eye.

The rest of the team had left around midnight, leaving them to mop up, and the cells were now occupied by all involved, with the exception of Sister Bernadette, who was escorted home by Kevin Monroe around 8pm. She had been the only one with a credible alibi but would be called for further questioning at a later date.

There was no doubt about it that Ivy Mason was in this up to her neck and was filtering the women through the system and on to Karen Lewis. They had interviewed her for over two hours and were sickened at how she had shown no sympathy or tenderness towards her victims and had no consideration at all towards the gravity of the offence. It was like she had no feelings, no emotion and was totally devoid of any type of compassion.

They still needed to interview Karen Lewis but had delayed this until the afternoon to enable them to catch up on all the paperwork. Jim and Dave had started the process the evening before but she had broken down in the interview room and the whole interview had to be postponed. "Stalling for time," Jim had declared. "Trying to get past the twenty-four hour period," he said, not having any of it.

"Morning," said Mel, stepping into the office. "How did it go?" she questioned, enthusiastically.

Mike had texted her earlier that morning telling her how much he had missed her and Jack, letting her know he would fill her in on all the details later and now she was chomping at the bit to be brought up to date.

Mike gave her a whistle-stop overview of the night's proceedings and then passed her a stack of case files for her and Karen to work through. "You'll hear all about it first-hand," said Mike, passing her the audio tape of Thomas Hamilton and Ivy Mason's interview. "Ivy's one is pretty sickening," said Paul, wincing from the memory.

"How's Jack?" said Mike, missing his little one and wishing things could be different.

"He's fine. Thought it was quite an adventure sleeping over at someone else's house so I made it into a game." Mike smiled, knowing how good Mel was at turning something unusual into something fun. "Thank you for having us," she said, turning to face Paul.

"Our pleasure," he said, knowing how grateful they both were. "Any time," he added, standing up to leave, so that they could have a few moments to themselves.

They had charged Thomas Hamilton at 9am that morning with 'perverting the course of justice' and he had been transferred to Holden Prison to await trial.

Ivy Mason's custody period had been extended to thirty-six hours from the usual twenty-four, due to the gravity of the offence and to enable additional questioning prior to charging.

Brent Carter's custody stay had also been extended to thirty-six hours, after striking out and assaulting Jim. He was now awaiting the arrival of his solicitor. Surprisingly, he was in fact the only one who had requested any type of representation.

Everyone was exhausted and Mel seemed to be the only one in the office with any vigour.

"It's so nice to see you smiling again," said Mike, enjoying the fact that his wife seemed more like her old self.

"Yeah, I feel much better," said Mel, perching on the edge of Mike's desk. "Mike, I know you're going to think this a bit soon but I would like to get some independence back," she said, looking down at her feet. "I would really like to see Liz this afternoon. I miss her, and in any case it will do me good. I realise that I'm not out of the woods yet, and I know the arrangement we have with Jane picking Jack up from nursery needs to continue for a while longer but I want to start being able to move around without a chaperone," she said, pleading her case.

"Where do you plan to meet her?" Mike quizzed, hoping she wasn't going to suggest their house.

"At home," she said, casually, knowing that this was going to be a challenge. "Look, I will be there with Liz, I won't be by myself," she said, looking at him with pleading eyes.

"Well, why can't you go to a coffee shop or something?" said Mike, feeling like he really didn't need this right now.

"Because I want to be able to go into my own bloody house when I want to," she suddenly snapped. "Sorry I didn't mean to bite your head off. I'm just really beginning to feel suffocated by everyone looking over my shoulder all the time. Mike, I'm not five years old!" she said, leaning forward and kissing him on the forehead, "I will be fine."

There was no point saying no to Mel, she was far too strong willed and he knew from experience that when Mel wanted to do something she would. He would just have to adjust his schedule so that he went home at a sensible time, so she wasn't left alone.

Mike took a deep breath as he watched his wife carry the case files and tapes across to her desk and then turned to face the window. He knew she was trying to get her life back on track, trying to move on from everything but the timing was far too quick for Mike's liking. He just didn't feel like she had given herself enough time to come to terms with everything.

The morning passed swiftly, filled with a million tasks that needed doing. Mike's mind was darting everywhere moving from work-related issues to personal stuff that was dear to him. He felt stressed and exhausted and worried about Mel and the thought of a beer or two with his mates Harvey and Bernie seemed really appealing right now. Somewhere to let off steam but there was no way there was time for that.

He looked across at the station clock and then decided on a quick sandwich before moving on to interview Karen Lewis. "Bridget, are we nearly ready for Karen Lewis?" he asked, taking a bite of a cheese and pickle sandwich.

"Nope, she's pulled another turn," said Bridget, looking down at her notes. "Doctors in with her know."

"For fuck's sake," said Mike, under his breath as he made his way back to his desk. "What a waste of time." He looked down at his mobile, resting on the edge of his desk and decided to call Jim. "How's it going?" he said, leaning back in his chair.

"Mike, we've just come across another room," he said, sounding a little shaky. "It's right up in the attic area," he said, giving him the details. "Looks like another operating theatre but much smaller," he said, coughing to clear his throat. "Doesn't look like it's anything to do with babies though. Looks like a dentist room to be honest. We've taken lots of photos and gathered up all the evidence," he said, reassuring him that they had everything they needed. "We are just about to head back now." They had spent the entire morning at the lodge with two other units and the whole site had been screened off until further notice.

"OK, thanks Jim, catch you later," he said eager to see what they had found.

He turned to face Mel who was typing away furiously and then went in search of Karen.

"Hey," he said, walking into the briefing room. "How are you doing?" She was standing in front of the case board, staring at all the photos with her hand resting on her chin.

"Anything else on Niko?" said Mike, as he took his place beside her.

"No, should there be?" she said, turning to face him. "Mike, I've done what you asked of me. Niko has not breached bail and there is nothing to suggest that he will," she said looking agitated. "You need to get Mel some professional help, Mike, you know that."

Mike nodded, turning to leave the room. He knew she was worried about the inspector but he also knew she felt he was dealing with Mel from the wrong angle.

Now, of course, Mel had decided enough was enough and was cutting ties with the agreement set in place and the whole bloody saga was strangling him like a noose.

He spent the entire afternoon working through the findings brought back to the office by Jim and Dave and the case board was brimming to overflowing.

Jim and Dave had photographed all the medical equipment found in the room and everything had been sent off for identification and analysis.

"What the fuck is that?" said Mike, holding up a picture of what looked like a drill piece.

"Dread to think," said Dave, closing the file.

Mike looked across at Mel's empty desk and wondered if she had left already. It was almost 4:45pm and he hadn't caught sight of her for a while.

"Has Mel left?" he asked, addressing Tina who sat near her. "Yeah, she left around 3:30pm," said Tina, "when you were in a meeting."

Mike walked over to his desk and sat down in his chair. He was really uncomfortable about Mel going home without him, he didn't like it at all. He picked up his mobile and scrolled for her number and then he swung his chair around to face the window.

He sat listening to her phone ringing over and over until it eventually went to voicemail. "Hey Mel, give us a call, so I know you're OK," he said, ending the call swiftly. He hated voicemail.

He sat staring into space and then he dialled again ten minutes later. Where the fuck was she and why wasn't she answering.

"Paul, I'm calling it a night and I suggest you do the same," he said standing up and grabbing his phone. "I've had enough for one day."

"Night, Bridget," he called out to her as he took the station steps two at a time. "See you tomorrow."

Why wasn't she answering, he pondered, selecting reverse and swinging round in the car park. She knew he would be worrying about her. This just didn't feel right.

The journey home to Westbury Fields was tiresome and long. He usually didn't mind the commute but today he felt impatient, he just wanted to get there.

He pulled onto his drive and jumped out of the car, catching sight of his neighbour waving at him.

"Hey Mike," he said waving a brown cardboard box in the air. "This was delivered the other day but I haven't seen either of you for a while," he said strolling down his pathway. Mike reached out to take the box, which had a picture of a paddling pool on the front.

"Thanks," said Mike, switching it to the other hand. "Thanks for taking it in," he added, turning to face his house.

"Yeah I tried to give it to your brother, but he didn't seem interested," he said, shaking his head.

"What do you mean my brother?" said Mike, spinning round to face him.

"The guy who's staying with you at the moment," he said, giving Mike a strange look. "I assumed he was your brother or at least a close relative," he said, starting to feel a little nervous. "He's been in and out of your house all week. I assumed he was a relative staying with you."

"What are you talking about?" said Mike, raising his voice. "What bloke, what did he look like?"

"Well, dark hair like you, leather jacket, looked a bit Greek actually, if I'm honest. He's in there now."

Mike dropped the package in disbelief. "Call the police," he said, charging towards his house. "CALL THE FUCKING POLICE!"

Eighteen

Twenty minutes earlier…

Mel pulled onto the driveway feeling really relieved. She had managed to shake off her chaperones and was going to have a lovely girly afternoon with her best friend Liz.

She had really missed their afternoons together and she knew that Jack really missed playing with Henry. She had decided to explain to Liz what had been going on, as she didn't feel it was fair to change their day-to-day arrangements without so much as a word.

She wasn't going to go into detail about the rape, as some things were far too private and no matter how fond she was of her she just didn't want to share something so intimate. She didn't want her looking at her with pity, tip-toeing around her. No, she wanted anonymity in that field. She was, however, going to explain that she had been assaulted seven years ago and that her attacker was out on bail and that she was a little nervous. She wanted to explain why she had suddenly stopped picking up Jack temporarily from the nursery and that things would be back to normal soon.

It was just going to be them today, no little ones in the background to overhear sensitive things that they were way too young to process. No, it was going to be a girly afternoon where she planned to explain, in not too much detail, what had happened all those years ago.

She had stopped at the shop for doughnuts en route knowing that this would be a welcomed treat and couldn't wait to see her friend's cheerful face.

She fumbled with her keys, trying to unlock the door with two overflowing carrier bags of shopping, and stepped into the hallway. "Phew," she said, out loud, knocking the front door shut by leaning back against it. She was home.

She made her way into the breakfast diner dumping both shopping bags on the countertop and turned to face the urn. "You won't be getting any more of me," she announced, in a firm voice, as if to say enough is enough. "It's over."

"Oh, I'm afraid it's a long way from over," came a soft whisper from behind her. Mel froze, rooted to the spot, her body paralysed with fear. She could feel her heart pounding against her chest, which was echoing through her entire body. She tried to take her next breath but felt like her body had shut down entirely. Oh my God I'm suffocating.

She tried to turn, forcing herself to turn round, she must see who it was. "Oh God, please don't let it be him," she said, slowly turning towards the door. She wiped the tears that were blurring her view, trying to make herself focus. She wiped them again, straining to see the distorted figure that stood in the doorway wearing denim jeans and a black leather jacket. She slowly lifted her head up towards his face. "No, please don't let it be him, please, please, please, don't let it be him," she begged.

A mop of greasy black hair, with the all too familiar quiff, slowly came into focus.

"Nooooo," she said, dropping down onto her knees. "Noooo"

Her body shook violently as she could feel herself convulse and then she threw up all over the floor.

"Now there's no need for that now is there?" he said, stepping fully into the room. "Don't go spoiling what I've got planned for you," he said, moving towards her.

Mel raised her head, not wanting to look at his ugly taunting face, as that would make it real. A face that had haunted her for the last seven years, that she never wanted to see again. But she needed to see it, she needed to see what he looked like now. She hoped he was frail and debilitated, decayed with rot, pieces of him dropping off onto the floor, as he shuffled along, dragging his leg, that's what she wanted to see.

She opened her eyes, willing herself to be brave. She had to see him.

"It's not you," she said, trying to comprehend what was happening here. "It's not you," she repeated, trying to get to her feet and stumbling forwards.

"Who are you?" she said, straining to get a better look at his face.

"Oh my God," she said, tears flowing down her face. "You."

Standing before her, dressed as her perpetrator, stood Joe Treville. He was wearing a black leather jacket, just like Niko had done and he had dyed his hair jet black. No wonder he had avoided capture.

She looked at his piercing green eyes and his fresh young complexion wondering how someone so handsome could be so ugly.

"Why?" she said, "Why me?"

"Why you indeed, my little beauty, Why indeed? Because your fucking husband has taken everything from me. Seven fucking years I waited to get hold of Linda and Rachel, seven fucking years of plotting my revenge and he comes along and takes it away in one fell swoop."

"But why do you want to hurt them?" she stuttered, wiping the tears from her eyes, trying to get her head around his reasoning.

"Because they're mine. They belong to me," he said, spitting the word out in spite. "They fucking owe me."

"But your father took everything from them. Their entire childhood, starving them and holding them prisoner for over a decade, how can they possibly owe you anything?" said Mel, trembling violently.

"Well let's see shall we," he said, sitting down on a bar stool. "what about the fact that they've got all my fucking money!" he screamed, his face purple with rage. He took a deep breath and looked casually across at the vase, lowering his voice. "Funny really, how you were so easy to manipulate," he said walking over to the vase. "You should learn to keep your patio door locked and your spare key hidden," he said, tipping the vase upside down.

"Watched you for hours pouring over this sad little letter," he said slowly opening it up. "Yeah, been watching you for weeks," he said laughing. "Not very private these townhouses, are they?" he continued to taunt.

"Yeah, really got me thinking when I watched you crying over this letter day after day and screaming at the vase. Yeah, I just had to see what it said." He opened the letter and read out the first line in a sickening soft tone. "It is my duty to inform you that Niko Dimitriou is due to be released on bail on the 4th May 2026. Well, well, well," he said, moving over to her. "How easy it was to become him, sneaking in when you were out of work. Moving things around to tease you," he said, waving her spare key around, which was dangling from his jeans pocket. "I learned everything about the case and what he had done. Got his description down to a fine art, wouldn't you say?" he said, spinning around in his crocodile shoes. "And how I enjoyed watching you pouring your troubles out to your pathetic husband night after night. Slowly unravelling bit by bit. How I relished watching you collapse in the side alley last week," he said, moving towards her. "God, I dined out on that for days. Anyway, seeing as I can't have them, I will have you," he said, pushing her down on the sofa. "I've got to be compensated somehow, don't you agree? Your husband has taken from me what was mine and now I'm going to take something from him that he considers to be very special," he said, towering over her.

"No you're not!" she screamed, kicking him in the groin. "You fucking get away from me!" she yelled, racing towards the door. He lunged towards her grabbing her by the hair, making her drop to the floor down onto her knees. "Get off me!" she screamed, sinking her teeth into his hand.

"You fucking bitch," he yelled, dragging her out into the hallway. "I have to say you're a lot more feisty than your little friend who came round earlier," he said, kicking open the toilet door and laughing. "Oh what fun we had."

In the middle of the floor, bound and gagged, was her best friend Liz. "Oh my God, what have you done to her?" she yelled, crawling towards her.

"Oh Liz," she said, pulling her blood-soaked hair away from her face. Tears streamed down her face as she watched her friend wriggle helplessly, as she fought against the rope that bound her hands. Liz's eyes flickered, as she looked desperately at Mel. "Why have you done this to her?" Mel said in a whimper. "What has she got to do with any of this?"

"Oh, think of it as a practice run," he said, in a smarmy way. "You know how I love auburn beauties."

"You bastard," said Mel, rising to her feet.

"Now don't go getting all silly on me," said Joe, leaning against the wall. "You really are a beauty, you know," he said admiring her long blond hair and voluptuous body. "Seems a real shame to have to damage any of your beautiful sculptured features. Why don't we see if you can entertain me without tarnishing your porcelain assets," he said, his face lighting up. "Now I want you to do exactly as I say," he said, sniffing the air and moving towards her.

He stopped in his tracks, disturbed by the sound of a key turning in a lock.

"Now who the fuck is this?" he said, stepping backwards out the room and turning to face the front door.

"Ah, it's your pathetic husband," he said, reaching into his inside pocket. "Must be all worried about his little wifey," he said, turning to look at her. "I'm sure he won't be a nuisance for long." He held the gun out directly in front of him.

"MIKE, DON'T COME IN!" she screamed, rushing forwards.

BANG

It was too late, Mike was lying on the floor in the hallway, blood dripping from his mouth, eyes wide open.

"Nooooo," Mel screamed, sheer panic rushing through her. "What have you done, what have you done?" she screamed, terror rising through her like she had never felt before. "Get out of my way," she screamed, struggling to get past him so she could get to Mike.

Joe grabbed her hair wrestling her to the ground, pinning her to the floor, so she couldn't breath. His laughing taunts cut through the air like a knife, as he ripped at her hair pushing her face up by her chin.

He held back her head, so her neck felt like it was about to snap and then he placed his mouth over hers. "You taste of vomit," he said, spitting in her face. "You had to ruin it, didn't you?" he said, turning her round, so her face was squashed against the floor. Mel struggled against his grip, pushing him backwards and catching him off guard. She tried to turn, she had to turn, she had to get to Mike.

He lunged again, pushing against her body, dragging her up to her feet and pushing her against the wall.

Oh my God, she could feel the gun. It was digging into her chest, stabbing at her heart. She was going to die. She knew she was. This was the moment when Jack would become an orphan, just like she had.

No, she couldn't let it happen again. She couldn't let Jack be dragged from one children's home to another, like she had. She just couldn't bear to let it happen all over again.

"Nooo," She screamed, pushing him from her and grabbing at the gun.

"Oh no you don't," he said, struggling against her grip, refusing to let go. He forced it from her, pushing her to the ground, smothering her with his heavy body.

"Stop struggling," he suddenly whispered, releasing his grip to unbutton his flies.

Mel lay there lifeless as she watched him lean down over her, his face getting closer and closer, so his breath was in her face. And then she lunged her head forwards, smashing at his head, taking him off guard, pushing him away.

"You bitch," he screamed, holding his face in his hands, as his cracked nose burst and blood shot over her. She could feel the gun, on the tip of her fingers, she was so close. She gave one last push, forcing him sideways, pushing him away.

She nearly had it, it was almost in reach – BANG.

She watched as his stunned expression changed to sheer unexpected horror, he clutched at his chest, falling forward while on his knees.

"Help me, somebody help me, oh please somebody help me," she whimpered, struggling as she tried to push Joe Treville's heavy body to one side. She was covered in blood, blurring her vision, as she crawled towards the toilet door on her hands and knees. She stopped, taking in the sight of Liz, staring up at the ceiling covered in blood.

She had to get to Mike, she had to see if he was alive while praying that Joe Treville was dead.

"Please let him be alive," she whimpered, crawling along the hallway.

She could see him lying on the floor, his head tilted to one side, so she couldn't see his face. His shirt was covered in blood and he was perfectly still.

She continued to crawl, unable to stand, feeling stripped of any strength she had felt before. She couldn't work out if she was seriously injured or if she was delaying finding out the answer but her legs wouldn't work.

"Mike," she said, touching him gently. "Mike, can you hear me? Please look at me, open your eyes. Mike, Mike," she said, shaking his body. "Oh my God, Nooo! Please Mike, open your eyes, you promised you would never leave me, Mike, you promised, you promised, please don't leave me," she said, tears flowing down her face.

She let out a piercing scream, so loud she wasn't sure if it was coming from her, as she shook his lifeless body.

"Mike," she said, clutching his body to her, "please don't leave me, please don't leave me."

Was that a siren she could hear?

Nineteen

Mel stood staring at herself in the mirror, despising what she saw.

She hated black and the large brim hat with the black veil covering her facial bruising looked hideous but she didn't care.

She couldn't care less what she looked like, what did it matter? She just knew she felt like she had died inside. A piece of her gone forever.

She dabbed at her eyes, tucking the tissue into her pocket and then she let out another sob.

"Mel, it's time to go," Paul called, standing at the foot of the stairs.

Mel took a deep breath, trying to step forward. She could do this, she had to.

"Coming," she said, tearfully, stepping out of the bedroom. "Won't be a moment," she added.

She made her way slowly down three flights of stairs, where Paul stood standing in a black tailored suit and coordinating tie.

She ached, not only in her heart, but every bone in her body hurt from Joe Treville's assault ten days earlier, but she had to do this, she had to say goodbye.

Paul opened the front door, holding it back so that Mel could exit first and then he closed it securely, after switching on the new alarm.

"Come on," he said, holding out his arm, "I'll help you to the car," he offered, trying to take the strain. Mel tried to smile, forcing herself forward. She could do this, she had to.

"It's all my fault," Mel suddenly blurted, reaching for her tissue.

"Why didn't I just go to a coffee shop like Mike suggested, why didn't I just follow the rules," she said, tears flowing down her cheeks.

"It's not your fault, Mel, you mustn't keep blaming yourself," he said, helping her into the car. "The only person responsible for this was Joe Treville."

He nodded at the driver and then reached out for her hand. "You will get through this," he reassured. "You will, I promise you."

The driver weaved his way through the Tuesday afternoon traffic, stopping at the foot of the hill. Paul stared across at The Sanctuary, the place where it had all started and let out a deep sigh. Seven years they had been working on this case, in theory, albeit intermittently, and it wasn't over yet, not by a long shot.

They still had to find Rachel.

"Are you ready to go inside?" Paul asked, as they made their way along the cobbled pathway leading to the vaulted doors of St. Mark's Church. Mel nodded, fixated on the graves and then she let out another sob.

"Yes," she said weakly, stumbling forward.

Paul held her hand tightly as he led her to the pews and then he stood by her side holding her hand.

"Please rise," instructed the reverend as the song, 'You're the Love of My Life' played softly as the coffin was carried by.

"Please be seated," he said. "We welcome you today to celebrate the life of Elizabeth Joan Turner, known fondly by all her family and friends as Liz."

Mel could feel her trembling hand tighten around Paul's as she caught sight of Rob, standing at the front, his head bowed, sobbing gently. What had she done? If only she had listened to Mike and done as she was told, Liz would be here now and she wouldn't be saying goodbye to her forever.

She coughed, catching her breath as she choked back the tears, watching Rob tremble. She couldn't hear the reverend, as the sound of his voice was drowned out by her grieving sorrow.

Why didn't she just grab the doughnuts and go, like she planned. Why did she start gathering extra shopping, delaying her arrival home. If only she had kept to her original plan, she would have been on time but instead Liz had arrived on schedule and rang the doorbell, assuming her to be in.

Why didn't she notice her car wasn't on the drive? Why did she step inside when he opened the door? He must have lied to her, she thought, staring down at her black shoes. He must have made out he was a house guest of sorts, showing her in and perhaps pretending she was in the kitchen or hadn't yet arrived home but was en route.

She gripped Paul's hand as she agonised over Liz's final moments, as she stared up at the sculptured ceiling. My God she must have been petrified, having no understanding of who he was or where he was from.

She took a deep breath as her eyes turned towards the coffin. I'm so sorry Liz I'm so sorry, she said over and over in her head. She looked at the yellow flowers draped across the top. Yellow Tulips, her favourite kind. Oh how Liz loved yellow tulips, as she said they were full of sunshine, letting us know that a new and brighter season was looming.

She knelt down as she felt Paul tug at her hand, releasing it, so she could pray. What she wouldn't give to have her friend back with her now, she thought, holding her hands together.

Her thoughts turned to Henry, her beautiful little boy, wondering how he was. What would they tell him? How would they explain that his mummy wasn't coming back, ever.

"Amen," she heard, echoing around the church.

Paul helped her back to her feet, as they retook their seats, so that Rob could read his eulogy. Oh no, this was going to be too much to witness, she thought watching the man, she hadn't yet met, describe his loving wife in the most sensitive and heart wrenching detail.

She listened as he described her so perfectly in every single detail. They way she made him laugh, the way she always saw the good in every situation, including every person she ever met. He described how he would miss her every single day for the rest of his life and that if he could do it all over again, he would do it differently, spending every single second with her instead of serving in the army.

It was totally gut wrenching listening to what he would do differently, given the chance. Sadly it was a lesson, learned too late. Perhaps something we should all learn from, she thought.

When he spoke about Henry, it was too much to bear, causing her a sharp intake of breath that she couldn't exhale. Paul squeezed her hand when she let out a gasp and then put a comforting arm around her.

She returned to her knees for the Lord's prayer and remained on them in despair as Liz's favourite song was played while the coffin was carried from the church.

"I'm sorry," Mel whispered as it passed her by. "I'm so sorry."

Twenty

"Mr Brugge, will you please keep still while I change your dressing," the nurse begged, unable to deal with her patient's desire to be discharged within the next twenty seconds.

"Just because you have been discharged by the doctor, it doesn't mean that you can hot foot it out of here without a clean dressing and the correct discharge papers. I also need to organise your meds, so you may as well sit still and let me do my job."

"Is he giving you trouble?" said Mel standing in the doorway, smiling.

"Ah, Mrs Brugge, perhaps you can have a word with your husband and wind down his need to accelerate," she said, with a wink.

"While we are all relieved with regard to his excellent progress," she said, removing her gloves, "we can't all work at a hundred miles an hour."

"I'll take it from here," said Mel, wagging her finger at Mike. "Leave him to me."

"How are you doing?" she said, moving in for a kiss.

"I'm ready to go," he said, raising his voice slightly, so the nurse caught his comments as she marched from the room.

"Yeah, I know how you feel there," she said, remembering how desperate she felt when the roles were reversed.

"But you've got to do as you're told, Mike," she said, then flinched from her words.

"How are you?" he said, grabbing hold of her hand.

"Funeral was tough," she said, giving his hand a squeeze. She stared up towards the ceiling, tears brimming in her eyes. "I kept thinking that I could have been burying you as well."

"Hey, it will take a lot more than that to keep me from you," he said, leaning forward to kiss her, then wincing from the pain.

"Mike, it could have been so different," she said, knowing it had been a close call. "Life is so precious, we have to make every moment count," she said recalling Rob's eulogy from the funeral service. "You had a lucky break," she said, looking at the sling supporting his arm and shoulder. The shot had gone clean through his shoulder and out the other side. The blow to his head on the front door, as he was blasted backwards, however, caused concussion and this had been the primary reason for his eleven-day stay in hospital.

"Well, the same goes for you," he gestured, stroking her bruised face gently.

"Your forehead looks so sore," he said, assessing her injuries. "How's the rest of you doing?"

"Well I'm still extremely stiff and I ache all over but other than that I'm tip-top," she said, tears brimming in her eyes again.

"Hey," he said, squeezing her hand. "You've got to stop blaming yourself. Joe Treville would have got in regardless of you being late," he said, holding her chin up by his forefinger.

"But if I had listened to you and gone to a coffee shop Liz would still be here," she said, breaking down.

"Hey, how could you have possibly known Treville was going to be in our house. The whole thing is total madness. Look, it was me he was trying to get to, through you. If anyone's to blame it's me for letting you go back there," he said, turning her so he could look her in the eye.

He handed her a tissue and kissed her on the nose. "This is no one's fault, other than that sadistic bastard and now he's exactly where he belongs," he said sternly. "Mel, can you do something about this bloody bandage?" he said, trying to pull it from his neck. It keeps catching on my wound," he said pointing to Julie Somers' aggressive bite wound on his shoulder.

"That area of your body's been under attack, recently," said Mel, trying to make him comfortable.

"Yeah, I will try to remember to turn the other way, next time I see someone heading for me," he said smiling.

"How's Jack," he said, standing up from the bed. "I can't wait to see him." He opened the bedside cabinet door in search of his trainers and then searched for a pair of socks.

"Let me help you with them," said Mel, reaching down to retrieve them from the bottom of the shelf. "He's missing you, obviously," said Mel, tying up his lace. "He's missing his buddy Henry as well. Rob did mention yesterday at the funeral that he thought it would be best if Henry returned to nursery as soon as possible, so that his usual routine could be re-established. I think that will give both boys the structure they need."

"What will happen to Henry when Rob returns to service?" said Mike, raising a very valid question.

"I'm not sure," said Mel, wondering about his long-term care. "I know Liz's mum lives in Australia," she said, suddenly looking all perplexed.

"Mr Brugge, your meds and discharge papers are ready," said the nurse, waving them in the air.

"Thank heavens, you've been really efficient," said Mike, in a teasing voice. "Come on, let's get out of here," said Mike, edging towards the door. Mel shook her head, smiling, God she had missed his ways. She gathered the two carrier bags of belongings from the bedside cabinet and followed him out to the desk.

"Mel, I'm planning on returning to the station tomorrow," he said, climbing into the passenger seat and pulling on his belt. "So before you go all political on me, telling me I'm not ready, I want you to know I plan on staying desk bound for a while, so there's no need to panic."

Mel smiled at him, as she selected reverse. "I wouldn't expect anything less from you," she said, looking over her shoulder. "I'm coming to."

Mike looked across at her about to challenge her decision, when he reconsidered his actions. "Well I will be keeping an eye on you," he said smiling.

"And I will be keeping an eye on you!"

They had both spent the last eleven days running through the events of that day. They had gone through every single segment of it, inch by inch. They had dissected it, debated different outcomes and challenged one another's decisions before finally laying some of it to rest.

The one thing that was definitely laid to rest was Joe Treville, who by now would be six feet under. Diane Treville had been given permission to attend the funeral on compassionate grounds and had been accompanied by two police officers and Paul. He had firmly stated that he could not rest until he saw him enter the ground himself and had made it his mission. He did actually say that, with the exception of his mother, there was no one else in attendance. Speaks for itself really, he had stated. Anyway he was gone and now Mike could bring good news to Linda's door.

"I think we still need Jane's help with Jack for the time being," said Mike, laying down some ground rules. "So, until we are both back to full strength, we will continue as before," he said.

Mel nodded knowing he was right. She wasn't ready to return home without Mike's support anyway, not only because of Niko but because her recent assault was so raw.

"Right let's go and get Jack," she said, smiling. She wanted her family back together. Tonight they would all go home together.

Twenty-One

"Mike, there're so many files to go through and each one gets more and more harrowing," said Paul, throwing a file down on his desk.

Mike looked up from the file he was reading, acknowledging their plight. "I know we are going to have to share the load," said Mike, looking across at Mel.

"One thing's for sure, they have all followed a similar path, most passing through Casio Grange and Danbury Manor. I've noticed some have come in from a home called Willow Place. Obviously it doesn't always suggest foul play but it would be interesting to know if there are any connections there," said Paul. "It's also hard to swallow, credibility wise I mean, how they all made such incredible progress all of a sudden. All the patients that were assigned to Ivy Mason and Karen Lewis all accelerated, obviously fast-tracked through the system, so that they would reach Keeper's Lodge," he added.

"Yes, and they are mostly lost souls, and by that I mean no family connections. They have all passed through a series of children's homes for various reasons, such as welfare issues, ranging from neglect to complete abandonment. Obviously some were foundlings, some orphaned very young, or have come from families with mental health issues, alcoholism or drug-related problems that have lost touch, or simply don't care enough. You would be amazed just how many children pass through the system," said Mike, turning round to face the window.

He thought about Mel and her brother Pete, passed from pillar to post when they were orphaned as youngsters. The stories Mel regaled were quite cutting, some chilling. It was a harsh world out there.

"Beats me how this went undetected for so long," said Paul, picking up another file.

"Well it's been carefully orchestrated, streamlined to perfection so it's seamless. Everyone along the chain is connected in one way or another, each doing their bit to progress things along the line," said Mike, spinning around to face him. "If you think about it, if everyone in the chain is involved, it's never going to be questioned. We need to work our way back to the source," said Mike, opening another file.

He had missed Karen Lewis's interview conducted by Paul and Tina, which he found a real handicap. He had read the report several times and had questioned Paul relentlessly but there was nothing like witnessing it first-hand.

He had been suspicious about her from the first time he met her, thinking there was more to her than her gentle, meek appearance. "It's always the little ones you have to watch," he had recounted to Mel on more than one occasion. "They're like whippets, look all endearing and then suddenly they've got you round the neck."

He was also amazed at their incredible likeness. There was something quite odd about the pair of them. Both were exceptionally small, tiny little pixie faces with oversized eyes. They could be mistaken for sisters. While Ivy Mason's plaited braids and boyish dungarees gave her a hillbilly appearance, Karen Lewis's look was more professional. However, her frame was so slight it did make it appear that she was a young child in grown-up clothing, like she was dressing up. Their similarities were beginning to haunt him.

"Paul, don't you think Ivy Mason and Karen Lewis look very similar?" he said, passing their photographs across the desk.

"Yes, I had been thinking about that," said Paul, reaching out for the photos.

"It's like they've come from the same rotten egg," Mike continued. "It would be interesting to get some DNA on them," he said, turning to face the window again.

Mike's thoughts were darting everywhere. He couldn't get their likeness out of his mind. It wasn't until they had been arrested and he saw them side by side that he had noticed their resemblance.

"It does make you question how long this process has been going on," said Mike, turning round again.

"What if they are sisters and were born into the institution, made for this very purpose," said Mike, pondering his suggestion.

"Jeez, Mike, that's some hunch," he said, straightening his pens.

"Well, think about it. We don't yet know how these girls are being impregnated. The likelihood is that it's artificial and, if so, they may use the same sperm donor over and over."

Paul looked up at the ceiling and then across at Mike. "Fucking hell, Mike, if this has been going on for over three decades and they use the same donor, or even if they have a few select donors on their books, it still makes for a lot of half and full siblings out there. It doesn't bear thinking about the consequences of that potential hazard."

"Yes, and if you mix inbreeding with people with inherited mental health issues the cocktail is toxic," said Mike, rising to his feet. "We need the blood results from these women," he said, walking across the room, "and Ivy and Karen too," he added.

He walked into the briefing room and stared at the board. He had a real sinister feeling about this case. This was an underworld like no other, a black market where everything was managed in-house, no outsiders so that every person placed along the chain was effectively from the same family tree. He felt certain of it. He just needed to prove it.

He really hated the fact that he had missed eleven days of the investigation. Keeper's Lodged had been completely shut down and all occupants had been reassigned to new institutions. Every single patient had to be re-evaluated, so that a new file could be drawn up with the correct medical records, albeit very patchy. Snippets of information were garnered from the files intercepted at the lodge but a lot of the case notes were phony leaving giant holes in their history.

Mike had requested blood DNA on all the babies that were born to the six women that eventually went into labour from this trimester and a team of officers had turned over Casio Grange and Danbury Manor.

Every patient assigned to Ivy Mason and Karen Lewis from both institutions had been reassigned to alternative homes and their case notes were now being examined.

Similarities from all the notes scrutinised to date had shown the same acceleration of progress and they were all heading in the same direction, Keeper's Lodge.

The team had also intercepted eight other members of staff that had turned up to work the following day. They had been taken completely off guard, totally unaware that the place had been turned over. He had read through Jim and Dave's interview notes, detailing their roles within the lodge, which concluded that they did employ kitchen staff, along with two nurses, a midwife and two cleaners. All eight were now part of the trial.

"Mike, I've been thinking about Brent Carter's involvement in all of this," said Paul, strolling into the room. "The guy lives like a millionaire and yet he drove these women into town everyday. It's bloody ludicrous, there must be more to it."

He sat down on a chair and crossed his legs. "His first interview with Jeff was basically written off as 'no comment'," he continued, "but Jim and Dave had a bash second time around and extracted a few extras, hindered by his solicitor of course who kept interrupting. Anyway, while you were in hospital I dug deep into his past to see how he made his millions but there's nothing on him. The guy's living in luxury but there is nothing to suggest he is a self-made millionaire. He owns nothing, no businesses, no shares in anything. The only thing his name is listed against is the property itself."

"Inherited?" said Mike, staring at Carter's picture on the case board.

"Well that's it, Mike, I've just received a response from my enquiries," he said, holding up a piece of paper, "and Brent Carter is listed as a foundling, no parental history at all. Mike, he's the perfect candidate, albeit male," he added, waving the paper. "What if he is a sperm donor?" said Paul, throwing his suggestion into the mix.

"That's a good call," said Mike, taking the paper from his hand. "DNA test him and compare result against the infants that have just been born," said Mike, adding him to the list. "We've got nothing to lose. Paul, I would like to pay Linda a visit," he said, knowing he was crossing the line. He had faithfully promised Mel that he would stay firmly behind his desk but he wanted to deliver this news in person. He felt that he had failed her previously and now he could reopen her world so she could return to her life and start again. Well at least he had some good news. He could definitely inform her that her perpetrator, Joe Treville, was six feet under and would never bother her again but they still hadn't identified Rachel.

Everything was dependant on the blood results and he felt like a fucking vampire-in-waiting.

They were also awaiting the result of the attic room analysis and what it was actually used for. It was masquerading as an on-site dentist facility but some of the tools were, without doubt, questionable. They had run tests on three of the women and it was concluded that their mesmerised state was a result of electric shock treatment, drugs and a degree of hypnotism. From their findings, with the exception of electrodes, there was nothing to suggest any type of surgery.

"Paul, there is so much to do," he said, feeling like he was drowning. "Until the rest of medical results start coming in, we are swimming in the dark," he said, walking from the room.

"I wonder how Julie Somers is doing?" said Paul, following him. Mike stopped in his tracks, pausing at his comments. "Yes, it's interesting how far we've come since first assuming that this had something to do with her father-figure alter ego," said Mike, remembering how they had made the ludicrous suggestion of climbing inside her mind to conduct an interview.

"We seem to have moved from an exorcism to vampire territory," said Mike, searching for some coins.

"Well you certainly look like you've been involved in some kind of altercation with the devil," said Paul, taking in the sight of his injuries. "How are you doing anyway in that department?" He had been actively trying to avoid asking too many questions relating to the shooting, as he knew Mike was struggling with the fact that he had left Mel exposed. He knew that his friend was battling with his conscience, that he had allowed his wife to return to the house unescorted.

"Yeah I'm OK," he said, looking down at his sling. "I will be glad when all this wrapping comes off. Coffee?" he asked, gesturing towards the machine. Paul nodded, leaning against the wall.

"It's Mel I'm worried about," he said, turning to look at her through the large double doors. "She pretends to be a tough cookie, making it appear that she is totally in control but to be honest I'm surprised she's standing up as well as she is. The anxiety of Niko's release and then Joe Treville's assault, one of those things alone would put most people out of action but a double whammy like that," he said, staring at her bruised face in the distance.

"Ah, and you forget about the fact that she nearly lost her husband," said Paul, adding to the list and then regretting it immediately he saw Mike's frown. "Sorry, I was just agreeing that she is standing up surprisingly well considering she has just lost a close friend as well," he said, then wincing from the realisation that he was digging himself deeper into the grave.

"Well, on that note," said Mike, pushing open the door while raising his eyebrows, "Shall we return to our desks and continue to dig where the need is greatest? Paul, let's go through everything with a fresh approach. Let's assume we are correct with our assumption that everyone in the chain of command is connected biologically. Let's work towards a common denominator, till we meet the devil himself."

Twenty-Two

"Hey, Mike, got something interesting here," said Paul, tossing the file across to him.

"What ya got," said Mike, leaning back in his chair and rotating his neck. He looked down at the file and then across at Mel and then he turned to face Paul.

"Some of the children were returned," said Paul, walking around to Mike's side of the desk. "Look," he said, pointing to a comment entered on the 25th November 2004. "It states here that a young girl aged eighteen months was showing signs of mental retardation and was returned to the clinic. Look, there's a detailed list of factors identified by the adoptive parents. Then in this file," he said, pointing to another file, "in 2005 there was a young boy aged two, showing signs of autism. Again the adoptive parents complained and the child was returned. Beggars belief really that you can just return a child, like you were returning a defective electrical item for a refund," said Paul, looking a little hot under the collar. "I mean surely the emotional attachment after two years of raising a child would mean you would love them no matter what. In this file there is a similar entry. In 2004 a girl aged three was returned, as the adoptive parents complained of antisocial behaviour and violence. Mike, something went wrong during this period, as there are several other files with similar entries," said Paul, pointing to a pile of files positioned on the right-hand side of his desk.

"They got the ingredients wrong," said Mike, rising to his feet. "If you impregnate women with mental health issues, its likely to be a deadly cocktail. Especially if the donor has similar problems. A lot of these conditions are heriditory."

"I wonder what became of the children that were returned," said Paul, continuing his way through the papers. "Some of them would be in their twenties by now."

"There is no mention of any children being returned in the batch I have run through" said Mike, retaking his seat. "I've covered 2010 to 2015, so far. So that suggests that they changed course," said Mike.

"Guys, the bloods are in," said Mel, walking into the room. "Ivy and Karen are related, they're sisters," she said, setting the papers down in front of him. "They share both parents," she said, shaking her head. "To be honest, I thought they would share one but both, that has surprised me."

"Well that explains their likeness," said Mike, reading the results. "Does it make you wonder what the parents look like though?" he said, imagining a pixie crossed with a midget.

"Perhaps Ivy and Karen were returned as infants, which would explain why they are still here. Maybe some of the other infants are now part of the breeding chain also, set to work to earn their bread and butter when they reached breeding age – or were readopted by parents with more morals," offered Paul.

"Hey look," Mike said, working his way down the list. "All six babies share the same father. So whoever was donating the sperm must have a good success rate." He turned to face Mel. "We discovered earlier that some of the babies dating from the millennium up until around 2005 were returned to the clinic with behavioural and mental health issues," he said, filling her in. "So I expect the sperm donors on their books now have been tried and tested since the cock-up – sorry, excuse the pun, wasn't intended," he said, thinking this was no time to joke. "However, how many deranged people could you gather together who would donate sperm under such horrendous circumstances? Not many is my guess. You're likely to get a few unscrupulous people if the payoff was high enough but the risk factor of being exposed to the outside world would be high, I should think."

"Yeah, it does point to the fact that they either use the same donor all the time or have a few trusted individuals on their books but then you are turning out hundreds of babies into the community that are related," said Mel. "Mike, the risk factor attached to that is huge. They run the risk of unknowingly inbreeding. How many victims have unknowingly had relationships with a half sibling, possibly gone on to have children?" said Mel.

"It's far greater than that, Mel. Some of these women have been impregnated again and again, possibly by the same donor. So potentially there could be couples out there that are full siblings. Then there's the underlying problem of mental health. All these mothers were here initially because of mental health issues." Mel looked up to the ceiling, the full realisation dawning on her. "Mike, this is hideous."

"Mike, Brent Carter is a donor," said Paul, pointing to his DNA and that of the six new babies. Jeez, that's his payoff, his millionaire lifestyle and all he has to do is drive the women to and from town, have an occasional wank, then sit back and wait for his pay cheque."

"That's quite a résumé," said Mike, cynically. Considering his route into the role. "So, we've established he was a foundling but we don't have anything else relating to his childhood. We need to find out how he was brought into the fold and did any other male donors come via the same path. Let's research the institutions he passed through because he obviously didn't reside at Danbury Manor because it's all female."

"Some of the victims came in via Willow Place," said Paul, remembering his earlier comment. "I'll check to see if that's mixed gender."

"It would be good to visit the lodge again," said Paul, gathering his papers together. "I really feel it would benefit us to walk around it without the place crawling with people," he added.

Mike looked at Mel knowing that she would explode if he broke his promise. "Well, perhaps we could all go," he suggested, smiling at his wife. "I'm sure you would like to see the place," said Mike, enticing his wife and leading the way.

"You know I would like to see it," said Mel, looking across at her desk. "Do you honestly think I would prefer to go back over there and type up notes when I could come with you?"

"Is that wise?" asked Paul, when Mel was out of earshot, collecting her bag.

"Probably not," said Mike, rising to his feet, "but I'm not going to get there otherwise, not without breaking a promise," he added, grabbing his jacket. "And in any case the place is empty and she will be right under my nose at all times."

They pulled into Keeper's Lodge at 2:15pm, stopping at the gate. "Evening," said Paul, leaning out of his car window to address the officer guarding the front entrance.

He held up his badge identifying himself and then proceeded forward as he released the gate.

"Wow it's quite something," said Mel, stepping out of the back seat gingerly and taking in the incredible setting. "Seems like such a waste," she said. "I mean what a retreat, if it was used for its original purpose." She nodded at the officer at the foot of the stairs.

"Told you it was special," said Mike, stepping around the yellow tape. It seemed really odd climbing the staircase and opening the front door without Thomas Hamilton overseeing the process.

"How did the visitors' book get missed?" said Mike, noting it on the side. "Bag it up," he snapped, feeling agitated all of a sudden.

"Hey," said Mel, reaching for his arm. "It must have been mayhem here that day, it's not surprising it got missed," she reasoned, walking along the hall. She stared at the oak panelling, marvelling at the stairs. "It's stunning," she whispered, wandering into the lounge. "Mike, it looks beautiful," she said, taking in the impressive sun lounge. "Totally idyllic. No wonder the place went undetected for so long. You would never consider this place to be one of cruelty and abuse," she added.

"Well, take a look upstairs," said Mike, "Might change your mind."

Mel wandered up the staircase running her fingers along the shinny banister rail as she went. "You coming," she said, suddenly feeling a little unsettled.

"Of course," he said, giving her a reassuring smile, "I'm not letting you out of my sight." He followed her up the stairs.

"It's odd how each room has a different level of home comfort," said Mel, comparing the room she just entered to the room she just left.

"Yes, we think it's either dependent on where they are along the pregnancy path," he said, recalling his earlier thoughts. "Or possibly to do with how fertile they are and how much profit they can bring in. Also, the room down here with eight beds, dormitory style, is possibly where the women stayed when they were between pregnancies."

"What suggests that?" asked Mel, her eyes darting around the room.

"See this name here," he said pointing to the nearest bed, that woman, Marianne Foster, is the one we spoke to at the drop-in centre, same goes with the one at the end. They work at the centre when they're not pregnant to keep up the charade. Come, I'll show you Thomas's room," he said, heading off down the hallway.

Mel followed silently, taking everything in. "Well, he's certainly very comfortable," she said, feeling surprised by its 'gentleman's club' image. Looks like he's been here thousands of years," she said, sniffing the musty air and taking in the sight of the overflowing bookshelves and piles of old newspapers.

"This is only the half of it," said Mike, pointing to the stack of papers by the window. "We've taken some for analysis, so we can establish their relevance, if any," he said, turning towards the door.

"Can I see the delivery suites," Mel asked, standing at the top of the stairs.

"Mel, it's very harrowing over there, I really don't think it would be a good idea," he said, edging her away from the stairs.

"Please, Mike, I want to see it and in any case I am a police officer not a fairy princess," she said, shaking off his hand.

"You're so bloody stubborn," he said, shaking his head. "Come on before I change my mind."

Paul was standing at the reception desk, flicking through the register. "Mike, it says here that on the 23rd July 2025, Julie Somers visited the lodge but it doesn't say who she visited," he said turning to face him. "That bit has been left blank."

"Are there any other entries for her?" Mike quizzed, moving in closer.

"No, that's the only one. The historical logs are at the station but surely that wouldn't have been missed," said Paul, closing the book. "I will run through them myself later."

"Who would Julie Somers be visiting here?" asked Mike, as he opened the front door. "I'm taking Mel across to the delivery suite," he said, stepping out onto the veranda.

Paul raised his eyebrows, shaking his head. "You sure," he said, as they went down the stairs.

"No," said Mike, looking over his shoulder.

Paul closed the front door and headed down the stairs after them.

"Mel, I think you should concentrate on the nursery area, as opposed to the delivery suite," Mike said, as they approached the block.

"He's right, Mel, it's really unpleasant and it's not going to make any difference to the outcome of the inquiry," said Paul, acknowledging Mike's challenge with his strong-willed wife.

Mike threw him a grateful look, letting him know he was up against it.

"And in any case, it's sealed off for forensics," he said, relieved, when he saw the tape across the door, saying 'DO NOT ENTER'.

Mel let out a sigh and made her way to the end of the corridor, turning right. She stopped at the viewing window, taking in the sight of the little transparent cribs lined up with pink and blue blankets and the two feeding chairs, set centre stage. Under normal circumstances a row of cribs would bring joy but knowing the intended purpose gave it a creepy feel.

"Mike, there's a small room here," Paul shouted, opening the door wide. "More of a cupboard really," he said, taking in the sight of the floor to ceiling shelving. "Looks like the team have taken most of it back for forensics," he said, looking along the shelves. There was a small desk at the far end with a single chair. A desktop monitor was positioned in the centre but the hard drive was missing indicating that it had been removed intentionally, either by the team or someone else. "Not much here," he said, emptying a few boxes of loose papers onto the desk.

Mike stared at some of the labels on the files as he ran his finger along them. "Paul, I think this is where they watch video footage of their patients' psychiatry sessions," he said, noting a file list on the wall. "If they're playing with their minds they must be evaluating the progress," he added. "Look, there's a list of recording sessions here with patient names. No one has mentioned this back at the station and I am certain if there was any footage we would have known about it immediately."

"But they wouldn't have had time to empty it out, especially mid-delivery," said Paul.

"Well, maybe this room is no longer in use," said Mike, turning to face the door. "The guys didn't unearth anything here, which is why it's not been mentioned. Paul, the footage must be somewhere else on-site, somewhere really secluded."

"What about the attic room?" said Paul. "The lads said it was accessed by a small set of stairs set behind a cupboard door."

"Mel, we're heading to the attic room," Mike said, grabbing hold of her arm and leading her along the corridor.

"But I haven't seen…" she said, cutting off mid-sentence, as he pulled her towards the door.

"Mel, we need to find the video footage of the psychiatry sessions," he said, opening the double doors. "We found a room where they used to store the tapes but it looks like they've been recently moved."

They made their way back towards the main lodge as fast as they could. "If we could find the video footage, we may be able to identify the person running this," said Mike, taking the stairs two at a time.

"We may also be able to identify Rachel," said Paul, hot on his heels.

The attic room, as described, was set behind what looked like a cupboard door. Even when you opened the door the mock shelving gave the illusion it was for storage only. It was so discrete, that he was surprised the lads had found it.

"Fucking hell, this is creepy," said Mike, making his way up an extremely slender dark staircase.

"It's like a winding turret, leading to a tower," Paul added, wondering if there was another way in. "There must be another way. How the hell would they get a dentist chair up here."

"Oh my God, I can see what the guys meant about it resembling a dentist's chair," Mike said, stepping into the room and looking at the chair, which was tilted in the backward position.

"Why do you suppose it's tilted like that?" said Mel, thinking it looked like they were hanging the patient by their feet.

"I dread to think," said Mike, turning his head round.

"The lads have obviously taken everything that was in sight back to the station, so we are looking for hidden treasure," said Mike, banging on the panelled walls. "It's got to be here."

"Mike, look, the chair is in that position because it can slide to one side," she said, pushing it across.

"Out the way," he said, dropping to his knees. "Paul, help me lift it," he said, struggling against the weight of a trap door against his injured shoulder.

Mel stood speechless, wondering if this was it or whether they had found something else even more sinister.

"This is it," yelled Mike, pulling out a box of tapes. "There's dozens of them."

"There in alpha order," said Mel, scrambling through the first box Mike lifted out.

"This box is A-B," she said, lifting it up onto the counter. "I've got Rachel's tape, I've got it in my hand."

"Put it in the recorder," yelled Paul, almost snatching it from her hand. "Put it in," he repeated.

Mel undid the box with shaky hands and slipped it into the recorder, positioned in the corner of the room. She pressed play and stepped back.

There was a pretty girl with blonde hair sitting in the dentist chair. She had her hands clasped, resting them on a petite pregnancy bump. She looked very frail with dark shadows under her eyes but she was smiling.

"Hello Rachel, or should I call you Anika?" a gentle voice asked from the background. "How are you today?"

"I'm OK," she said, stroking her stomach. "I think I may have eaten too much," she said, pointing to her bump. "Sarah thinks I'm getting fat," she suddenly spouted, angrily. "What do you think?" she questioned, innocently.

"I think you look perfect," said the gentle voice again. "Just as a woman should look," he added, gently.

"I know that voice," Mike suddenly whispered.

"What?" said Paul, not sure if he heard him correctly.

"The doctor's voice," he said, the wind knocked from him completely. "Oh my God," he said, sitting down on a chair, the realisation seeping through him like a deadly virus, "It can't be, Paul," he said, turning to face him. "It just can't be. But I know that voice, I just know it," he repeated.

Paul stared at the screen, willing the doctor to speak again.

Doctor Gyllensvan stepped from behind the camera, moving swiftly across the screen. He patted her bump gently.

"I think you look perfect, Rachel," he repeated. "Just perfect."

Twenty-Three

"I just can't believe it," said Mel, scrambling through some of the records, as they made their way back to the station. "How could this be?" she questioned, pulling out another file, shaking. "We trusted him, we trusted him," she repeated. "Mike, we handed the girls over to him seven years ago and he must have been working towards this ever since," she said, unable to believe what she had just witnessed.

The hidden storage had housed every single secret about the lodge. Boxes of files contained not only camera footage of psychiatric sessions but detailed logs of adoptive parents, giving names, addresses and payments received. Over six hundred babies had been sold on the black market over a twenty-five year period.

There was no doubt about it, Doctor Gyllensvan was going down for life and that was a done deal.

Mike had made the call to Jim, ordering him and Dave to arrest the doctor forthwith, so that he would be waiting for them at the station. This was going to be, without doubt, one of the biggest trials he had ever been involved in.

"We now know that Rachel was sometimes called Anika during her time here," said Mel, reading through her file, with a shaky voice. "That's why we couldn't see her listed on the log, the day the women were rescued," she said, turning the page.

"Yet he called her Rachel during the psychiatry session," said Mel, opening the window for some fresh air.

"Guess it didn't matter how he addressed her in a private psychiatry session," said Mike, looking round at his wife. "She had so many personalities in her head with different names."

"Or maybe he did call her Rachel, but remember Rachel didn't identify with her own name because she had been known for half of her life as Anika, during her captivity. So when they were taking the names of all the women that day, perhaps she offered the name Anika because that's who she believes herself to be. Also, half of them didn't offer last names either, like they didn't even know who they were," Miked added.

"So," said Paul, selecting 5th gear. "We need to establish what home Anika Doe got transferred to?" he said, putting his foot down.

"Paul, I need to call Jane to explain the hold up," said Mel, worried about Jack.

"I've already called her, she knows we're going to be late back," he said, reassuring her that Jack was absolutely fine. "But she did ask if we would be dropping you back and I took the liberty of saying yes," he said, wincing.

Mike stiffened waiting for her to challenge this decision and then relaxed, relieved that she had agreed with this decision.

"Yes, I don't want to put any extra stress on Jane," said Mel, thinking about her fragile status. "She's been so supportive and helpful but she is pregnant after all."

They arrived back at the station at 6:15pm, after dropping Mel off en route. "Jesus, Mike, the doctor must have been rubbing his hands together the day you brought Linda and Rachel to him for treatment," he said, passing Mike his coffee.

"Makes me cringe," said Mike, searching his drawer for extra sugar. "To think the path was set for them seven years ago, when I walked through his door."

"My guess is," said Mike, rising to his feet, "that Linda was an unlikely victim because she was too intellegent, but Rachel, with her identity disorder, was an ideal candidate. "I expect at first he thought he had a double win."

"Bridget, let me know as soon as Jim and Dave are back," he said, popping his head out of the double doors.

"I can't believe it," said Mike pacing back and forth like an expectant father. "How could someone like Doctor Gyllensvan, specialising in mental health disorders be responsible for something so abhorrent? I have to say, Paul, this has totally blown me away."

"Yeah, it makes you think about Julie Somers' involvement in all of this," said Paul, swinging round in his chair. "Is she a victim or is she part of the chain, after all, she was on the visitors' log," said Paul, remembering her entry back in August 2025.

"My guess would be part of the chain," said Mike, retaking his seat. "I'm not sure he would have sent her off on a sabbatical if she was a victim."

He thought back to her fragile status back at Arlington Terrace. "I can't get my head around that to be honest. She suffered a total meltdown fusing her own identity with that of Rachel's after years of studying her case. Where does Miss Somers fit into this?" said Mike, spinning round to face the window.

"Mike, they're back," said Bridget, popping her head around the door.

Mike held up his hand in acknowledgement, turning to face Paul.

"Are you ready to go back twenty-five years?" he said, rising to his feet.

"You bet," he said, following him out the door.

Twenty-Four

"I'm so nervous," said Mel, as she climbed into her car. "I just don't know what to do with myself."

"Well, just as well I'm driving," said Mike, selecting reverse and looking over his shoulder. He caught sight of Jack playing with two dinosaurs in the rear mirror and then he stared at the empty child seat to his right. He could feel his heart pounding in his chest and he felt certain it had missed a beat.

This was the day they had been working up to for the last three months. It had become very quickly apparent after Liz's funeral that Rob and Liz's family members were very few and far between. Liz's mum lived in Australia and her father had passed away the year before. She was an only child.

Rob, on the other hand, had no family members at all. His father had died in action in 2010 in Afghanistan, leaving behind a great gaping hole. His mother, unable to come to terms with her grief, suffered multiple breakdowns and was eventually admitted to West Park Mews, a retreat offering assistance to veteran's spouses, coming to terms with their loss. She died four years later.

Rob had followed in his father's footsteps joining the army when he was eighteen. He had a real hunger for action and loved travelling the world. He had met Liz at a military dance five years prior and they married six months later.

Mel hadn't realised the fragility of Liz's family ties and if she was honest having no family ties herself, hadn't really noticed the absence of grandparents. Liz had occasionally mentioned her mother but in no great detail and she knew they weren't close. She had attended the funeral by zoom and they had heard nothing since. Liz had mentioned that she had had her late in life and was almost seventy.

Mel had poured her heart out to Mike, sharing her fears of what might become of Henry's future with a military father and no other family members. They had met with Rob, initially in shared grief, but he had opened up pouring out his heart and his fears.

Mike and Mel had spent hours discussing the possibility of them stepping in as guardians while Rob was away, enabling him to return to service. Rob had been overwhelmed by their kind gesture, breaking down on his knees. He had nowhere else to turn and was desperate, his only other option, leaving service. He had battled with his heart and his conscience knowing he could never place his son in care.

Their offer was a lifeline thrown to him while drowning and he had accepted their offer with heartfelt indebtedness.

"I can't thank you enough," he had gushed, then burst into heartfelt sobs. "I don't know what you must think of me, leaving my son with someone I've only just met, but what sort of father would I be?" he cried. "Liz did everything for him, I don't even know how to be a good father. It's easy when you drop in a few weeks at a time. I guess I'm selfish," he had sobbed, through his tears. "Liz told me so much about you and what wonderful parents you are to Jack. For Henry to have a secure life with you means the world. I will of course visit whenever I get leave," he promised.

Mike had been sceptical at first, laying all his fears on the table. But they had worked their way through each and every one agreeing that it needed to be done legally, to ensure that the arrangement would be permanent and that the authorities wouldn't step in and remove him from their care.

Anyway it was now official, Henry was to come and live with them and his father would visit as often as he could. Jack had been beside himself with excitement at the thought of having a brother and had especially chosen a dinosaur so that Henry could have one of his own.

"What do I do if he starts calling me Mummy?" Mel had asked Rob, desperately not wanting to overstep the mark.

"You will know what to do in your heart, when the time is right," Rob had answered, making her cry.

"Right, we're here," said Mike, pulling onto their drive.

"You ready?" he said, turning to face her.

"No," she said, trembling. "Give me a moment." She took a deep breath and then followed it with another. "I'm ready." she said, stepping out of the car.

"Right, little fella, let's get you out," he said walking round the car. He stopped, staring at his wife, as he reached the other side. "You look beautiful," he said, reaching out to her face. He brushed his hand gently down her cheek. "He's a very lucky boy, a lucky boy indeed."

Mike lifted Jack out of his seat and kissed him on the cheek. "This is a very special day, Jack, when Henry comes to live with us."

"You ready?" he said, popping him down on the floor.

"Yes, Daddy," he said, giving him the cutest smile.

Mel looked up to the sky, a tear rolling down her cheek. "I promise to always love him, Liz, and I will do my very best to make you proud. I love you my dear friend, with all my heart. Rest in Peace."

Twenty-Five

The 24th November 2026 at Holden Central Magistrates Court.

Judge Ronald Williamson residing gave the following verdicts:

Doctor Gyllensvan was sentenced to life imprisonment. It was a unanimous vote. In view of his age, it was unlikely that he would see the light of day again.

Thomas Hamilton was sentenced to ten years imprisonment for perverting the course of justice.

Ivy Mason and Karen Lewis were deemed to be unfit for trial due to their birth origin and the fact they had been programmed and coerced. They were to receive psychiatric help through the state and monitored until further notice. Their medical licences had been revoked.

Brent Carter was sentenced to fifteen years for knowingly fathering two hundred and fifty children. No parole was offered.

Julie Somers' DNA revealed she was the biological daughter of Doctor Gyllensvan, aged 35 years, increasing fears that he was practicing these atrocities for many years. She remains in Holden City Hospital psychiatric unit.

The fate of the children born to this establishment was handed to the authorities for further debate. It was considered by some to be detrimental to the welfare of all victims to remove them from potential loving homes. The case continues.

Four female bodies were recovered from the grounds of Keeper's Lodge eighteen months later. The search continues.

Niko Demetrio was found hanged in his flat on the 25th December 2026. The verdict was suicide.

Inspector Mike Brugge was promoted to chief inspector, following the retirement of Inspector Lawrence Dhillon.

Linda was finally reunited with her sister Rachel four years and three months after the night of the fire at Victoria's Retreat. Mike had recounted that the moment was tender and heartfelt.

They have yet to meet Baby Blossom, who's future is still under review.

Also in this Trilogy

Book One:

On a cold blustery November night, Detective Sergeant Mike Brugge and his partner Detective Constable Mel Bailey come across a girl, age unknown, in the parkland in Gordon Square. She was frail, malnourished, dirty and was covered in excrement.

What had happened to this girl? Why was she cowering down, shielding her eyes from the light, with a look of horror on her face? She appeared to be non-coherent, totally unengaged and would not speak to anyone. Nothing could penetrate the world where her soul had taken solace.

Mike and Mel set out to find out where she had come from and what had been her plight. Revealing hypnosis sessions allow them to glimpse some of her pain and suffering. Follow their story deep into the horrors that unfold, causing chaos and turmoil among their own lives.

The detectives are about to discover a horrific, gut-wrenching story, that spanned over four decades. But will it end?

Book Two:

It was probably not the most obvious choice for a three month sabbatical but to Emma coming to Holden seemed totally idyllic. She had heard so much about it and could picture every single segment etched in her mind like braille. Now she wanted to fill in the dots and bring it to life so that she could see it for herself first hand.

It was April 2026 and she had secured a three month, off the record, sublet in a beautiful apartment called Arlington Terrace. The apartment with the black front door. It was totally perfect for her, required no references and no questions were being asked as to why she was there. In fact no one even knew she was heading that way, so she could slip in unnoticed and live incognito amongst the locals.

So how was it that Julie found her again, when she was so careful not to leave a trail and why was it that she didn't feel alone, ever? Was she going mad or was she simply being paranoid. What could she do to stop these tormenting acts from happening and make people believe that she was the one being persecuted.

Detective Sergeant Mike Brugge, Detective Constable Mel Brugge and Detective Sergeant Paul Osman are back at the heart of yet another investigation deep in the heart of Holden City Central. Follow them as they try to unravel a crime that intertwines their lives taking them back to a gut wrenching case that has infected yet another generation and into the horrors that emerge from beyond the grave.

Hello, Reader...

I hope you enjoyed Keeper's Lodge and that it brought closure to this dark and harrowing story.

If you have enjoyed reading this book, I would really appreciate it if you would leave a review for potential readers to see.

Take care, and I hope to entertain you again soon!

Best Wishes

Tracy Martin-Summers

Printed in Great Britain
by Amazon

76502347R00161